by Geoffrey Household

Novels

THE THIRD HOUR

ROGUE MALE

ARABESQUE

THE HIGH PLACE

A ROUGH SHOOT

A TIME TO KILL

FELLOW PASSENGER

WATCHER IN THE SHADOWS

THING TO LOVE

OLURA

Short Stories

THE SALVATION OF PISCO GABAR

TALES OF ADVENTURERS

THE BRIDES OF SOLOMON AND OTHER STORIES

For Children

THE SPANISH CAVE

Autobiography

AGAINST THE WIND

OLURA

OLURA

a novel by

Geoffrey Household

An Atlantic Monthly Press Book

LITTLE, BROWN AND COMPANY · BOSTON · TORONTO

LIBRARY OF CONGRESS CATALOG CARD NO. 65–18134

Fourth Printing

ATLANTIC–LITTLE, BROWN BOOKS
ARE PUBLISHED BY
LITTLE, BROWN AND COMPANY
IN ASSOCIATION WITH
THE ATLANTIC MONTHLY PRESS

Published simultaneously in Canada
by Little, Brown & Company (Canada) Limited

PRINTED IN THE UNITED STATES OF AMERICA

A La Lamia del Iturrigorri

OLURA

$$\text{\small ₷₷₷₷}$$

Memorandum of Henry Sequerra

I CONSIGN these informal records to my safe without corrections or omissions in case they should ever be required as evidence in a Court of Law. I have every reason, however, to apprehend that justice has been done and that it will never be seen to have been done.

The opening document is the first half of the narrative of Dr. Philip Ardower, which I have chosen to place on top of the file because it presents a lucid picture of his involvement with my dear ward and goddaughter, Olura Manoli, as well as the distressing and ultimately dangerous predicament in which these two supposedly responsible people became entangled.

The second document is Olura's own story. When I flew to Spain in response to her obscure and censored appeal, her answers to my questions appeared emotional, overexcited and inclined to attribute importance to a variety of circumstances which had none whatever. A woman's accuracy differs from that of a man, and it is often hard to establish the sequence of events when she considers a mood more vital than a fact and a half-truth more revealing than cold exactitude.

That was the reason why I requested her to write down with the utmost sincerity exactly what had happened. I must admit that I did not require such sincerity to extend to unnecessary details of her personal life, though, knowing Olura, I should perhaps have expected it. Initially her account covers the same facts as Dr. Ardower's; but one might be forgiven for failing, here and there, immediately to recognize that indeed they are the same.

The third set of papers is the remainder of Ardower's narrative, which reveals his very natural anxiety for Olura and the consequences of his chivalrous imprudence which made my intervention as difficult as it was urgent.

During his life Theodore Manoli was closer to me than a brother. Since his death the welfare of his only daughter has been the first responsibility of love. I will not say it has been easy to discharge. Upon reaching the age of revolt — which seems an imperious necessity to the more intelligent of the younger generation — Olura chose passionately to reject Theodore's environment, while preserving his sense of duty, his integrity and his devotion to those he loved. The Establishment was anathema to her. She referred to it with thin lips, like an Orangeman forced to mention the Roman Church. As for me, her godfather, guardian, trustee and — to carry on my simile — a cardinal not only of the Establishment but the International Establishment, I was endurable only because the darling had become attached to me at an early age.

As I reread these documents I perceive recurring in Olura's character a quality which at the time I put down to her essential femininity, never realizing that she had inherited it from Theodore. Indeed the most perfect illustration of it is her own christening.

Theodore's handwriting was unintelligible — a fact which even I hesitated to point out to him. Far from being slipshod or undecorative, it was so imposing that a reader attempting to decipher it for the first time invariably blamed his own stupidity. Even when Theodore, to avoid all possible error, wrote in printed capitals he joined them together with such luxuriance that the essential word seemed to be engrossed in the priestly script of some high and vanished civilization.

Upon the birth of his daughter he registered her name as Olivia. For once he was particularly careful with his capitals, and there could be no conceivable doubt that the name was Olura. It was early in the war, and Theodore was sleeping on a camp bed in the office; so the first he knew of what he had done was at the christening. I remember the loudly whispered protest of her mother when the parson pronounced the name. Theodore did not turn a hair. He said that it was charming and congratulated his secretary on so delicious a typing error. I am compelled to accuse him of preferring to accept a mistake rather than the truth about his handwriting; but at the same time I applaud his extraordinary power of instant decision. He never failed to exploit any totally unexpected situation which was obviously desirable.

Nor indeed did she, on the occasions when she was free to act. I see that inspired inconstancy in her change of — shall I call it? — objective in the Hostal de las Olas, in her impulsive but often profitable reactions thereafter, in her instinctive realization that Ardower must be dead and her admirable choice of the right witness to suborn.

That perhaps is the least of the illegalities which I feel bound to record in my personal statement, the fourth and last of these documents. My motives were in no way public-spirited. I do not share the opinions of Olura, humane and liberal though they are; still less do I share those of the Alliance des Blancs which have no base but hysteria. When, however, such activities as theirs grossly disturb the peace and happiness of the individual, mere defeat is, I feel, insufficient punishment, and my qualms of conscience are allayed.

Narrative of Dr. Philip Ardower

AT our first meeting it seemed to me odd that a woman of obvious sophistication should insist on dressing like Red Riding Hood. I remember arguing it out with myself — for want of anything better — as our two solitary figures approached each other across a waste of sand which should have been glittering particles of reflected sunlight and in fact was a melancholy yellow under the stormy sky.

The cloak and hood were, I admitted, practical enough when one had packed only summer clothes and yet foresaw the probable need of something warm and decorative. So what was wrong? Too conspicuous. But women liked to be conspicuous, provided they did not achieve originality by being out of fashion. A good point for her. So long as she looked attractive she didn't care whether she was in fashion or not. Very well! But had she any right to sail among the mediocrities of the hotel like a great lady? She was too young to be a great lady. The crimson cloak and hood suggested Disneyland rather than a Duchess.

She had arrived a couple of days before, and since then had kept very much to herself. Already she was plainly adored by the maître d'hotel and her waiter, but to the rest of us she gave no more than shy smiles in passing. I formed the impression that she was on her guard rather than shy, that she faintly resented the interest she aroused. She looked courageous, but as if she couldn't afford, even in that easiest of hotels, to leave the necessity for courage in her bag upstairs.

She was walking up the estuary, in full sail over the deserted beach with the gusty northwest wind behind her. I was plugging along towards her with my eyes half-shut against the stinging squalls of sand above high-water mark. As we passed I wished her a good morning without shortening my stride, and was surprised when she stopped. It was reasonable enough that she should; but I had been overimpressed by her air of hesitant privacy. I expected nothing but the shy smile.

We chatted for a moment about the hotel and the weather, and then she asked me what was at the head of the estuary. I had found, I told her, nothing but marsh; it was impossible to cross over to the other side without swimming or going miles round by the road.

"I see why you wanted to," she said.

The little village of Maya across the water beckoned an invitation, and not merely because it *was* across the water. Outcrops of rock had forced the estuary into a curve. At the bottom of the loop was a small new-moon beach with boats drawn up on it. The anchorage was so sheltered and the sands so steep that there was no necessity for a quay. Two gay villas, of the type you can never buy because the owner's grandchildren would be so disappointed, crowned

the rocky headlands, and a single street of red roofs strag-
gled up from the comfortable quadrilateral of the water-
side inn. It had a little terrace with a green awning over
it, and announced its specialty to be Prawns and Lobsters.

"I'm told one can wade across easily at low tide," I answered. "But the channel is still too deep to tackle without
a swimsuit. I was looking for a shallow higher up the
river. They say the prawns are marvelous at that pub."

She asked when low tide was. In something less than a
couple of hours, I told her. And even then the wind at the
mouth of the river would add another foot to the depth.

"It looks as if we could get over just upstream from that
boat," she said.

It didn't look like anything of the sort. There was a
quite considerable fishing launch anchored in the channel, which had not yet begun to heel over though the keel
was probably touching sand. But she wanted to go. Therefore it was possible.

"Let's try!" she said.

It is never any use arguing about wind, tide and the
clock when a woman has decided that you are unenter-
prising and that they will all obey her. I observed, perhaps
dryly, that I saw she was a romanticist.

"And you?" she retorted. "Weren't you looking for a
crossing too?"

"But that was greed."

"Oh, was it? Your prawns are going to taste exactly like
any others!"

The intelligence behind that reply was exciting. So, outside the hotel, was she. Shorten her a good six inches, and her graceful, high-breasted body could be compared to that of some lovely Latin peasant with a jar on her head. One couldn't call her slim in the sense of those revolting, so-called vital statistics, with their dead, unmoving 34s and 26s like the readings on a pressure gauge, which are flung at us by every newspaper and advertisement and mean absolutely nothing to me. The figures were irrelevant to her as to classical Greek sculpture or to one of Lely's provocative lovelies at the court of Charles II. For the rest, I took notice of that fairish hair in some fashionably thick arrangement, the large gray eyes, the straight but utterly unaggressive nose. The mouth might have been a little too full for some, and the upper lip a little too long for others; but any of them at any age would have been enchanted to look at a nonexistent river crossing with her.

I told her to wait while I rolled up my trousers and tried out the channel. It was three feet deep; soft, sticky sand at the bottom added another six inches.

"You could do it if you took them off," she said.

"Well, but what about you?"

"Oh, I was hoping for a swim."

She took off the crimson cloak and rolled it into a bundle. She was wearing a severe blue swimsuit with a loose sweater over it.

"My shirt," I pointed out, "is very short, and . . ."

"I don't mind."

"I wasn't thinking of you. I was thinking of highly shockable Spaniards on the other side."

"I see."

"And I refuse to sit at a café table in soaked trousers and this gale."

"Put my cloak on," she suggested, "and hold it up as high as you can without shocking Spaniards."

I was most unwilling to be watched on an open beach — for villagers, though invisible, are always fascinated by the antics of foreigners — while putting on a woman's red cloak and taking off my trousers under it. But I had to. I am sensitive to making myself in any way noticeable. She didn't seem to give a damn. I tried to square her free and easy manners with her reserve in the hotel and verged, I think, on the right answer: that if she felt something was worth doing, she was completely uninhibited in her approach to it.

We crossed — she splashing along confidently, I looking like an old woman going out to pawn her husband's pants. Behind a convenient rock I returned to masculinity and handed back the cloak.

She was wrong about the prawns. They did *not* taste like any others — as you, Sequerra, will agree. Possibly for her they did. She had no interest in food and drink.

We talked easily but without intimacy. She appeared to have a mind of high quality, though untrained. She cared too much about vague service to her fellows and too little about knowledge, like so many of the generation ten years younger than my own. Opinionated? A bit of a prig? Well, if she was, I could hardly distinguish it, for she possessed all the social graces.

There was a continual roar of speech and laughter from

the bar behind the terrace. The crew of the *María de Urquijo*, the launch now high and dry in the channel, were drinking away their leisure while fishing was impossible. She thought the racket extravagantly loud. I may have replied that I was glad there were still men in the world who did not care how much noise they made. Basques when speaking Spanish, as these were, are more full-mouthed than in their own language.

We stayed an hour and crossed back to our home sands by a knee-deep paddle. On the open beach the wind was too fierce for conversation and too cold to stop and watch the savage seas meeting land for the first time on their journey from Labrador. In any case we had seen all we wanted of that frustrated fury from the hotel windows. Plainly she thought so too, especially as rain was now pouring down.

She went straight up to her room to change, and I might have imagined that she had had enough of me as well, though she thanked me sweetly for prawns and my company. She had put on again her manner for public places, as if she had been too shortsighted to be sure of any of us and taken refuge in a comprehensive smile.

The Hostal de las Olas was a hotel with some pretensions to luxury: one of the showpieces of the Spanish Tourist Office. The guests were pleasantly cosmopolitan, pleasantly prosperous, without belonging in any sense to what I believe is called the International Set for whom the prices of the Hostal would not have been enough. They were far too high for me. Mere longing for a hot bath took me there in the first place, and a windfall in the shape of unexpected royalties from the paperback of my *Iberian Migrations* enabled me to stay on.

I had been wandering about from farm to village *fonda* in the remoter valleys of Vizcaya, and had then spent a couple of weeks at Eibar. I speak and write Euzkadi — Basque, that is — with ease and purity, but I had noticed that in discussing the techniques of modern industry I was sometimes unsure of the form of Spanish loan-words. That was why I chose busy Eibar where such discussions are hardly avoidable. I deprecate philologists who are content with book knowledge. If my subject were English Literature I should feel a fraud unless I could converse without effort in idiomatic Elizabethan.

A succession of gales, confining us to the hotel lounge and bar when we should have been dispersed along the beaches, enhanced that easy pleasure which we took in our fellow holiday-makers. Sea and a shade of boredom produced that eagerness to talk and be talked at which is more common on board ships than in hotels. There were an affable German publisher with his pretty wife and daughter and a number of genial French families with a papa who had arrived near the top of his profession and could afford to do himself well. The handful of English and the few Spaniards kept as a rule to themselves, through fear, I think, of being forced to speak a foreign language — though in fact some of them may have had far more fluency than the rest of us, who misused each other's languages atrociously but in the best of good humor.

My most frequent companions were two unattached

Frenchmen. Major Vigny, a parachutist, had been a security officer in Algeria and had, I gathered, been forcibly retired by de Gaulle. He spoke excellent Berber, and this — my tastes being what they are — compensated for his political opinions, which were some thirty years out of date. His constant companion, introduced to me as des Aunes, was more reserved. He had a very courteous air of authority and I suspected that he might be a general. In the absence of any experience entitling me to recognize French generals, it is probable that I was merely going by the respect which Commandant Vigny paid to him.

When I came downstairs after changing damp shirt and sweater, I found Vigny in the bar, endeavoring to be polite to the weather while leaving no doubt that he thought it a deliberate insult to the French. He had the same attitude to the lunch hour. He complained that eating at 2:30 made him drink too much too early. Evidently he had only recently arrived in Spain. Des Aunes, on the other hand, had no more objection than I to lunching even at three, which suggested that he had been longer in the country. It was a fair speculation that he might have belonged to the O.A.S. and found it healthier to live in exile.

I joined Vigny at the window, placing my *fino* on the sill alongside his Cinzano.

"I see that you are very English after all," he said. "You can amuse yourself in the rain."

"In our cloistered existence," I replied, "we keep our first youth longer than the military."

"Take it from me, Professor — you won't have any luck."

It was never any good explaining to him that I was not a professor, merely a Fellow of my College. And I dislike the everyday use of the doctorate, especially when on holiday among the English. One tends to be cornered at the bar by comparative strangers and asked secretively if any reliable remedy is known for piles.

"I haven't given a thought to the possibilities," I said, not quite truly. "But why shouldn't they be there?"

"Her tastes are notorious."

I was surprised that he knew anything about her. He had never made any remark when he saw her passing through the lounge.

"You don't read your papers then?" he asked.

"Recently, no."

"You should have seen her photograph often enough in the last three years."

"I have an incurable habit of reading. It leaves me little time to look at the pictures. Who is she?"

"Olura Manoli," he said.

"Olura. Let me see. Yes. She sits in the street, and her father is a wealthy Bolivian. Or is she the movie star who is so remarkably casual about having babies?"

"She does sit in the streets. Her father was Sir Theodore Manoli. And she has no babies."

"My dear Commandant, that's not my fault," I said, observing that my ignorance of Miss Manoli had thoroughly annoyed him. "And I have at least heard of her father."

"She is a lot more important than that old plutocrat."

It was my turn to be annoyed, for I remembered that Sir Theodore was a rich Greek shipowner who had taken British nationality some time in the nineteen-thirties and had splendidly deserved his knighthood, which no doubt meant far more to him than the rest of us. He had worked himself into the grave for his adopted country and had — or so his biographer maintained — direct access to Churchill on any question of merchant shipping during the war.

"At her age importance can depend only on the effrontery of one's public relations officer," I replied.

Vigny gave a short military laugh and looked as if he would like to spit.

"I endure you," he said, "only because your smile reminds me of the more unpleasant portraits of Voltaire."

"Another Cinzano?" I suggested.

"Thank you. No."

"Well, what's she famous for?"

"She has a marked sympathy for Africans."

"Political or personal?"

"Woman is never wholly a political animal."

A typically closed and Gallic remark! I shouldn't have invited it.

"Africans should be encouraged to see the pleasantest possible aspects of our civilization," I said, "if, as it appears, they insist on adopting it. Personally I hope they will invent something of a more genial simplicity."

"Such as new forms of famine and disease, for example? But there appears, thank God, to be some lunch," he said and left me.

Lunch did not hold for me its usual unthinking pleasures, when between courses — excellent though somewhat denationalized to suit the palates of foreigners — I could chat with Vigny and des Aunes on my left or exchange more formal courtesies with the large round table on my right which just accommodated a Portuguese family. The Frenchman were uncommunicative. The family was distracted by its too prettified six-year-old daughter, who refused to eat because she was not getting enough attention. She got it all right.

Olura sat opposite me some twenty feet away. I could not take my eyes off her. I kept on staring and trying not to be caught like a child, and eventually received a child's rebuke. She rested her head on her hand and stared me down with a half-smile as much as to say: take a good look once and for all, and get on with your lunch. I felt absurdly angry with myself and with her, and let her leave the dining room first so that I should not have to pass her table. I swore that wealthy socialites were not for me.

Des Aunes and Vigny, who never missed a trick — the French in any summer hotel have a positively feminine genius for detecting everyone's embarrassments — watched me with discreet enjoyment. Vigny managed to say *I told you so* by a mere cock of the eyebrow. I took to drink. It seemed to me that my waiter had a sympathetic air of comprehension as he replaced the empty bottle with a new one. By this time I was oversensitive to deaf-and-dumb language.

After a long siesta I found that the gale had gone down and that the evening was gray and still. The surf was formidable, thundering in under a light mist of its own making, for there was no wind to blow away the spume. This was inviting, so I went out along the beach for a bathe. There was not a soul in sight except a Pair of the Civil Guard who made soundless, frantic signs for me to come in. No doubt my seal-like play with the waves looked foolhardy from a distance, but I know when the surf — it was worse than the night which you will remember — can be made to do my work for me. I was brought up as a boy on North Cornish beaches.

I returned to the hotel, spent an hour or two writing up my notes on traces of Arabic in the spoken Basque of Álava, and went down to the lounge at the beginning of dusk. I noticed that the few British were huddled together near the bar under protection of the usual barricade of chair and sofa backs. They seemed singularly sheep-like, and I looked around for the wolf. It was, of course, Olura.

She sat in the opposite corner, chatting gaily with a shadow and exquisitely dressed in white. That extremely expensive simplicity is as obvious to any man of taste as to a woman; we are capable of appreciating the picture, while knowing little or nothing about the brushwork. When I looked again at the shadow, I saw that the darkness against the folds of an undrawn curtain was due not to dusk but to race. I was pretty sure that I recognized that distinguished head and beard. If so, Olura's exceptional elegance could be explained. It was the correct gesture towards a prime minister.

Social confidence being now restored by waves and work, I gave her a formal bow and a more comradely smile. She at once beckoned me over and introduced me to

Leopold Mgwana. He was taller and lither than I had imagined him. The pointed, black, closely-curled beard was
a more integral part of his fine, bony head than it appeared when lovingly exaggerated by the charcoal of car-
toonists; they also made him a forest Negroid, which he
wasn't. His nose and cheekbones showed a strong Nilotic
strain. Power in the flesh and power as one expects it to be
are never the same; but there was no mistaking the air of
purpose, benevolence and integrity which always won for
him a sourly admiring press in spite of his somewhat personal interpretation of democracy.

As we chatted, it became clear that Olura had been
waiting for him, that it was she who had selected the hotel
and had come down ahead of him to assure herself that it
really was the sort of place where he could relax. Vigny's
uncharitable suggestion passed through my mind, for
Mgwana was only in his early forties. Even though ruffled
by slight jealousy, I was inclined to disbelieve it. Olura's
attitude to Mgwana was not unlike that of a first-class personal secretary to her boss. Between them was easy and
genuine friendship.

His tranquillity impressed me. He did not in the least
withdraw himself; but he was impassive as a shield of
black steel, behind which roared a conveyor belt accepting, rejecting, always obedient to a pattern of press but-
tons which his own deeper self had set. The pattern, I
should guess, was defensible even when wrong. No politician, after all, can be sure that his objectives are socially
and economically valid. We in the universities are better

qualified to tell. But what we cannot do and he can is to put such power into a creed that it digests his errors without doing much harm to the ideal.

Olura and he were sipping tomato juice — a drink which to me suggests recovery from a hangover or a rarefied atmosphere of conscious virtue. On that first evening, a little unsure of his surroundings, he had probably left the choice to her. My own refreshment during the protracted Spanish evening is invariably brandy and soda. By the time I had finished my second I found enough impudence to tell Mgwana what I had heard of him from the last Governor-General of the colony.

He had been sitting next to me at a college gaudy, rejoicing in his retirement from the cares of office but missing his Africa and eager to talk about it. He told me that when he had been forced to put Mgwana inside — the law being what it was — he had been afraid of going down in history as a minor second cousin of the obstinate Pharaoh. Not, he said, that there was anything whatever holy about Mgwana. Far, far from it. But the man was a powerhouse for all Africa, and his name would endure.

"I couldn't hate him," Mgwana said with a deep chuckle. "I knew that soon I would be responsible for law and order myself. And I too had my secret fears. I wouldn't have liked to go down in history as the leader whose followers had cut Sir Horace into pieces and sent little baskets of him round the villages."

Olura protested that he was exaggerating, that his followers would never have thought of it, that his own example was enough to prevent it.

"But you must sometimes have felt hatred," I remarked
to lead him on.

"Yes, I did. The stupidity of policemen. The resent-
ments. I still hate the — the polite condescension."

"There can't be much of that left."

He smiled, but didn't answer me. After all, he was fresh
from a round of conferences and probably suspicious that,
as soon as he left the room, European ministers would recover a sense of ease and get on with the job on an old-
boy basis.

I ventured to touch on the question of the Portuguese
colonies — my fondness for the Peninsula often makes
me an untimely propagandist — suggesting that Portugal
alone, with the example of Latin America close to its
heart, was genuinely trying to create a multiracial society.

That instantly revealed Olura for me. Just as the loyal
secretary loathes the rival firm more than the managing
director does, so she would not even try to see the argument. But Mgwana by no means rejected it out of hand.

"They should have tried to make their Brazil faster and
earlier," he said. "I grant that the ideal is sincere, but I am
bound to fight it. Do you find any dishonesty in that?"

I did not. Yet later in the evening of that stimulating
day, when Olura and Mgwana had dined and gone out, I
did feel that he had missed a subtle difference between
European nations which I could never tactfully explain.

The Portuguese family who were my neighbors at table
were fascinated by Mr. Mgwana, and wanted to know who
he was. I sensed that the color of his skin was to them as
unimportant as the color of his shirt. In their gay, bird-

like discussion of the lovely English lady and her obviously distinguished friend there was absolutely no undercurrent of Beauty and the Beast. The British, however, who belonged to the same class of bourgeoisie in prosperity and education, were uneasy. Their women verged upon prurient curiosity. I would have liked to add to my field ethnology some further examples of weary French cynicism, but Vigny and des Aunes had paid their bill and left the hotel.

The next day was glorious from dawn to dusk, and the sun truly Spanish rather than Atlantic. After idling over breakfast on the terrace and still seeing no sign of Olura or Mr. Mgwana I strolled westwards along the beach, aiming for the delicious complex of miniature islands and peninsulas on the way to the Maya Estuary, where one could choose sun or shade and take one's sea calm or rough according to mood.

When I turned round to look at the attractive front of the hotel with its three tiers of stone balconies, Olura was leaning on the balustrade outside her room. I had put all of a quarter of a mile between myself and the hotel, and only a third of her was visible; but I knew very well who it was. I had discovered — let us call it sentimental curiosity — that her room was separated by two balconies from my own.

I waved to her, without much expectation that she would notice. She waved back at once. I went on my way with a faint hope that Mr. Mgwana was recovering from his political exertions by staying in bed till lunch and that Olura might accidentally choose my patch of beach. High-minded though she was, she was not at all averse to admiration — and I was the only person, unattached and of the right age, to give it.

Half an hour later I was ashamed of that cheap "accidentally." Another woman might have come a roundabout way or settled in some half-hidden crescent of rocks where she could be sure I would find her. Not so Olura. She was always true to her self-imposed frankness. She walked straight up to me and merely remarked that she knew I would be there.

She was quite dazzling. No Red Riding Hood that morning. Not much, in fact, of anything at all. What there was seemed to be constructed of petals of pale green, with a wholly frivolous thigh-length wrap of some material utterly unknown to me, white, pleated, and very possibly unique.

She swam, I observed, violently, using far too much energy. When we had settled down to sun ourselves, I congratulated her on choosing an original spot for Mr. Mgwana.

"What did you think of him?"

I replied that he was a remarkable man, and that I saw what his last Governor-General had meant.

"It was wicked to treat him as a criminal," she said.

"The poor Governor was only doing what Whitehall told him he must. And even with a leader like Mgwana his people weren't really ready for independence."

"Who is?" she asked. "But it's a right. Look at ourselves! No country which is prepared to use the Bomb deserves independence."

I laid off that one, for I always find myself in complete agreement with both sides of the argument, and can't help showing it. In the heated nuclear atmosphere that does not increase one's popularity.

"Independence is, I suppose, a right," I agreed, "but it would have been hardly fair to hand over the government to Mgwana without first making sure that he had something governable."

She rolled her delicious body over to face me, drawing up one smooth and intoxicating thigh to support it, and accused me of talking like a civil servant in the Athenaeum. I reminded myself carefully that there might be a whole week ahead of us and that it would be unwise to point out too academically that she had no more idea than I of civil servants' small talk in the Athenaeum.

"I don't know enough about you, Miss Manoli," I said. "Is your interest in politics active?"

"Yes. But it's an interest in humanity. And Olura, please, not Miss Manoli."

The musical name came very easily to my tongue. I had been repeating it rather too often in private.

"There is so much I can do, you see," she went on. "It isn't sensible that these fine men who are deciding the fate of a continent should have to put up at cheap joints in Bloomsbury. It isn't right that they should experience nothing between —" her words came tumbling out, and she had the grace to smile at herself "— between chops and chips and Lord Mayor's Banquets. So I entertain them. I try to get for them everyone they want to meet —

editors and tycoons and those horrible Public Relations
Officers."

"I thought yesterday that you would be a marvelous
P.R.O. yourself," I said.

"Yes. Perhaps it does describe how I try to help the helpless."

"Which helpless?"

"The emerging nations."

Oh dear and damn! That sounded like a prefect of seventeen at an English girls' school or an American do-
goodess of forty. Leopold Mgwana might find her wealth
and enthusiasm useful, but he wouldn't like being described as helpless. He might even agree — if he ever
drank more than tomato juice — that an African politician in London was a deal less helpless than the unfortunate Minister of State who had to negotiate with him.

"They must all think you are an angel," I said, getting
safely onto more personal ground.

"Yes?" she answered coolly. "Do you?"

That put me on the spot much too early. Her remark
was ironical rather than inviting. At the same time I did
not rule it out that she might be probing — with some enjoyment — to see how much of a fool I was.

"I might be doubtful about your technique of flying, but
the wings are very lovely."

"A fairy in a Christmas pantomime?"

"No. Lovely meaning lovable."

That kept it on a high plane, even if somewhat em-
phatic. What I was really thinking about — if it could

be called thinking — was the fascinating effect of sun-flecked golden down on untanned surfaces.

"You don't know me at all."

"But I want to. And if I sound patronizing, it's just my professional manner, which I can't help. It only means that I feel protective."

She was a bit doubtful about that one. I suppose a good many men had presented themselves as likely to protect her and her money.

"What are you?" she asked. "A barrister?"

"A comparative philologist, with an interest in ethnology."

"Cannibals and canoes?"

"No. My special subject is the peopling of Europe. Migrations and so forth. I have a theory — generally considered to be unsound — that evidence imbedded in vocabulary and grammar is as significant as that of skulls, pottery and midden heaps. I know nothing about Africa south of the Atlas, but our interests touch in Algeria where the inhabitants had a lot more fun than they do now."

"What sort of fun?"

"Hunting over the great plains of the Sahara."

"You call that fun?"

"Yes, if it means dinner for the family. No — with reservations — if it means killing for kicks," I answered boldly. "And I'll bet you Mgwana agrees with me."

"I do not always accept Leopold Mgwana's tastes," she said rather haughtily, and rolled over on her back.

So there I was in the dock alongside criminals like Mas-

ters of Stag Hounds! On the other hand, hadn't there been
a faint appeal to me to take Olura for what she was and
lay off the supposed public image of Miss Manoli? When
again she rested herself on one elbow, conversation was
easier and more intimate — perhaps because it did not
concern ourselves. She proposed to show Mgwana as
much of the Basque Provinces as could be seen in a long
afternoon's drive and wanted my advice on the route.

I have put down all this because you asked me for the
utmost frankness in explaining my relations with Olura
and Mr. Mgwana. And you are right. Considering that I
had known Olura for only thirty-six hours, my recklessness, sympathy, devotion — whatever you like to call it —
is inexplicable without its full background.

It would be absurd to claim that I had fallen in love
with her. She was in another world, and her character far
too complex and difficult for a don with half his mind on
relics of prehistory in the Basque language. About the
other half of it I have been crudely honest. I was very
much aware that she was in a holiday mood, unattached
except for her duty to Mr. Mgwana, and that if she were
feminine enough (she certainly was) to look for relaxa-
tion in captivating some casual male companion, I was
available, sexually excited — a revolting phrase to express my enchantment — and reasonably presentable.

On that disastrous evening of July 21 I remember
with astonishment that I was bored, and missed Vigny
and des Aunes. Olura and Leopold Mgwana dined in Bilbao and did not return till after eleven. On arrival she
went up to have a bath. He was more interested in a long

and tinkling drink, for the night was like a steam room. He appeared most grateful for the afternoon's tour. Having seen only towns, England, his own tropics and the desiccated coasts of Egypt and North Africa, the abrupt savagery of those green mountains plunging to the Atlantic was strange to him. Half modest, half uneasy, he said that there must still be so many currents of European life which he did not understand.

He told me with one of his deep chuckles that Olura considered me a member of the Establishment, but still with a soul to be saved. He was too practical a man not to be amused by her overenthusiasm. Yet, like Vigny, he thought her a person of importance, a mover of public opinion. I couldn't believe he was right. In these days there is no salon influence corresponding to that of the great Victorian and Edwardian hostesses. Olura's entertainment of the citizens, prominent or promising, of new countries was well conceived and undoubtedly useful. But it was not an exercise of power. It remained a generous and ambitious eccentricity.

Mgwana left the lounge a little before midnight, saying that he had a couple of hours' work before him. I read the local paper and then went up myself. Looking along the line of balconies, I noticed that Olura's light was still on. I remember thinking that she was not the type to draw curtains automatically and that, since there was nothing but the Biscay swell between Brittany and her bedroom for three hundred miles, she would certainly prefer casements opening on the foam.

I was in a first half-sleep, obsessed with pots of cactus

and miniature orange trees — association with the sort of balcony Olura would have in London and the difficult choice of a seat which would face Keats's nightingale — when I heard my name being whispered. I sat up, and there was Olura standing just inside my own magic casement.

"Don't turn the light on!" she said.

The situation looked very hopeful. This approach fitted her self-imposed sincerity, and she was very scantily dressed so far as I could judge in the liquid, dark-blue shine from the sea behind her. I slid out of bed and asked her to come in.

"No. Philip, I need you in my room immediately. Along the balconies. I've just done it. The bedroom windows are all shut."

Her voice was steady, but there was something wrong with her breathing.

"Are you ill, Olura?" I asked.

"No, no! Come at once and don't let anyone see you!"

Obviously this was not an occasion for dressing gown and pajamas. What was up I couldn't begin to guess; but whether it was a large moth or burglars or a violently overflowing lavatory cistern, action had to be taken. So I grabbed beach shirt, trousers and sandals. After reconnoitering all visible balconies in case some romantic was leaning out to have a look at nothing, I slipped across to her room. One of the wrought-iron barriers on the way was impassable except by way of some nasty spikes on the outer edge. She certainly had not climbed that just from alarm at insects or plumbing.

The heavy curtains of her room were now tightly drawn, but the window behind them was open. My first mental snap was of Leopold Mgwana standing in the middle of the room with his hands behind his back and an air of Savonarola about to be burnt at the stake. I hoped to God that I had not been called in to rebuke him for unwelcome approaches.

His presence in Olura's room seemed, however, to be explained by common interests in work. Her portable typewriter was on a chair. Two other chairs were drawn up at a table covered with papers. More papers had overflowed onto the bed — a fairly convincing sign of innocence. Olura must have been playing the private secretary though hardly dressed for the part.

With the clear-sightedness brought on by mild rivalry I suspected that she ignored convention — of course with her usual high-mindedness — and then accused the opposite sex of coarseness because it couldn't adjust itself immediately to the pure atmosphere of a nudist camp. All splendid! All setting an example of modernity free from inhibitions! But she would not have been so determinedly progressive if she had not been well aware that she was very beautiful.

"Philip," she said, "we want to know what to do. I am not going to drag you into this. But I must know what to do."

This time her voice was on the edge of hysteria. Mr. Mgwana, still immobile on his pile of faggots, said:

"I, too, should be grateful for your advice, Ardower. I

give you my word of honor that I will never mention your presence here."

I liked his use of my surname, unconsciously implying that whatever the differences of power and ancestry our education and traditions were the same — or at any rate similar enough to treat some impossible emergency with an imperial pretense of coolness.

I asked with a show of heartiness but in a low voice what the trouble was. The strained atmosphere suggested that some gorgeous, idealistic folly of Olura's had put him on the spot. But why climb along balconies?

"Go into the bathroom, Philip."

The bathroom door, wide open, was in the far, left-hand corner of the room — from my position by the window, that is. The bed more or less faced it. I passed Mgwana and looked in. What I saw instantly reminded me of a Punch and Judy show, of the recurring tableaux in which the upper half of a puppet, Judy or the Hangman, droops over the edge of the stage after being whacked on the head by Punch.

The bathrooms of the Hostal de las Olas were the latest word in luxury, but Spanish capitalists and their builders like to economize. Each bathroom had a frosted window, about two feet high and eighteen inches wide, opening into a malodorous shaft. The sill of the window was some five feet above the floor, and in Olura's room — though not in mine — it was to the right of the bath, opposite the door into the bedroom. From this window drooped the upper half of a man with a camera hanging down beyond his head, its strap caught under his coat collar. The bar and

thumbscrew at the top of the window, which normally
prevented it from opening more than ten or twelve inches,
seemed to have broken.

Olura's gray eyes, distended by shock, were fixed on me
in a sort of desperate question — not so much panic-
stricken at what had happened as apprehensive of what I,
as the first arrival, might think had happened.

When there is no reason for acting, one can never tell
what one's own face shows or how. Without a word passing between us, her tension relaxed. I did not know much
about her character; it was possible that her surface manner concealed an explosive temper. But I could not con-
ceive that it would ever express itself in violence. She
thought twice before squashing a mosquito. It was unbelievable that she would squash an impertinent photographer.

Mgwana's character, however, was unpredictable. I
could not tell how far away he really was, in all the con-
fusion at the bottom of his two cultures, from using an
assegai on any deserving object. Yet surely self-control
must be second nature to so balanced and patient a politician.

"He didn't!" Olura exclaimed. "I swear he didn't!"

I never saw anything look so dead — the puppet, I
mean, not Mgwana. But in case he had just fainted, humanity compelled me to feel his heart.

I explored further. The base of the skull and back of the
neck felt anatomically odd. One doesn't have any certain
knowledge of these things without medical training. For
purposes of comparison I ran my hand over the back of

my own neck. It seemed more solid, however much I relaxed the muscles. The question had to be settled one way
or the other, so I stuck my fingers and thumb well into the
puppet's flesh and found a lot of hard things loose. I then
had to pull myself together by severe personal exhorta-
tions and a splash of cold water from the tap.

"When did you find him?" I asked Olura.

"Just now, when I went into the bathroom."

"The door wasn't open?"

"No. But who is to tell it wasn't?"

I had not altogether realized the setup till then. What I
myself believed might be a relief to Olura; but what was
the world going to believe when the story broke? It was
probable that Olura and Mgwana could prove their innocence — medical or other evidence must surely be in their
favor whenever police investigated the incident — but by
that time, after columns and columns of front-page fiesta,
they would be degraded forever.

The objective of the photographer needed no explanation. He hoped for some salable demonstration of affection between Olura and Mgwana. But why had his confederate, whose existence must be assumed, killed him?
A deliberate attempt to get Mgwana convicted of man-
slaughter, ensuring even more scandalous publicity? I
gave it up.

Mr. Mgwana entered the bathroom, at last breaking his
tortured silence.

"We must accept what is coming to us, he said, "and
you, Ardower, must go at once. We have no right to drag
you in."

This stoicism in face of the unknown wouldn't do at all; after all, he was a man experienced in action and I was not. I reminded him that he had had a stormy journey to power and that he must sometime have been faced — in the jungle, say — with an awkward corpse.

"In Government House, too," he answered frankly. "But I control the police. Obviously I could keep a . . . an incident like this quiet if the interests of the country demanded it."

"Wouldn't you be laying yourself open to blackmail?"

His admission disturbed me. Since I had invited and expected it, that was absurd. Possibly I foresaw even then that a man accustomed to disdain the conventional processes of law was unlikely to keep a plain citizen's sober balance between alarm and overconfidence.

"In a young country a politician is always open to blackmail," he said. "But there are means of dealing with an individual. And one can shut down a . . ."

He left his sentence unfinished. In the presence of Olura, with her ardently liberal convictions about the Freedom of the Press, it would not have been tactful to mention the shutting down of newspapers.

I made them both sit down. Whoever was waiting for the shriek, the excitement, the summoning of the manager, could damned well wait.

"Tell me about press photographers, Olura. Are they really a nuisance?"

"Not when they come from reputable papers. It's the French and Italian free-lance photographers."

"But would one of them go as far as climbing in by a bathroom window to get a . . . well, if he had reason to think . . ."

I found it difficult to express what I wanted to say. Olura, however, had no inhibitions.

"If he believed that the relationship between Leopold and myself was sexual? Yes, he might," she answered without embarrassment. "I don't think any paper would dare to publish more than a kiss. If there were anything worse I would be invited to pay to get back the negative."

"Then this is all in the day's work from the point of view, say, of a sub-editor paid to bring in the dirt?"

"Yes. I remember that when I took a dancer to Rome because I felt he ought to be imaginatively directed in a film I was pestered by photographers. He was a Negro from Mali, and so he was News. I could have smashed their slimy faces and their cameras."

I advised her not to tell anyone else that, and asked Mgwana if he had any suspicions.

"In my own country I could guess who was behind this," he replied. "But not here."

"Was it widely known beforehand that you were coming?"

"No. That good man, Prebendary Flanders, recommended the hotel as a place where I should find peace and privacy. So Olura booked a room for me and made sure I would be welcome. There was nothing official."

"But your political sympathizers in London knew you would both be here at this time?"

"Probably. Why?"

"Because unless this is some appalling accident, it must have been planned well beforehand."

"It was not planned in this form," said Mgwana, at last getting the politico-gangster half of his brain to work. "Whoever arranged that bathroom had to kill a man to do it. Nobody would take such a risk. It is not worth murder just to compromise Olura and me. There is only one explanation. The photographer may have been brought here to create a scandal; but he was killed for some reason that does not concern us. And then his body was used in this way."

That seemed to fit the facts, while avoiding a great many questions. I said that I wondered what would happen if we simply shoved him back through the window.

"You can't!" Olura cried, appalled by the brutality of my suggestion. "You can't!"

"It is most unlikely that a fall of one story could produce such a wound," Mgwana pointed out. "Even if the postmortem was not very thorough and took the fall for granted, I think the police would soon receive an anonymous letter."

"But who is to know he fell from here?"

We pulled him in and looked cautiously through the window. Any detective would spot at once where he fell from. The ladder up which he had climbed alive or been hoisted dead was still in position. Two of the bathroom lights were still on, showing that guests were awake or careless, but none of them could look out into the shaft. The base of the sliding bar of Olura's window had been unscrewed from the sash. That could easily be done from the outside, but not from the inside.

We stretched him out on the bathroom floor. He was a little fellow with a muddy, dark complexion which suggested — unless it was a result of the blow — that his profession seldom took him into the open air. Mgwana, now away from the stake and into his memories of sedition, recommended that we should put on gloves. We hadn't any, so did our clumsy best with two pairs of Olura's stockings. She was utterly overcome, and had gone back into the bedroom.

He had half a dozen press cards on him — some from highly respectable papers, to which, I am sure, he was not accredited. His passport gave his name as Alberto Livetti, born at Naples in 1935. Profession: Press Photographer. Mgwana, who knew his way around the scattered and unintelligible stamps of passports, said that he had entered Spain by Irún six days earlier. He took a few quick notes of Livetti's other movements.

Even without the camera slung from his neck there could be no doubt of Livetti's objective. Nobody in the hotel was News except Mgwana and Olura. A screwdriver and the screws he had removed from the window bar were in his pocket, together with a plain iron key which was probably that of the door at the bottom of the shaft.

"If you could be proved innocent in a week or two," I asked, "would the temporary scandal still damage you?"

"In my own country, not seriously. In London, I suppose it would be disastrous for us both."

I said that locally we might be able to avoid publicity,

that although I had no friends in high places I had a lot among the useful middle class. It was true. I could call on a fund of exaggerated good will in Vizcaya, for even my name was absurdly in my favor. With a slight change of stress, it means "wine" in Euzkadi and naturally encourages the ripening of friendship when casual acquaintances try to find out whether I possess the Basque's capacity for Rioja as well as his language. I felt sure that I could count on help in trouble and a blind eye — at police sergeant level — to any reasonable illegalities.

"You will find that steps have already been taken to prevent us keeping it quiet," said Mgwana gloomily.

It was my thinking of village, mountain and sea, and of the sturdy, classless inhabitants who had accepted me as one of themselves, which led me towards my lunatic proposal. I asked Mgwana if he thought it likely that anyone was watching what we did.

"From a distance, perhaps. But not here, close to. Think of the risk! Anyone on the spot, anyone acting suspiciously, is going to be questioned. When the hunter has set a trap, he goes away and leaves it. He doesn't stand by it."

"Could we move this across the balconies to my room?"

Mgwana picked up the puppet by its shoulders. I had the impression that he could have dangled it from one hand. He was a little shorter than I, but he had longer and far stronger arms.

"Easily," he said.

It would not be fair to imply that, writhing in the hunter's trap, he had forgotten his determination not to allow me to be involved. Defeat, I think, was such a challenge to this able and highly educated son of unprincipled chieftains that it was not in his nature to reject an ally. I am also sure that anxiety for Olura counted.

So away we went, with Mgwana's boom-like arms passing Livetti carefully and silently round the spikes of the balconies until we had him safely in my room. For the moment I put him in the wardrobe, locked it and pocketed the key.

"I wish the bar were still open," I said, as I drew the curtains and switched on the lights.

"I have a bottle of the best palm toddy in my room," he suggested, "forced upon me when leaving London by one of my constituents."

It seemed a welcome plan in more senses than one. His room was a floor up. It could be approached by the wide and imposing main staircase, or by a service staircase which started outside my room. If any confederate or hotel servant had been posted in the passage to keep an eye on Olura's door and ensure that she did not escape the vilification which was coming to her, he would not see us slipping up the back stairs.

As we returned with the bottle of African rotgut, down the main staircase and along the passage, we passed the open door of a pantry and a floor waiter sleepily packing together the debris of somebody's late supper. It seemed to me that he should have finished that job long ago. We said good night to him — thus creating a worthwhile complication, though hardly an alibi — and knocked at Olura's door. Since she was expecting us to come back through

the window, she was alarmed. Her response of *Who's
there?* sounded as high-pitched as that of a child in an
empty house. I hoped that it would pass, if heard by the
waiter or anyone else, as the reaction of maidenly modesty.

If that palm toddy was the best Africa produces, I am
appalled to think what the suffering masses consume; but
taken in a tumbler of water it relieved my dazed sensation
of dashing to and fro like an experimental rat in an emergency. Mgwana, too, it must have helped, for he sighed
and then showed his gladiator's teeth in a grin. I cannot
remember how much we actually talked about what must
be done. Little, I think. The next move was so obvious.

The back of the hotel was supported on concrete pillars,
and the space beneath acted as a garage for the guests'
cars. The door giving access to the shaft had to be there,
for it certainly was not in the resplendent and terraced
front. So long as we didn't make a noise, there should be
no great difficulty in getting our puppet into Olura's car
unseen.

We asked Olura to stay in her bathroom in case of need
and then went down the ladder. The key from Livetti's
pocket was indeed that of the door to the shaft. It was unlocked, so I locked it. Just as we were about to move the
ladder Mgwana whispered that we ought to replace the
screws in Olura's window frame. I agreed reluctantly,
for we would cut off our only way of retreat if someone
started hammering at the door; but I could not help admiring Mgwana's potentialities as a careful criminal and
thinking that it was just as well for the Governor-General

that he achieved his country's independence without having to use violence.

That done, the rest was an interminably long job. It was pitch-dark in the shaft, and we could not tell where the devil my room was. So back went the ladder to Olura's window. I tossed my key through the now discreet opening and asked her to go to my room and hang out a towel.

As soon as it appeared we followed the technique which we had learned, and unscrewed my window bar. A desperate task it was, too, for one of the screws had rusted in. Then I passed the lower half of the puppet to Mgwana, and somehow managed to support the upper half. We took such precautions to keep ourselves and our burden from scraping or falling that it seemed like five minutes before we had negotiated the mere fifteen feet to the bottom of the shaft.

After replacing the screws in my window and laying the ladder on the ground — God only knew where it ought to be — Mgwana opened the shaft door and reconnoitered the garage and the back of the hotel. He then helped me to curl Livetti up inside the boot of Olura's car. Having left the door unlocked, with the key in it, I drove away. Mgwana meant to stroll about the terrace for a bit in statesmanlike meditation and go in casually by the front entrance, without, if possible, disturbing the night porter.

I had originally intended — in mere visual imagination, quite unplanned — to drop Livetti into the dark water at the bottom of an abandoned iron mine; but we had taken so long to remove him from Olura's bathroom and the hotel that I had no hope of reaching the mine before

dawn. Some temporary solution would have to be found,
and his final disposal left till the following night. I had
little fear that we could now be involved in his disappear-
ance. What did trouble me, and especially Olura, was the
possibility of the body being found and of someone —
not, I mean, the real criminal — being accused of murder. Then the whole lot of us would have to confess, with
a poor chance of our innocence being believed.

Driving south along the deserted, winding country road,
heading inland for the mountains, I tried to make some
sense out of all the vague notes which my mind had registered when there was no time to think about them.

Since Mgwana and I had managed the operation in re-
verse, it was obvious how Livetti, alive or dead, had been
introduced into the shaft. The back of the hotel was a
fairly busy spot. Besides the open garage, there were the
washhouse, a staff lavatory, the garbage cans and an
empty bottle store. But to anyone who knew the excited
chaos of a Spanish hotel, invariably understaffed, at mealtimes, with every employee intently rushing on his or her
own business, a quick move from car to shaft door was
reasonably safe. So long as you kept clear of the kitchen,
the passages and the wine bins, you could run a funeral
parlor outside and nobody would have the time to notice
it.

At dinner, then. Say, between ten and eleven, taking an
average between early foreigners and late Spaniards. But
since Olura had taken a bath between eleven and twelve,
Livetti must have been pushed through the window after

that — indeed when she and Mgwana were actually in the bedroom.

There was no certainty, however, that they would be. I could understand Livetti's waiting up his ladder on the off chance that he would get his compromising photograph; but to kill him and stage the revolting scene when it might be useless was crazy.

Very well, then. The decision to kill Livetti could only have been taken after the murderer was sure that Olura and Mgwana were in the room. That fitted, for nobody would hang around with a corpse longer than he had to. So Livetti had entered the shaft alive, accompanied by his employer or confederate, and Mgwana's confident opinion that the murder had nothing to do with the business in hand was untenable.

He seemed very sure, that unknown companion of Livetti's, that Mgwana would not leave Olura's room until he or she had visited the bathroom. Well, if their relations were as intimate as Vigny believed, he could count on that. This bit of rumination nearly sent me over the edge on a hairpin bend. It was a shock, for I had liked Vigny. Even the most casual acquaintances have no right to be murderers. Yet Vigny could well be the unknown companion, or, if he wasn't, he knew who was. Who but Vigny had been so slanderously certain of Olura's tastes? The rest of the hotel, guests and staff — and I had talked to most of them — had shown curiosity about her without any recognition of her past and identity.

But that evidence which was convincing to me was not

really evidence at all; at the most it might make a very
intelligent policeman think. In any case I had no interest
in bringing Vigny and des Aunes to justice for killing an
unsavory press photographer, if they did. All I wanted
was to get rid of him.

For that uncharitable thought I was promptly punished.
Olura's car stopped. I discovered that she had finished
her long run of the afternoon on the reserve tank and in
all the excitement had never thought of telling me. I had
nearly reached Amorebieta on the main road from San
Sebastián to Bilbao. Once across it and on the edge of the
high sierras, I had every hope of finding a temporary hiding place for Livetti and of returning to the hotel garage
before anyone was up to see me come in. As it was, I was
stuck on a fine stretch of open road. The headlights
showed bare agricultural land ahead of me. So far as my
memory of the road in daylight went, it ran through one
of the few parts of Vizcaya without a tree or a rock.

A couple of miles back I had passed a Pair of the
Civil Guard and noticed — to my horror — that they
were of two minds whether to stop me or not. They must
have remembered in time that it was government policy
to treat holiday-makers and their cars with the utmost
respect and that it was no business of theirs what I was
doing on a minor road at 4 A.M. But I knew very well that
when they caught me up and offered their assistance
they might look at the car's papers and mine, ask me if I
had permission to drive it and very politely take the opportunity to look in the boot to assure themselves that it
contained only a tourist's baggage.

Up to then I had been pleasantly surprised to see myself a man capable of cool, competent action. That delusion, I have observed, is regrettably common among the young. I felt uneasily that philologists in their early but responsible thirties might not be free of it either. That sinister Pair in gray-green cloaks was steadily tramping towards me through the night; and they were sure not to be Basques — for it is the policy to station a civil guard far away from his home — with whom I could talk myself out of almost anything.

Behind the bank which bordered the road I found a field of maize. It would have to do. I hauled Livetti out of the boot. He was beginning to set in his fetus position, and it was difficult to drag him through the first few rows of tall stalks without knocking them down. Worse still, the farmer had been growing runner beans between the rows, using the stalks as supports. I left a track which the powerful flashlights of the Civil Guard could easily pick up. Myself, I hadn't a torch at all; or, if I had, I couldn't guess where Olura chose to keep it.

Panic was complete until some part of my brain which wasn't busy putting the blame on Olura began to work. There was just enough slope for the car to run backwards. I turned off the lights, heaved and jumped in. We trickled down the slight gradient for a hundred yards and scored up another fifty on the flat. The Pair could now examine the verges of the road as much as they pleased.

They did — on the off chance that I had ditched something. They also requested me to open the boot. I saw that in my hurry I had left Livetti's camera there, but that did not matter; it could well have been mine. They had the remote and severe air of the Guardia, which is partly responsible for its unpopularity, but were most helpful. Yes, there was a filling station on the main road which would open soon after dawn or earlier if there were a lot of holiday traffic on the road. They would see that someone drove out with a can of petrol.

I gave the Pair ten minutes and then walked after them. Already there were pinpoints of light in the upper windows of the farms. At first I could not find Livetti. That seems incredible, but I had done a thorough job of hiding him. Add to that holes left by a blasted cow which had been barging at some time into the beans, the impatience due to abject terror and the fact that my landmarks were no longer blocks of black but definite shapes of dark gray.

At last I got him. He would not fit on my back in his acquired form and was too heavy for me to carry in my arms like a baby. Partly I dragged him and partly I hugged him. When he was safely back in the boot, I felt faint and sick. His cold cheek had touched mine too often.

Waiting in the growing light for petrol, I had time to think out my next move more responsibly. The wild immensities of Vizcaya, with its abrupt and forested mountains and its rivers racing through shallow gorges, presented to the eye a perfect landscape for the getting rid of unwanted burdens. But I knew the life of the countryside too well to take that gamble in daylight. The roads follow the valleys; and the valleys, though often appearing empty, are well populated. You cannot see the forester, or the farmer walking ahead of his draft oxen down the deep-cut lanes, but from his higher ground he can see you.

Away from the roads and on the bare green tops of the huge hills, bogs and falls of rock offered plenty of discreet possibilities — but all useless since there was no way of packing Livetti on a donkey. Then there was the sea. Beaches and the busy corniche roads were ruled out; but there ought to be places, though I didn't know one, where a car could be driven close enough to the merciless brown cliffs between Arminza and Lequeitio. That was the easy solution, and I suspected even then that it might have to be taken. I did not like the sea; it held no finality. It could heave him anywhere, but it could not unfortunately put any water into his lungs. No, my deserted iron mine was by far the best, and till nightfall the safest hiding place for Livetti was the locked boot of the car.

It was nearly five when Amorebieta's only taxi came out to my rescue with petrol. I knew its proprietor well. He was a gnarled Vizcayan called Echeverría, whose face looked as if it had been cut out of teak by a do-it-yourself sculptor with a heavy hand and an odd sense of humor. He had driven me from the station to the Hostal de las Olas when I first arrived, and had lectured me — as one honest Basque to another — on the folly of dressing up like foreigners on holiday and wasting money on flunkies and sons of bitches when there were half a dozen decent taverns where I would be taken in and treated as a brother. Like many of these plain and sturdy charmers, he flattered himself that he had far too much common sense to

be fooled by anybody. When he found that he had been,
he enjoyed the joke so thoroughly that his affection was
won.

He read me another lecture now: on my carelessness
in running out of petrol, which was the sort of misman-
agement to be expected of Castilians, but not of Basques
and Englishmen. I explained that I had come from San
Sebastián, taken a roundabout route after a considerable
evening out and lost my way. That amused him. He
wanted to know what I had been eating and drinking and
whether there were any girls; so I invented for him a
surpassing local menu and a nightclub singer. He had a
protective attitude towards me, like that of an indulgent
father whose son had risen out of the working class and
could always be trusted to produce eccentric entertainment.

After paying Echeverría the fare he would have
charged his next-door neighbor, I drove straight back to
the garage under the hotel. So far as I could tell, my arrival was unobserved. Cautiously I tried the kitchen door.
It was open, and the service stairs took me up to my room.
The key, I then remembered, was with Olura. I did not
want to alarm her or perhaps waken her from an exhausted doze by tapping at her door, so I called on
Mgwana. He took a bit of rousing. He had the politician's
trick of snatching some sleep in spite of anxiety.

He was a remarkable presence in scarlet-and-gold pajamas and a clashing dressing gown of imperial purple. I
suppose that when at last he could shut his door against
the world he pleased himself by a return to tropical mag-

nificence. When I told him that I had come back with Livetti he was relieved. He said that he never ought to have allowed me to drive away, that we had been far too impulsive and that he had been worrying over the intolerable risk. He mentioned the awkward inquisitiveness of dogs. I had thought of that, too, but probably not so anxiously as someone accustomed to the habits of vultures and hyenas.

On the other hand he was far more shocked than I by Livetti in an open garage. What about the risk of some sneak thief breaking into the boot? He wanted to go down at once and keep watch on the car. I wouldn't have it, assuring him of my very real faith in the honesty of the local population. So far as the hotel was concerned, we had slept the night away, innocent and undisturbed. It seemed a pity to spoil so clean a sheet by sitting in the car without any imaginable excuse and arousing curiosity. Luck had been with us even when he came in from the garage; he had found the night porter asleep and had tiptoed past him.

There's nothing like the prospect of standing together in the dock for breaking down the inhibitions of black and white. We could not possibly sleep, so we talked; or rather he did. And it was the best kind of talk — not the flowery tripe which he handed out at public meetings and the United Nations, but getting down to the real day-to-day working troubles of bringing a nation of primitive agriculturalists out of the Iron Age into the twentieth century. In his own country he had little use for the rights of the individual, but he was forced to pretend for the sake of opinion abroad that he had. The rights of the individual were prized by just those people who kept alive the evil conscience of the West, and that evil conscience was of enormous value to him. No, he didn't think it was unjust.

I delicately brought up the question of Olura and her gang, and found a most forgivable inconsistency. Though no one knew better than he that well-meaning enthusiasts must not be allowed to interfere with government, he worshiped Olura and all that she stood for. He was full of gratitude and overestimated her importance because he loved her dearly. Not passionately. Not quite as a father. More as a favorite nephew, extraordinary though that may seem. At least I remember feeling something of the sort for a young aunt of mine. She was all-powerful. She was beautiful. And, though I used to dream of rescuing her from untold dangers, there was not a trace of conscious sexuality.

"Chivalry, yes," he said to me. "I don't know if you grant us that. We have it, but in a rather different form: reverence for the woman who can serve and command. It's not unlike the knight's worship of a queen — if that ever existed outside literature — but religion, superstition, whatever you like to call it, comes in."

Well, so it did in the twelfth century. The Cathars. The troubadors. And read any fairy story with the eye of an anthropologist!

Then he was encouraged by our intimacy of common disquiet to reveal a bit more of himself. He wanted to know whether I, as a fairly broad-minded European, really felt superior to the African.

"Of course I do," I replied frankly, "but in fifty years' time my children will not."

No, he explained, he didn't mean the obvious, present-day differences of culture and education; he meant physical repugnance which he admitted was widespread. But was it deep-rooted or just the normal human prejudice against anything unfamiliar?

"Do we in fact, to you a neutral and intellectual, bear an insulting resemblance to apes?"

I said that to judge from what I had read the white man of some discrimination had always been impressed by the physical splendor of some tribes and the animality of others. Speaking for myself, knowing little of Africans, I could well find repugnant the face of some jazz musician empty of everything but coarseness and false good humor, while feeling humble before that of a sensitive, brave and kindly fisherman.

"There is a type of businessman around the Baltic," I told him, "which bears an insulting resemblance to a pink pig. But what matters to me is the spiritual quality of a human face. It appalls me to think that some people, black or white, might have an immortal soul, and it saddens me that others might not have."

I could see that I had shocked him. In a sense he was a hypocrite. In all but name he was a dictator. But he was an earnest Christian of missionary simplicity. Peculiar in a black Napoleon, yet reassuring! I had no doubt that

Leopold Mgwana was of vital importance to the future. I felt for the first time that I cared very much for his reputation, quite apart from Olura's.

At half past eight we called on her. She was in pieces and defenseless after so agitated a night. There was a tired-little-girl quality about her which I found adorable. I gave her a short account of what had happened and asked her to drive the car — since she would attract less attention than I who had never been seen in it — round to the side of the hotel terrace, where one of us could always keep it under observation from the balconies.

She cried out that it was horrible, that it would be better if we all confessed and that she couldn't bear it. Her lack of courage disappointed me. It may be that I had treated with too obvious heartiness the question of the empty petrol tank. The trouble with Olura was that one had to fall over backwards to avoid making her feel guilty, since she was dead certain to be feeling guilty already, usually without reason.

I said at once that of course I would take the car out of the garage and that it didn't matter. She gave me a look of extreme dislike, including the silent Mgwana in it, and instantly went out to drive it round herself.

Mgwana posted himself on his balcony and took the first watch. Meanwhile I tried to get some sleep and probably got some. When I went down for lunch I stopped at the bar and was boldly accosted by a new guest whose trim buttocks suggested that her skirt was designed deliberately for an interminable succession of bar stools.

Her face was over-repaired, but intelligent. I might even

have granted her an immortal soul, which goes to show what nonsense one can talk when there are no facts on which to base opinion. She had an entertaining line of patter which would have appeared very sophisticated if she had not assumed that because we were both English we were confederates against the world. I found myself compelled to offer her a drink — since I needed another myself — and she then decided, sliding off the bar stool and revealing for my benefit a jellied leg very well molded, that we should take our glasses to a table.

"Tell me," she asked, "has anything been happening here?"

"Nothing more than some filthy weather. I hope it clears up for you."

"I don't think I shall stay more than a night," she said.

I replied politely that it was a pity, and where was she going on to?

"Back to Madrid. I live there. I'm the correspondent of two of our Sunday papers."

"Have you come up to see Leopold Mgwana?"

"I might as well, now that I'm here. I'll ask him what he thinks of Spanish women or something, though as a matter of fact —" she gave me an elegantly smutty glance "— I expect he's fully occupied."

I was just about to deal with her as she deserved and leave her to pick up the pieces when I remembered what the experienced Mgwana had said: that "they" would see we couldn't keep it out of the news.

"You mean Miss Manoli?" I replied. "Of course one has to be broad-minded about these things, but . . ."

"Do they seem a happy couple?"

"I don't know. I never noticed."

"Isn't that like a man!" she exclaimed gaily.

She asked how long I was staying, and when I said that I would be at the Hostal de las Olas another week she gave me her card and invited me to telephone her if I saw or was told anything out of the ordinary.

"But what sort of out of the ordinary?"

"I don't know," she said. "Anything to do with La Manoli can be News. I had a hot tip that I should drive up here at once if I wanted a scoop. It sounded like a society scandal."

"How do you clever girls get your information?" I asked. "I mean, anybody could telephone and send you off on a wild-goose chase."

"They do, but not twice. This was just an anonymous telephone call to tell me that Mgwana was here with some society girl. I checked the information with a source in security police, and couldn't make him say yes or no. But I had a hunch, and here I am."

"Why the police?"

"Well, Mgwana is an important person. I supposed that if he were really here, he would have a guard."

She certainly knew her way around. A secret police source would be most useful. And no doubt her source occasionally got his reward. He could always have a bath afterwards.

The implications of what she had just told me needed sorting out. If anyone at all were keeping an eye on the security of Mgwana he was pretty inefficient. Whatever little book of rules he had would surely include the checking of bathroom windows. And wouldn't he make himself known to Mgwana?

I was prepared to bet that the police had not yet taken any action. Mgwana's visit was unofficial. His inexperienced embassy in London might never have thought of dropping a note to the Spanish Embassy. As for Olura, who had arranged the holiday, it was not in her character to communicate with an undemocratic government to request the discreet services of its brutal secret agents. So it was possible that Madrid had known nothing of Mgwana's arrival until a leisurely report was received from Frontier Control.

Another hypothesis was tenable: that a security guard had arrived soon after Mgwana, and that he had connived at last night's atrocity. I ruled that out. The secret police might be a sinister lot when dealing with Basque or Asturian miners, but I knew them to be conscientious and hard-working from the point of view of the State. No agent would allow himself to be suborned by a pair of dubious foreigners, especially since he would have to explain how a murder took place under his nose.

"Have you found out if the police have a man up here?" I asked.

She had not. But she did have, she said, a contact in the hotel, a man called Araña. The name had been given to her by her anonymous informant. I offered to help her to find Araña and to act as an interpreter in case she did not speak Spanish.

"I do," she claimed.

It was a fair conjecture that Araña would turn out to be the floor waiter who had been packing up that late supper, well posted to listen for sounds of alarm from Olura's room. I took my little Sunday pornographer upstairs, and found the man in the pantry on Mgwana's floor — which was surprising since there was never any room service during lunch. I had not looked at him closely during the night. Now that I did, I doubted if he was the type to take a bribe for anything plainly dishonorable. There were half a dozen young waiters sliding smoothly about the terrace with drinks, any one of whom would be a far more likely choice. This fellow was unshaven and looked as if he hadn't washed or slept, but he was middle-aged, fatherly and reliable.

I turned her loose on him, and never in my life heard worse Spanish. She used a torrent of verbs in the infinitive and assumed a French accent — on the grounds, I suppose, that it ought to be more intelligible than an English one. But I must admit that this hideous jargon, when accompanied by a too understanding smile and a general air of comely flesh all a-twitter, did get results.

Even at his age he could not resist the synthetic charm which was squirted at him and did his best to understand her as she driveled away about the excellence of Spanish hotels and how poorly paid the staff was. But when she asked him outright if anything of interest to a newspaper had happened to the English señorita during the night, he looked at me for permission to talk.

"We have no secrets from the lady," I said.

"Nothing happened," he told her, "nothing at all except

that this gentleman and the black Excellency came downstairs together and called on the lady about two o'clock with a bottle."

I grinned at my dainty journalist. She shut the half-open bag which had been a hint that hundred-peseta notes were to be found in it, and looked at me with a set face in which was puzzlement as well as irritation. She got out of there as fast as dignity and her skirt allowed. She may have thought that I was Mgwana's shadow and bodyguard.

"By the way, friend," I asked when she had gone, "what's your name?"

"José Arizmendi."

I switched at once to Euzkadi.

"Who told you to hang about in the passage, Arizmendi?"

"The manager."

"And what the devil does *he* want to know?"

"He told me that it was on orders from Madrid. Somebody has to look after your black man until a trained guard arrives."

I said that I was very glad to hear it, which I wasn't. I could have extracted some useful information if the waiter had been employed or bribed by Vigny.

"And the sooner he comes, the better," said Arizmendi. "By God, Ardower, I tell you I'm not cut out for the police!"

There are no "sirs" in Euzkadi. We democratically use the surname, whatever the difference of status.

"One can see that," I assured him.

"Thank you. All the same, there are plenty of good fel-

lows among them up here. I had a second cousin who was
a sergeant in Vitoria. But what I was going to say to you is
that my job would be easier if you and the Minister would
tell me his intentions. Look! It's not decent to stand outside a guest's room, so I stay in the pantry. Last night I
was on the floor below, for I knew this African uncle was
in the lady's bedroom."

He stated the fact without even an innuendo in his eye,
for which I gave him full marks — though I suspect that
his unconcern was due to the fact that he took the immorality of politicians for granted.

"But then you and he come downstairs at two in the
morning," he went on, "so he wasn't there at all. Good!
Now you are all three in the lady's room, and a little later
she comes out with your key to get something from your
room. So you are still there, and at breakfast time I am
still on duty in the pantry. And again you two come down
from upstairs. It's like a farce in the theater!"

I said that we had moved very quietly so as not to wake
up other guests, and he admitted very readily that he
might have been dozing. I am sure that movement along
the balconies never occurred to him; there was no conceivable reason for it.

I promised that in future the Prime Minister would
make the job of his amateur security guard as easy as possible, and then I asked him if he knew anyone in the hotel
called Araña.

"Yes, the outside man," he replied. "He does the odd
jobs and the garden. An Andalusian with all their gypsy
tricks. He cuts little bunches of flowers and presents them

to the old ladies. You should see him mimic them afterwards. He's always good for a laugh and free with the drinks."

Well, there was the man who had almost certainly provided Livetti with a ladder. No wonder he had been recommended as a rich source for any newshawk trying to fill in the details of a juicy scandal.

All this had taken the best part of an hour. I joined Mgwana on his balcony and told him what I had discovered.

"I asked our people to let the Spanish Embassy know where I was going and when I should arrive," he said. "But they are too busy learning how to use fish knives and leave the proper cards. I can't blame them. Conventions aren't as useless as they seem. Just a year ago the Ambassador was a schoolteacher and the First Secretary a bank clerk."

God, how the man must have needed that week of rest which Olura had arranged for him!

She came up from lunch and asked why I had not been there. I explained that I had been busy pumping a female Livetti.

"Yes, I saw her in the restaurant and spoke to her," she said. "She's Mary Deighton-Flagg and was at school with me. She wasn't a bad feature writer, but if she goes back to London she faces an action for slander. It isn't her fault that the Law is four hundred years out of date."

I replied emphatically that the conversation of Miss Deighton-Flagg made me thank heaven for Her Majesty's judges.

"So far as I can see," I added, "your Mary thinks that

any woman of character and originality has to be a nymphomaniac."

"Meaning me? But I don't care what she thinks, Philip, and I'm sorry for her."

"I hope you weren't sorry enough to give her a story," I said, and refrained from pointing out that I admired her charity more than her taste.

Only twenty-four hours earlier I had been looking forward to a promising holiday from erudition, islanded in luxury with the lovely eccentricities of Olura and the exotic intelligence of her black man. But now, hard behind that curled-up puppet in the boot, came so much more humanity with alien purposes: the Deighton-Flagg woman, a specialist in poking round the bend of lavatories on the pretense of cleaning them; the puzzled Arizmendi; the unknown Araña; and now at last the security guard who might have been some use the night before but could be only an embarrassment in our present emergency.

That was my first meeting with Lieutenant Pedro Gonzalez. He had come from Zarauz, where he had been keeping his polite eye on the children of some German prince whose matrimonial adventures with one millionairess and two fashionably deformed movie stars had left some doubt in the eyes of the Law whose bloody baby was whose and why. He spoke perfect French, which wasn't much good to Mgwana, who had only English, so I was called in to translate.

I liked Gonzalez at once. He was thin, wiry, and had a mobile face which he kept under control — sometimes with an effort. He wore a bow tie and a black summer suit, and could have passed as any bachelor enjoying a respectable holiday. Except for a twinkle in his eye and a bulge on his hip — so discreet that it would have been unnoticeable if not for the exactitude of Spanish tailoring — he might have been a clerk at a consulate or the serious, young under-manager of a first-class hotel.

He wanted very little from Mgwana: merely that he should keep in sight when not in his room, and should allow himself to be accompanied when traveling by car. He had no reason to suppose that His Excellency's holiday would be disturbed, but we must understand that Spain was a welcoming nation and could not avoid receiving people who might abuse such hospitality. He believed — with a bow to Olura and me — that we, too, with our great tradition of offering political asylum, found it had occasional disadvantages. I got the impression that Gonzalez's chiefs had given him more precise information than he was giving to us, but all policemen like to surround themselves with an aura of mysterious importance.

Olura treated him distantly, seeing in him a member of Franco's secret police with a habit of torturing honest workingmen on his day off. But he was nothing more than a citizen of excellent education who conceived it his pleasure and duty to keep the peace. He would have served monarchy or republic as loyally as the government of the Caudillo.

The evening passed without incident, one of us continually keeping an eye on the car. I was determined to dispose of Livetti alone. I could easily have been persuaded to take Mgwana along, but that was now impossible. As for

Olura, I knew that her sensibilities would be outraged. However much I needed her company and such physical help as she could give, I felt that she would never want to see me again afterwards.

Yet she insisted, and nothing could shake her. She must have balanced her duty to the living individual against her guilt at desecrating the dead, and decided in my favor.

At half past seven I went to her room. It was pouring rain again, and I wanted to start early in case we were held up by mud or flooding when we left the main roads. She was ready, and wearing the Red Riding Hood cloak. I exclaimed impulsively that it wouldn't do.

She smiled and asked why not. I wondered myself why I had blurted out anything so silly, and then saw the answer. Because it was the essence of our first meeting. Because it should not be associated with this cold-blooded crime which, the night before, had seemed merely a desperate solution and now grew with every moment to be more disgusting, more immoral and more inevitable.

"No, I'm wrong," I said. "The cloak will be quite black at night and hides you. But please promise to stay in the car when we come to the point."

"I won't promise anything, Philip. Last night I came to you only for advice. But you didn't give it and go back to bed."

"It didn't seem an occasion for only advice."

"That's what I feel now."

We hesitated over the irrevocable step of leaving the room and going down to the car, not talking very much but at ease with each other.

"He has a home," she said.

"I suppose so. But anyway he is never going to return to it."

"I hate this!"

"So do I. But don't you believe Mgwana is worth it?"

She looked at me gratefully. Keeping Olura happy sometimes reminded me of arguing with a professor of ethics about the ultimate good.

She had just lifted the hood over that dark gold hair when Mgwana came in. His expression made us both sure that Livetti had been discovered.

"You mustn't go," he said. "Not yet! Will you watch the car from the window while I tell you what has happened?"

It was not, after all, the worst; nor was it wholly alarm which had given his face a patina of purple-gray. That dull darkness was a cloud of anger and humiliation.

He had just received a telephone call, he told us, in his native language. A white man had been speaking — not at all fluently except for his command of insult in vocabulary and inflection.

The voice, sure that it could not be monitored and understood, had challenged him with what he was concealing and where it was. Mgwana naturally assumed that our movements had been observed. In fact, as I now know, they had not. The accusation was an intelligent guess. After all, we could not possibly have hidden Livetti in the hotel to be discovered at any moment by the host of eager chambermaids.

"You will leave the hotel, boy," the voice ordered, "taking the body with you and driven by your . . ."

Mgwana, translating for us, was hoarse with sup-
pressed fury. The unknown speaker must have referred to
Olura by some barbarously disgusting term for a whore,
even coarser than ours.

". . . driven by Miss Manoli," Mgwana went on. "You
will leave the hotel at 9 P.M. precisely, and we shall assist
you both to dispose of the body. If you do not obey, the
police will be informed and advised to open the boot."

"But how did the caller know you still had it?" I asked.

"I think now that he didn't know," Mgwana replied,
"and that he was fishing to find out. But I was so surprised
and outraged that I gave it away."

"Then there was no mention of me and last night?"

"No. I'm sure they do not realize that you come into it at
all," he said.

Olura tried to be masculine and calm. She pointed out
that the man behind the voice was a murderer and trying
to force us to help him. He was in serious danger, whereas
we had only questions to answer and a scandal to face.

Mgwana considered that in a long silence and shook his
head.

"There was some proof that I did not kill Livetti so long
as his body remained in the window," he said. "There is no
proof at all now. The motive is just as weak or as strong as
it was before, but the evidence of guilt has become over-
whelming. I think I must obey."

Looking back in cold blood, I believe that Mgwana
ought to have confided in Gonzalez, and immediately
opened up a line direct to the Minister of Justice and the
Head of State. In that way it might have been possible to

keep the whole affair secret during investigation. But he
was new to the ways of the West. How far would his word
be trusted? Wasn't it likely that color could count against
him? Even if it didn't, would they remember his early
tribal youth, and forget Balliol, the London School of Eco-
nomics and his influence at the United Nations? He was
not yet sure enough that the diplomatic old-boy network
applied to him.

Olura was too lost in all this naked brutality to remind
Mgwana that civilization continued to exist outside it. I
myself, who should have known better, accepted the situation as it was, and put my faith in a trained mind accustomed to distinguish clearly between conflicting hypothe-
ses. In fact I considered all this criminal impertinence as
a challenge.

"I suggest that you and Olura obey the instructions," I
said. "But they will find when they follow the car that
there are two unexpected men in it — myself and Gonzalez. That will save us from any annoyance."

What I meant by annoyance — and it was not lost on
Mgwana — was any attempt to assassinate more than his
reputation. Who was involved besides the highly probable
Vigny I could not know; but it was abundantly clear that
they did not like Mgwana and did not stick at murder. If
they were so obliging as to dig a secret grave for Livetti,
they could easily make it large enough for two.

Olura again protested that I ought not to get involved
with two people who might be arrested at any moment.
And what was the use of our all taking an evening run in
the car and returning with Livetti?

I explained my plan to them. It was unlikely that our followers would dare to stop us; but they might very well carry out their threat of tipping off the police. If they did, our Lieutenant Gonzalez would show his pass and deal with any wretched cop who wanted to search His Excellency's car. When we reached Amorebieta we would all stop and order dinner. There was a café, I said — just to give them confidence in the objectivity of all this — where the wine was excellent, but I could not answer for the food.

Gonzalez, Mgwana and Olura were to remain at our table and take a taxi back to the hotel. Meanwhile I would try to get clear away with the car. I assured them that I knew the roads, the language, the people and a taxi driver and that if we all kept our heads and grabbed any opportunity which Amorebieta offered, it could be done. Gonzalez, whose sole duty was to guard Mgwana, had no interest in my movements.

Olura's expression was untranslatable. She looked as if she opposed my scheme but had nothing better to offer. Mgwana retired into that impressive air of martyrdom which really meant, as I now realized, that he was waiting motionless in the jungle with ears spread until he saw which way to charge. At least he had given me a quick smile at the mention of Gonzalez, which showed that he appreciated the main point.

At nine we collected our tame secret policeman and played the capricious foreigners on holiday who couldn't stand any more of the hotel in the rain and were going out for a drive. I sat alongside Olura. Gonzalez and Mgwana were in the back. It had been a muggy day, and it seemed to my guilty conscience that the boot was not quite airtight.

No car followed us. It was unnecessary. For the first few miles there was only one road we could take. Then after we had passed the first crossroads and were swinging up the hairpin bends of the coastal hills I looked down on the headlights of a car keeping half a mile behind us. While we were on the flat in the wide valley which seemed so empty at night and so full of scattered red-roofed farms during the day, the car accelerated and passed us. For a second it forced us to slow down and almost instantaneously increased its distance. Undoubtedly the intention had been to stop us and give us our orders; but the sight of three men with Olura instead of one imposed caution. The car was a big black Seat with a Spanish number. Two people whose faces I could not see were in it.

In Amorebieta we parked openly outside the café. Here we had the choice of three roads — to San Sebastián, Vitoria, or Bilbao — so that anyone who proposed to follow us had to stay pretty close. I deliberately ordered a meal which would take time to prepare and then left the other three at the table on the excuse of going out to see if the local *estanco* had any good Havanas. I found the black Seat almost at once.

While we were settling down at our table, it had been parked in the darkness of a narrow lane which ran along the side of the café — an effective choice for jumping out hard on our tail wherever we went. I could not see if anyone was actually seated in the car, for I had no wish to

show too open an interest, and still less to explore the
shadows and doorways far down the lane. It looked as if
boldness had paid off and the Lord, without any complicated miracles, had delivered the two into my hands — or
rather Echeverría's, if he was in.

He was. He greeted me as an old friend and suggested a
game of billiards with the local worthies. He wanted to
put his Basque-speaking Englishman on exhibition. I explained regretfully that I hadn't even time for a cup, that
my adventures of the previous night had ended in astonishing success and that I now had the cabaret singer
under my wing. Unfortunately we were being followed
closely by her . . . I nearly said husband, but remembered in time the extreme respectability of the middle-
class Basque. So I made it impresario, leaving him with a
gallant impression that Olura's beauty and talent were being exploited by dirty foreigners in San Sebastián.

Would he, I asked, come to the café in half an hour in
order to drive her, together with a black gentleman and a
plainclothes cop, to the Hostal de las Olas? I was about to
romanticize my colored friend when he interrupted me to
ask if it was not Mr. Mgwana. He not only knew from the
local grapevine that Mgwana was staying at the Hostal,
but quite a lot about his career. Like so many Basques, he
was surprisingly well informed through the small, sound
provincial papers.

I had not time to fit Mgwana into the story. If I had
foreseen Echevarría's knowledge, I could have told him
something closer to the truth. But it didn't matter. When I

went on to ask him to park in the lane and break down there, he was eager to help.

The excuse had to be better than a puncture, for two men were likely to start pushing him out of the lane the moment he looked like settling down there. Wheel? Clutch? No, he shouted jovially, no, he could do better than that. It was the lousy garage, run by an incompetent bunch of coons from Barcelona. He told me at length what he thought of them; they had wrecked his hand brake. He had given up taking it to them. He had discovered that a hearty sideways kick at the base of the lever invariably released it when jammed. It would, he thought, do excellently for our purpose. The more excited helpers tried to pull the lever out of the floor boards, the worse it would stick.

All this took a long time. I had to control my impatience and keep on assuring myself that Lieutenant Gonzalez, with all the police of Amorebieta at his disposal, could deal with any unexpected emergency. When at last I returned to the café, Olura was picking at the first course and looking a little set and pale. I could see no reason for it. Her car was in full view, and none of the crowd of customers in the café was paying any attention to us. There was an obvious foreigner leaning on the bar who had not been there when I left — a powerful chap with a large, round face wrinkled and tanned by sun, and a colorless mop of hair on top of it. He was very noticeable, for that type of parched complexion usually goes with thin features.

After we had chatted a while in English and cautiously indicated to Mgwana that I might leave at any moment, Olura and I switched to French, which she spoke very fluently, in order to bring Gonzalez into the conversation. I told him that the Minister and Mlle. Manoli were feeling tired and would return to the hotel after dinner; they would take a taxi as they had promised to lend me the car. This weak story was made even weaker by Olura instantly denying that she was tired and announcing that she would go with me. There was nothing that I could do about it.

Echeverría passed the window and reversed into the lane. I saw the man of the open spaces quickly pay for his drink and go out. He had at once spotted the possible traffic problem, though I doubt if he realized that it was deliberately planned.

There was no time to bother about what an experienced policeman would make of our erratic movements. I got up, leaving Mgwana to pay for the meal, patted Gonzalez cheerfully on the shoulder and bolted. A glance down the lane showed me that Echeverría was playing the obstinate and angry taxi driver to perfection. I recognized Vigny by his uninhibited gestures. Echeverría was on the pavement, solidly detaching himself from his hand brake. He was probably telling the two that they could try to take it off if they liked, but that he would hold them legally responsible for any damage. He had little facility for expressing himself with his hands and an almost English contempt for so volatile a practice.

Olura was already in the driving seat. I told her to make for Bilbao. It was the road which our followers would probably choose as soon as they forced a way past the taxi, but on so good a surface we could reach the western suburbs and be lost beyond finding before they had a chance of overtaking us.

"Why did you take so long?" she asked.

"There was a lot to arrange."

"You might have warned me."

"I couldn't."

She replied coldly that Gonzalez must have known we were up to something, that she liked to drive her car herself and that she would not be treated as a sort of helpless Andromeda.

"You'd look very well in the part."

"Does it ever stop raining in this damned Basque country of yours?"

A thoroughly bad-tempered remark, but I picked up the association. A cold and wet Andromeda. And Perseus tactless enough to want to kiss the drops off? However, it was hardly the moment to develop red-hot fantasies of the male imagination, even if they had rather more charm than usual.

"If you want to take risks, it's O.K. with me," I said, as she got herself boxed in behind a truckload of gravel.

"With that in the boot?"

But she passed the lorry on a blind bend with her horn screaming in the best Spanish manner. I did not have to ask her to do it again, for we could now swing left up the

valley of the Nervión towards Valmaseda. Of all the turn-
ings we could have taken it was a hundred to one against
the black Seat choosing that one.

I must now give you some local color if you are not to
suppose that my plan was crazy and unworkable. Iron, I
imagine, begins to interest you only after it has reached
the smelter or the blast furnace. Here it is part of our life
and landscape. Between the limestone of the Cantabrian
Mountains and the sea, where the colors of Vizcaya
change from misty greens and white to emerald and ma-
roon, the ore can be quarried almost anywhere. The only
problem is to transport it to the market at an economic
price in spite of the steep, broken country of the coastal
range.

In the busy industrial valley of the Nervión the ore
comes down by aerial cableways, much like ski-lifts, to the
foundries and the quays. To the east, as far as the boun-
dary between Vizcaya and Santander, any little estuary
with deep water or any promontory beneath which a
coaster can ride at anchor in calm weather serves as the
terminal of a cableway. A chute is built out from the cliffs,
themselves of iron, and the ore goes roaring into the hold
forty or fifty feet below. Why it does not go slap through
the bottom of the ship I have never understood.

The quarries carve away the hills, leaving a skyline of
fantastic mounds and pinnacles above the distorted quadrilateral of a ravine, which, as the cut deepens, may become a massive shaft with a squared entrance big enough
to hold a house. When the workings are abandoned because of landslide or flood, these ravines, their brown

sides melancholy with sparse scrub and weeds, their floors an untidy maze of puddles, tips and rusty trolley lines, suggest a Wellsian picture of vanished civilization whose last survivors took refuge in the dark tunnel, grand and sinister as the main gate to the pit of hell.

It was in one of these deserted galleries, which always held a black pool of stagnant water at the end of the cut, that I proposed to sink our puppet. I knew it well, for there were pre-Roman workings in the hillside above the shaft. That had been the limit of my interest. I did not know if there was any night watchman — it seemed unlikely — or how near one could approach the quarry by car without arousing curiosity in the scattered miners' cottages.

Now free of all pursuit, Olura and I drove at leisure up and down hill as country roads led us from one little valley to another. There, among the roots of the mountains, where foreign tourists might well lose their way but could hardly be engaged in any illegalities, we were safe from inquisitive policemen. I won't say that we felt it. Each lonely figure we passed was a potential danger.

We crossed the main Santander road outside Somorrostro, and headed down to the coast through the driving spatter of a Biscay squall, which, while it lasts, is aggressive as a slap on the face. When we came to the iron company's road, leading to the old workings and the active quarry, known as the Garay Cut, alongside them, I asked Olura to stop on a hard-rolled patch of gravel under the oaks while I explored on foot. I assured her — since she seemed touchy on the point — that I should not be more than half an hour.

It was soon obvious that the car could not safely go any farther. A little way down the road on the right was a row of three or four cottages. Lights were out, but that was no guarantee that everyone was sleeping soundly. Two hundred yards on was the entrance to the Garay Cut. There was a light in the gatehouse and some activity around the crushing plant, where coke was being shifted from a dump to the boilers.

The track which had once led down into the ravine of the old workings left the road well short of the gatehouse and ended at a tip. I slid down the steep slope in an avalanche of iron dust and gravel, and waited to see if the whoosh had attracted attention. Nothing happened. The sound might have been common enough in heavy rain.

At the bottom of the ravine I followed the old working face which I knew would lead me to the shaft. It was like walking the length of some vast derelict ship from the open stern to the cavernous forecastle. I could not go wrong so long as I used my flashlight to avoid tripping over rocks and rusted ironmongery.

When at last I entered that loathsome tunnel, I found it eerie and difficult to endure. But hard necessity is a remarkable cure for superstitious shiverings. The pool was not far from the entrance, coiling its dead surface back into the darkness and silence of that dripping hellhole as far as the beam of my torch would carry. I should guess that there might already be a corpse or two rotting under the motionless water. Those places must have been well known to executioners of both sides during the Spanish Civil War.

Just outside the shaft, on what one might call the starboard bow of the empty derelict, was the tumbled mass of the landslide which had finally made the workings unsafe. The years certainly hadn't made them any safer. I could see — for the cloud cover racing past the half-moon was now wispy — the black cracks in the overhanging hill.

The debris of the landslip promised a route to the top. Rain had eroded the loose earth and gravel, and the rivulets now pouring down from puddle to puddle of orange scum had cut out between the larger rocks a slippery but practical zigzag. I was all in favor of trying it, for I doubted whether I could ever climb out of the ravine over the loose ore down which I had come.

The upper part of the slope turned out to be a rubbish tip, domestic and industrial. It was crisscrossed by tiny tracks — probably made by sheep or children, though I wouldn't have allowed either there myself — and easily climbed. At the top I found myself close to the fence of the new quarry. I could watch the night shift working around the power plant under the naked lights swinging in the wind.

Decision, right or wrong, was forced upon me by an abandoned wheelbarrow. It was lying upside down at the top of the rubbish tip, its bottom rusted through except for two bars. I was still determined that Olura must not be allowed to help me with the puppet. Yet if she did not, it would be a slow and exhausting job. The wheelbarrow at least offered an easy method of getting him as far as the tip.

I righted the barrow and began cautiously to push it along the lip of the ravine. I couldn't possibly be seen. To the men on the other side of the fence it would be blackest night outside the pool of high lamps. But, by God, I could be heard! Unless the wheel was kept dead straight it squealed like a wounded hare. I muffled it with a bit of sacking and my coat, and left the rest to the wind. Every loose fence slat and notice board was creaking, forming a faint, shrill background noise for the shovelings and wheelings of the quarrymen.

There was no rhyme or reason in the tracks, since they had all been made originally to serve purposes which no longer existed. I would have been hopelessly lost if the lights behind me had not given a sense of direction. Near the main gate of the Garay Cut I chose a footpath at random. It turned out to be most convenient, passing through the woods, avoiding the cottages and entering the road nearly opposite the point where we had parked the car.

Olura was out of it, and on the edge of the trees. I think she believed the muted squeals to be proceeding from some defenseless animal and was preparing to interfere with nature. Heaven knows what I looked like, soaked, covered with red mud and pushing that sinister wheelbarrow. She did not think it humorous when I remarked that I entered pursued by a bear.

I turned the barrow upside down and anointed the axle with the car's dipstick until it was reasonably silent. I did not much want to come to the point. Livetti had been twenty-four hours in the closed boot. I told Olura that there was not the least point in getting wet and that the job was now simple. Her answer to that was to unlock the boot and take Livetti's heels.

My pushing of the wheelbarrow may have been a little impetuous. That was understandable under the circumstances. With Olura following close behind, I took my cargo through the woods and then out along the edge of the ravine to the rubbish tip. My eyes were now used to the darkness, and I could make out the former tracks of the wheel. It was risky to flash a torch so close to the new workings, and unnecessary.

The barrow became heavier and I realized that I was pushing it up a slight slope which ought not to be there. A moment afterwards it wasn't there; it had dropped, turf, surface and all, a couple of feet. I had gone charging past the rubbish tip and into the split levels of the landslide. The little platform on which I was standing felt like a jelly balanced on a point. I leapt instinctively to safety and then actually returned to retrieve Livetti and the barrow — an act which illustrates my underlying terror at losing control of his destiny.

The subsidence was silent except for the sudden crash of stones on the hard bottom of the ravine and Olura's not too stifled cry of alarm. Both were heard in the new workings. Two men jumped the fence, one of them carrying a lantern. Another, after exchanging shouts with them, picked up an emergency telephone on the wall of the power plant.

Olura and I lay flat. I had just time to turn the wheelbarrow upside down on top of Livetti. But the two men scrambled down the rubbish tip into the ravine without looking to right or left. They must have thought that the woman's voice had given a loud scream at the bottom of the cut rather than a muffled one at the top.

We were on our feet at once and trotting back behind the barrow on the now familiar path. But that telephone call had worked. Three lanterns appeared from the gate-house, cutting us off from the woods and the car. The men stopped at the edge of the slope of ore and yelled to their two companions, who were stumbling about the bottom of the cut.

Olura asked me why they were so excited. I whispered back that there had recently been a crime in the old work-ings. Some woman had been murdered, and they were on the alert lest it should happen again.*

"Can those three get down to the bottom from there?" she asked.

I replied that they could, and that it was the route which I had first taken.

She vanished before I could say a word. I couldn't call out after her, nor imagine what she was up to. I just waited in desperation, terrified lest she might miss the path and fall over the edge. At last from the direction of the rubbish tip and well inside the ravine I heard two piercing screams. They sounded to me too clear, musical

---

* The body of a young girl had been found a week earlier. I learned the details afterwards when the arrest of her assailant — who, I am glad to say, was not a Basque — was reported in the local press. Sexual crime of this sort is much rarer than in north-ern countries.

and Kensingtonian for any local girl in trouble; but the effect was immediate. The three men crashed down the ore pile to the rescue.

She rejoined me minutes later. By that time all the lights in the ravine were bobbing towards the shaft and its pool. We ran along the now unguarded path, still with the barrow, and reached the woods.

"Brilliant! But what a gamble!" I exclaimed. "It didn't sound as if it really came from the bottom."

"I don't suppose it did," she said. "But once men have got something firmly fixed in their heads they don't think."

We sat down to get our breath back. There could be no argument over the next move. She must get the car away at once. I was sure that those sturdy quarrymen would have put through a call to the Civil Guard or police. As for the incubus in the barrow, it was a disheveled, muddy nightmare to be got rid of. It could not conceivably be returned to the boot. The events of the last twenty minutes had accustomed us both to forget that it had had any previous existence.

The sea must take it. The pylons of the cableway, glimpsed now and then in the clear gaps of the racing sky, had already suggested a solution which I regretted that I had not tried in the first place, though perhaps beyond my strength single-handed. Olura could only accept, for she had to get the car away. Her weary face under the dark, dripping hood had lost all its air of slightly mocking pride. There was only a helpless misery in her eyes as if she would never see me again and it was all her fault.

I hurried her off, telling her to drive around for half an hour and then to park inconspicuously in the nearby village of Pobeña, on the road between the houses and the little seashore hotel. This catered to the transient tourist, and the place was full of foreign cars. In the unlikely event of being questioned, she could always answer that she had been unable to find a room and was sleeping in her car till dawn.

Between the quarries and the bay was a formidable headland. The line of the cableway crossed it by a saddle and then dropped straight to the cliff. I found a stony, steep farm track leading in the right direction, and pushed and pulled the barrow up. The blasted thing seemed to weigh more than Livetti. By the time I had reached a crossing of lanes halfway to the top I was utterly exhausted. Leaving the wheelbarrow in the care of a sleeping cow, I explored with increasing hopelessness until at last I found a pylon. After that it was fairly plain pushing, for a path ran downhill beneath the cableway.

A mile away to my right was the beach of Pobeña and a few scattered lights in the village where that adorable, impossible woman would by now be sitting in the car. Below me was the attack of the sea, little plumes of white on top of the breakers signaling for the main assault on the beaches while the flankers spouted and thundered as they swept along parallel to the cliff.

Myself and the puppet still more or less intact, we skidded and rolled down the last heather-covered slope to the ore dump. The arm of the chute slanted downwards and outwards from the top of the cliff like the boom of a great crane. At the end was an oblong cradle some fifty feet above the sea. Livetti and I descended the chute faster than I intended. There was a revolving belt on it worked by gravity, and we weighed enough to move and accelerate the well-oiled rollers. As we approached the cradle I hoped to God that the bottom flaps were shut when not in use. I remembered that I had seen quarrymen sitting in it and fishing with long lines on a Sunday afternoon.

Gravity and grease delivered us into the cradle. The flaps were shut, or I should not be writing. But my nerves and patience were at an end. I was standing in a space the size of a small truck with no more visible connection to earth than an airplane, while that inchoate menace below hurled up curtains of spray between the cradle and the cliff. Trembling with panic and inefficiency, I filled Livetti's pockets with lumps of iron ore and stuffed some more inside his shirt. Most of it fell out as I threw him overboard.

I need not have descended so quickly. On one side of the chute was a narrow, slatted band up which I could walk so long as I did not look down. Once safely on solid masonry again, I recovered some power to think and decided not to leave an inexplicable wheelbarrow about. So I let the chute carry us both to the cradle, and tipped it into the sea as well.

It was quick and easy to rejoin Olura, for a broad cliff path ran back to Pobeña from the top of the chute. As I walked back, I began to feel frozen with cold. I was plas-

tered with squelching mud from head to foot, covered
with bruises from the barrow and with both hands raw
from the rusty handles.

When I left Olura in the darkness I had not realized
that she too was in the same condition. Apart from the
cloak, she had not been dressed for violent activity. After
that anonymous telephone call to Mgwana she had, to
avoid any suspicion, changed into a light woolen frock of
the type which fashion writers — if faced with the problem — might well have described as suitable for dining
with a black prime minister, a secret policeman and a di-
lapidated don. The skirt of this enigmatic frock was now
held together by a safety pin and mud. Her legs were
bleeding in several places, and there was a nasty cut on
one arm. Her impulsive and successful charge halfway
down the rubbish tip and back had knocked her about
badly. The cloak, now a spongy mass thrown on the floor
of the car, had at any rate kept her dry.

We drove back the way we had come; not that I had any
fear that the black Seat would still be cruising in search of
us, but it seemed wise to avoid the center of Bilbao and the
bridges. We could not afford to be seen entering the hotel
as we were, so we waited till dawn, the heater of the car
making my dampness tolerable, and then drove to the
spring of Iturrioz, where the water shoots out of a cleft
in the limestone into cascading pools, with tall, white
heather springing from the pockets of mossy soil.

Olura was an efficient traveler, well equipped with rags
and sponges. I washed out the boot, removing all traces of
its vile cargo, and then reduced the mud in the inside of

the car to an amount which might reasonably have been deposited by any rainy journey. Meanwhile Olura was at the spring, carrying out running repairs to herself.

You have asked me for absolute frankness, which I have given you. I refuse, however, to put unnecessary details, which in no way illustrate the difficulties of our plight, on exhibition. Olura's account, which, you said, is in your possession — God forbid that I should ever see it! — will, if I know her, nakedly describe her first serious love affair. I will not comment upon my choice of those two adjectives.

Certain personal details may, however, help you to assess my motives and the reliability of my story. As a man of the world — if I may be allowed that vulgar but expressive phrase — you will rightly maintain that forty-eight hours, however agitated, do not offer sufficient evidence for a man, inoculated by pleasant and varied memories of fornication, to fall very gravely in love. Until I saw Olura returning from the spring I did not for a moment admit to myself that I had done so. I considered my reactions to her presence to be, on the whole, a compound of lechery restrained by tact. I was attracted by her, exasperated by her, shy both of her enthusiasms and her social position.

Shall we perhaps consider the picture postcard element? The sight of Olura emerging from branches of white heather in the first of the sun would, I grant you, hardly guarantee the permanency of my affection. But it might very well trigger off self-knowledge. There had indeed been a moment when I returned to the car at Pobeña at which our eyes had met with intention, but the alarm of

each at the appearance of the other was inhibiting; and I
rather think that both shrank from any sort of physical
contact while the ghost of Livetti still dwelt in the boot.
But now our longing for each other was no longer complicated by pity and fear. I will leave it at that.

We returned to the Hostal de las Olas soon after nine,
and tried to preserve our respectability by entering separately. Olura, carrying the beloved cloak rolled up under
her arm, made a swift dash for the stairs instead of the lift
and at least confirmed her reputation for shyness. I myself, observing that the terrace was empty of waiters and
breakfasters — for the sun which had consecrated us had
again vanished — sneaked through the open windows to
the lift and was fairly caught by Mary Deighton-Flagg.
She looked, sounded and smelt the worse for liquor.

"My God!" she exclaimed loudly. "Have you been in the
sea?"

"I have," I answered. "The tide was right for shrimping."

"Did Olura enjoy it?"

She disappeared into the dining room, wiping her dagger and flaunting that doubly tight little bottom. She must
have made it her business to keep tab on our movements.
Once she had seen Mgwana and Gonzalez come home
without us she was perfectly capable of staying awake —
with nips of brandy and a revolting pile of pink cigarette
butts — to see when and in what condition we returned.

Mgwana was in his room, fuming with anger and anxiety. He certainly worshiped Olura. Had danger threatened her in his own benevolent republic, I think the con-

ference with his police would have made one of Hitler's
sound like a wedding breakfast. He swung to the other extreme of confidence and gratitude as soon as he heard my
story. It must be exasperating to be a man of action when
one is debarred from any action whatever.

However, in one respect he came up with the fruits of
his experience.

"Don't bandage those hands of yours," he said, "if you
can bear it. Just keep them closed so that nobody notices
and asks questions. And both of you must give me your
shoes, which I shall keep locked up with my papers."

At the end of the day, after we had all got some sleep
and fed at leisure and started to feel that we were no
longer outlaws from civilization, he decided to fly back to
London and home to Africa. He had no fear and he was
well accustomed to relaxing even when guarded, but he
was out of his depth as a tourist in Spain. He could never
believe — he told me so — that the painstaking Lieutenant Gonzalez was as efficient a companion as a detective-
constable from Special Branch. That amused me, and
confirmed my opinion that the true bond of the Commonwealth is a kind of Bournemouth/Torquay complex which
is ill at ease without the comparative honesty of British-
trained police and hot colonial puddings for dessert.

He was still disturbed at the lack of any obvious motive
for the murder of Livetti. He repeated that nobody would
take such a risk simply for a fifty-fifty chance of creating a
front-page, international scandal. Myself, I considered the
actual happenings of that night unguessable. As good a
theory as another was that Livetti had tried to blackmail

his accomplice. But I admitted that the more one tried to reconstruct such a quarrel, the less sense it made.

Olura and I had returned to the only relationship which Mgwana had seen between us — due, no doubt, to slight embarrassment on her part, and on mine to the sudden insecurity of the male animal in love. When his intentions are strictly dishonorable, he has a pretty clear picture of them; but when his emotions are deeply involved, he can find a hundred reasons for refusing to accept the evidence of his ears and eyes.

Mgwana wanted her to fly back with him, but she pointed out that she could not leave the car in Spain; she would drop him at the airport and then drive slowly home through France. The decision was sensible and I could not oppose it. Anyway I had no chance. We were never alone except for disturbed moments while the chambermaids were moving my things to her room and hers to mine — an exchange which I ordered without consulting her, knowing that she would protest that I couldn't endure the room any more than she could.

She said just that. I replied that in any room of hers my imagination would be so fully occupied that I wouldn't care if devils danced in it all night. She received this confession with one of her steadfast looks which might have meant that she knew it already and approved, or that she was searching, with some difficulty, for the right file in which to put so coarse and clumsy a remark.

And so next morning, July 24, I got out early from that room to say good-bye to them. Gonzalez knew his job. He refused to allow either of them to say where they were going and he would not let Mgwana book his flight in advance, assuring him that the Spanish Government — who only wished that more notice could have been given them of his distinguished arrival — would see that he got a seat on any plane which suited him. It was another slight indication that Gonzalez's superiors suspected a possible source of danger, though I was then far from guessing in what direction their fantasies would develop.

I was hurt that Olura should choose to say good-bye to me in the lounge while Mgwana was paying his bill.

"You're not moving on as soon as we leave?" she asked.

Well, no, I wasn't. Neither my personal charms nor my political opinions were likely to tempt anyone to invade the privacy of my bathroom. So I proposed to stay out a second week at the Hostal de las Olas, and then to continue my linguistic explorations from one village to another.

"Don't try to make Calais in less than three days," I said. "You're still too tired."

"Oh, I'm not going home yet. The house is shut up, and I'm not expected."

"What are your plans?"

"I don't know. I'm not coming back here, Philip. Suppose you took me out to lunch at the prawn place for a start?"

So began the most radiant, the most undeserved days of happiness. What cause is there? How does a mere biological compulsion become such unity?

Genes? Bilge! My genes, if in fact they do control my behavior, have been delightfully compatible with those of

thoroughly unsuitable partners too many times for me to
have any trust in them at all. Shall I fall back on similar-
ity of acquired characteristics? But Olura's social upbringing was very different from mine. Our view of life? But
my acceptance of human depravity is hopelessly opposed
to her insistence that it can be reformed. Our values,
then? Different in all nonessentials. I see that begs the
question and gives a pointer to the right answer. In essen-
tials our values are the same.

Still, that offers only a base for unity. It does not explain how I can say *I am we.* Values and culture have
nothing to do with it. There is no more devoted mate than
a gander. Another pointer, perhaps. Could it be that so
entire a love descends from high antiquity and is now a
rare survival among civilized men and women like the
compass sense of direction?

Rare? But all lovers think their experience unique! And
reasonably enough at the age of twenty. But you, my good
Philip, are thirty-four. I know I am, and so I have standards of comparison. When paradise is paradise, I recognize it; and that's more than you can say for most
people.

Well, let it go! Memory, I fear, tends to exaggerate
when there is little hope of paradise regained. I will leave
this unscholarly speculation and continue to record the
facts.

After Olura had seen off Leopold Mgwana, she said
good-bye to Pedro Gonzalez — having at last decided, I
gathered, that he was an endurable policeman, though a
secret one — and drove hard for Maya. She arrived in

front of the inn a little after two, looking more carefree and irresponsible than I had ever seen her, car and expensive baggage giving the usual impression of an elusive fastidiousness rather than outright wealth.

After lunch Elena and her husband showed us over their inn, which was larger than I had thought, with half a dozen clean and simple bedrooms and a recently built, very showy bathroom which did not open on a shaft. In fact it was excellently placed over the kitchen, where the effects of Spanish plumbing, always more optimistic than orthodox, were entirely overwhelmed by appetizing odors.

There was a room free on the first floor, with a window looking up the twisting river to the cloudy mountains of Álava. I did not dare suggest it, having no idea what simplicities were acceptable to Olura and what were not. The answer, I have since discovered, is any and all, provided she approves of herself.

She took the room joyfully. I was careful not to inquire for another, since I was reluctant to force myself upon her. My apparent lack of enterprise was perhaps common sense. To set one's hopes on mere proximity is to show distrust of all else. In any case by the end of that day such irrelevancies as trust and distrust had ceased to exist.

I remained at the Hostal de las Olas, for there was no other accommodation readily available in Maya. I did not waste time looking for it. Our Hero and Leander act had a delicacy which suited the flowering of Olura, and it never occurred to either of us to try to improve upon perfection.

Every morning I walked the mile along the beach to the
edge of the water which separated us. Sometimes it would
be she who swam or waded across opposite the inn, sometimes I. On other days I would see red cloak or white cape
already far up the estuary and turn south over the powdery sand until we stood facing each other with the deep,
transparent ribbon of the tide between. Then we would
solemnly exchange our good mornings and endearments
until one or the other, overwhelmed by this half-deliberate
frustration of the sense of touch, dived in and swam
across. For all that week the sun shone, and our privacy in
the miniature coves and bays of the river was never disturbed.

This exquisite girl was so full of sheer goodness. True,
it sometimes displayed itself as goody-goodiness. Her human sympathy was genuine, soundly based in character
and training, but guilt at possessing so much wealth
tended to exaggerate the expression of it. She was so determined to find opportunities for service that she could
dig them up when they didn't exist or were completely
worthless.

I think, too, that guilt formerly extended to her own
physical beauty, as if she had no private right to it. I write
"formerly" because idiocy of that sort goes up in flame.
When a woman sees that her lover is intoxicated by her
beauty to a point of tears and poetry, she can hardly go on
thinking that she ought not to have it. But I admit that I
do not really understand such an oddity in my adorable
and passionate Olura. It is somehow connected with that
air of being chosen for a sacrifice, which, when I first saw

her in the hotel, gave me the impression that she lacked vitality.

As I rejoiced in her day after day, I felt — carefully hugging the secret to myself — that she was returning to what nature intended her to be: a gay, robust, sensuous creature, for whom world politics would not be half so important as what she was going to have for dinner. She had not anywhere near reached that point, nor ever will, nor would I wish her to, but she was coming along nicely.

We had, I remember, one furious row over her idol, Prebendary Cyril Flanders, who made far too many appearances in her conversation. I have only seen that anarchistically-minded churchman smirking and evasive upon the television screen. I felt that he had the furtive single-mindedness of a tycoon, making it his business to corner the market of protest whenever an excitable minority could be persuaded that the Government should take some action which it was manifestly impossible for any government to take.

Something of the sort, being made overbold by lunch, I mentioned to Olura one afternoon when we were leaning upon her windowsill, idly picking out among the wooded headlands and scoured sandbanks exactly where our hidden beaches lay.

"Philip, can't you ever admit that any serious thinking goes on outside Senior Common Rooms?" she asked.

"By God, I do! Far too serious! Which means that it's generally more emotional than exact."

"Sometimes the people can get their way only by direct action."

I said that when the people thought they knew what they wanted, politicians were only too delighted to give it to them at any cost. That was how elections were won.

"Then what's wrong with making them realize what they want?"

"Nothing — so long as it isn't just what Prebendary Flanders wants. What does he?"

"Everything which is fine and generous. Justice for political prisoners, nuclear disarmament, sympathy and help for the colored peoples."

I said that I could see no one principle in all that, and that I myself would much rather be governed by a benevolent Mgwana than alternating juntas of incompetent conservatives and ignorant socialists.

"But if British police and administrators were as efficient as Leopold Mgwana," I went on, "you would all be lying down in the streets from Trafalgar Square to Hammersmith."

"Leopold doesn't like it," she insisted. "For the moment he has to."

"And no countries like threatening the rest with atom bombs. They have to."

"If everybody refused to obey . . ." she began.

"But they won't. I remember my mother asking what would happen if everybody wiped their noses on their coat sleeves."

"At least Cyril is ready to suffer for what he believes!"

"I'm sure he is. With relish."

She said, "I hate you!" and went out and slammed the door. I was in that detestable state of uncontrollably twitching lips because one feels like crying and wants to laugh, when she opened it again and told me that Prebendary Flanders was a Saint. She then slammed the door once more. But the partition walls of small Spanish inns are not built for displays of emotion from young women trained in violence by lacrosse practice before breakfast. The door frame fell out in a cloud of plaster, and she collapsed into my arms, at first slightly hysterical, then rippling with laughter.

Slapstick she could not resist. And she could hand out, with effective quietness, the verbal slapstick of wit. Humor — well, it depended on what one was refusing to take seriously. At any rate, it was not hard to encourage the habit of laughter to grow. I hope she never forgets again, whatever my own fate is, the gaiety which is natural to her.

It was eleven in the morning of August 1. I had left Olura before dawn and was just setting out to meet her on the banks of our river when the telephone announced a gentleman to see me. Might he perhaps go up to my room? It was the manager himself speaking; the inflections of his voice sounded as if he were personally introducing some banker or real estate agent. The unexpected visitor was obviously known and respectable, so I did not hesitate to ask him up. It was astonishing how clean my happily engaged conscience had become.

It felt instantly loaded with guilt as soon as the district chief of police entered my room. I knew him well enough to nod to. The fact that he had not announced himself under his own name was worrying. It looked as if he wanted to observe my face when he walked in on me without warning.

"Nothing. Nothing at all," he said soothingly, as soon as I had given him a chair and exchanged the usual compliments. "A very simple question. What were you doing in Miss Manoli's car on the night of July twenty-first?"

The hell of a simple question! I had never thought out an answer to it. And which was the twenty-first? The first attempt or the second?

"Which day of the week?" I asked to gain time. "On holiday one loses count of dates."

"Wednesday. Or, more strictly, early on Thursday morning."

"She asked me to find out what was wrong with it."

"And what was?"

"Nothing but damp on the plugs," I replied, and added hastily, "The fact is, I couldn't sleep. So I thought I would see to the car. But I didn't check the petrol."

"You asked the Pair of the Guardia to send some out to you?"

"Yes, I did."

He shot straight at me, not allowing me a moment to anticipate the question:

"Have you ever known a man called Livetti?"

But my imagination had played with that possible inquiry and come up with an answer which would conform to the reaction of perfect innocence.

"Livetti? Now, let me see! Yes. Wasn't that the Roumanian who was interested in gypsy dialects? I'm afraid a scholar cannot avoid all contacts behind the Iron Curtain, Chief. But I assure you I have no political affiliations."

"The man I mean was Italian."

"I don't think he was."

"A press photographer."

"No, Chief. Something in Bucharest University."

"His body was washed up on the beach at Pobeña."

He waited for comment. I wasn't giving it. I could not decide whether I ought or ought not to know where Pobeña was. I say "decide" but my brain was unrecognizable. Swamped with adrenalin, it was working as fast as a computer, rejecting, accepting and producing the answer without thinking in words at all.

"He had been swimming?" I asked.

"He appears to have been killed at least twenty-four hours before entering the water."

I made some conventional remark, and waited for worse.

"Close to the point where you ran out of petrol, Livetti's passport was found by the side of the road."

So that was the only connection with me! I prayed that my face had not shown relief. His passport must have dropped out of his pocket while I was carrying him back to the car. The usual carelessness of the panic-stricken criminal!

"What a curious coincidence!" I said. "I don't wonder that you wanted to interview me."

"You didn't see or hear anything suspicious?"

"A cry for help, you mean? No. Anyway the Pair was

patrolling the road. If there was anything to hear, they
would have heard it."

He seemed to be perfectly satisfied, and left me with
many apologies and thanks. But I was far from happy. It
was natural enough that when the passport was found,
the police should call for a report from the Civil Guard;
and that had involved me. But how far had investigations
gone before somebody decided that I ought to be grilled?
It occurred to me that this visiting cop had dragged
Pobeña into the conversation abruptly and had been
watching me closely.

I trotted off along the sands, upset at being late for our
daily rendezvous. When delight is of unknown duration,
to lose five minutes of it is to lose a year. But there was no
Olura, for which I was illogically thankful. A little later I
saw Lieutenant Gonzalez leave the inn and drive off. Then
I watched her hurrying upstream along the Maya side of
the estuary, hugging my joy, uneasy though I was, at the
rare blend of grace and determination in her movements.

When I had swum across, it was a rather still and stat-
uesque Olura who greeted me. She told me that Gonzalez
had been most friendly, excusing his sudden call by explaining that he had to compile his official report on
Mgwana's short visit. He had, however, asked her one
question: what was I doing with her car on the Wednesday night?

"Oh, my God!" I exclaimed. "What did you say?"

"That I didn't know you had taken it out. I pretended
that I thought they wanted you for stealing it, and said
that I'd given you leave to use it whenever you liked."

Brilliant! That didn't clash with my own story. I told her how I too had been asked the same question at the same time, and assured her that we should get away with the mischance of the dropped passport and hear no more. I am not sure how far I really believed it, but I was not standing any further interference from Livetti. He had done his duty in bringing us together.

I should have remembered — if I hadn't been too enchanted by the present to worry about the future — that Livetti was a foreigner and connected, however disreputably, with the press; that meant that his case would be ruthlessly investigated. When a country gets half its foreign exchange from tourists, it is more sensitive to a foreign than a native corpse.

Gonzalez, as I knew, was not normally employed on criminal investigation; but Leopold Mgwana and Olura were V.I.P.s and called for tactful handling. Since Gonzalez was personally known to us and himself a witness to oddities in our behavior, he was the obvious choice to put us through a preliminary interrogation.

He was on our tails again in the evening, which showed very clearly that we were under surveillance, though I had not noticed a following car or a plainclothes cop. I doubt if anything less than an armored troop carrier on either side of us would have distracted my attention from Olura. I had taken her out to dinner in Santurce at the entrance to Bilbao Harbor. When we left the restaurant, Gonzalez bobbed up.

He had the decency to express surprise at meeting us. Since it was so, could we give him five minutes of our

time? Wherever we liked, of course. But the offices of the
Port Police were close and very comfortable.

They were, and conveniently empty except for the night
duty staff. When Gonzalez had provided us with coffee
and cigarettes, and polished his French by a few courtesies to Olura, he said how sorry he was that we were being
unnecessarily bothered by this affair of Livetti; but — just
to clear it all up — what *had* we been doing in Pobeña on
the night of July 22 after we left him in Amorebieta?

There was a shocking guilty silence from which Olura
was the first to recover.

"Have I got to say?" she asked with a charming helplessness straight out of drawing-room comedy.

This was the devil. I couldn't even start to guess how
much they knew. The disturbance in the quarry on the
night before the body was washed up would certainly have
been reported by local police; but how could investigation
of it lead to us? Anyway, the legal pathologists had established that Livetti had been dead for at least a day.

"It would be as well," Gonzalez recommended.

"M. Ardower was being very difficult."

"But, excuse me, Mademoiselle," he murmured in some
embarrassment, "you meet daily and appear to be on intimate terms."

"We were not then on such good terms, Lieutenant."

"And what made you choose Pobeña?" he asked me.

I put down these questions and answers verbatim, for it
is the easiest and most concise way to give you a clear
picture of what I have been asked, what I have admitted,
and when and why I have deliberately misled the police.

Me, too, it assists — for the hardest task of a suspect is to keep tab of his own lies.

"I knew there was a tourist hotel where one might find a room," I answered.

"And did you?"

"But no and no!" Olura interrupted indignantly. "I told M. Ardower that if he was not prepared to treat me with respect he could walk home."

"And you started to do so?"

"I took a stroll round to let her cool off."

"What shoes were you wearing?"

I had been wearing rope-soled *alpargatas* which do not slip on wet turf or rock. But he might not have noticed what the soles were made of, for on that hasty journey to Amorebieta his professional attention was fixed on the more distant surroundings of Mgwana, and my unimportant feet were generally out of sight in the front of the car or under the table.

"I don't remember," I replied, "but you should. You must have seen them when we were together."

He let that pass, to my infinite relief.

"What time did you arrive in Pobeña?"

Olura answered for me that it was about 2 A.M., as it was.

"What had you been doing since leaving Amorebieta?"

"I think you had better ask *him* that," she replied, as if some disgust at my behavior still remained.

"Just going from place to place," I said, "until she threw me out."

"I see. Now, M. Ardower, what was the reason why you

persuaded a taxi driver named Echeverría to block the passage of a black Seat car which was parked alongside the café?"

I had given no thought at all to Echeverría. Mgwana told me that on the way back from Amorebieta to the hotel the taxi driver and Gonzalez had chatted amicably together, and that he hadn't understood what they were saying. It was improbable that Echeverría would then have gone into any details, for he was not the type to chatter about the private business of someone he considered to be practically a fellow Basque. So it looked as if he had since been forced to make an official statement.

Gonzalez therefore knew that my sudden departure with Olura had been deliberately plotted. But an ardent lover, when on holiday and unaccountable to anyone, might be expected to indulge in eccentricities. It was quite believable that I had tried to get Olura away from some former and jealous admirer and to prevent him following.

So I took a chance that Vigny had in fact been in the black Seat. My story could then be made to fit, more or less, into the vague and preposterous yarn I had told Echeverría.

"Mlle. Manoli had made another conquest in the hotel," I said. "A Frenchman called Vigny. He was very determined that I should not be alone with her."

Gonzalez nodded approvingly, as if to say that he was glad I had told some of the truth. Then to my alarm he switched the conversation into Spanish which Olura did not understand.

"Don Felipe, if you are not what you appear to be, it would naturally be a help to tell me."

"No, there's no mystery about me," I replied, wondering what on earth he was getting at.

I knew there might be some distrust. Any foreigner who speaks Catalan or Euzkadi inevitably hears a good deal of wild separatist talk from his friends. It is, in fact, mere talk, for no one has any intention of renewing violence. But the police like to keep an eye on foreigners who might not be aware that the Civil War is over.

"Perhaps we should have been working together," he hinted.

"But I am not in any way in your business."

"In England we know it is organized differently."

The reputation of our older universities! It all started, I suppose, with Hogarth and Lawrence in the first war and gathered force in the second, when the Government very sensibly stuffed its intelligence services with dons. Naturally they made efficient and imaginative staff officers, but I have never read that higher education contributed anything notable to the arts of security. However, once a legend, always a legend.

"Who on earth gave you that idea?"

I got some of it out of him. He had certainly been asking a lot of questions before he tackled us direct. One of his informants was Miss Mary Blasted Deighton-Flagg. Well, I had only myself to blame there. Then Arizmendi had confirmed that I stuck closely to Mgwana and was always popping up where I wasn't expected. Gonzalez hinted at yet another source of misinformation. Possibly Vigny himself? The French can never rid themselves of the vice of seeing British agents under their beds.

It occurred to me that our safety was far too critically in the hands of the occupants of the black Seat, whom I had never expected to hear of again. Gonzalez must have memorized the number of the car when the driver overtook us and suspiciously changed his mind about stopping. Echeverría would have repeated the same number. So it was a fair bet that the sunburnt man in the café had been identified and interviewed, and probably Vigny too. True, they did not dare tell whatever the truth was, but their frightened lies were unpredictable and sure to be ingenious. And they might well wonder why I was conveniently on the spot, and so ready to protect Mgwana and Olura.

That was what had been in the back of Gonzalez's mind: I could just possibly be Mgwana's unofficial bodyguard — though it must have seemed damned unlikely in view of my movements before I arrived at the Hostal — and I might have had a good reason for killing Livetti or keeping quiet about his death.

Well, the police could have as many conferences as they pleased over that theory. In the end they were bound to reject it as absurd. As soon as they had traced the background, career and antecedents of Livetti, it would be clear that there was no conceivable connection with any of us.

Gonzalez gave up, expressing his regret that a series of

coincidences had compelled him to question us. That offered a useful opening, and I said that I couldn't see why the police had not accepted them as mere coincidences.

"After all," I added with such innocence as I could manage, "if somebody followed us to Pobeña, he must be able to confirm what we were doing."

"Unfortunately nobody did follow you."

"Then I don't understand."

And indeed I did not. Quarrymen? Vigny? Police? Who in God's name could have trailed us? Yet it was so simple.

"There are valuable cars parked in the village," Gonzalez explained. "As a matter of routine, the *sereno* takes a list of numbers every night. When this body was washed up, his list became of interest."

Knowing the educational attainments of village watchmen, I said, probably irritably, that I was surprised the list was legible.

"It was not," he admitted. "But one of the GB cars could possibly have been Miss Manoli's. And since you were good enough to confirm that it was . . ."

So a bold lie right at the start would have saved us! I have always wondered why criminals when arrested deny everything and later confess what they must; it seems such devastating proof of guilt. But experience counts. After all, one hears nothing more of those cases in which blank denial has succeeded.

As Olura and I were driving back to Maya, we decided that the police must already have suspected something like the truth and rejected it. The Pair of the Civil Guard had — by a blessed sense of duty — thoroughly examined the boot and interior of the car on the night of July 21, and found them empty.

Still, we were very uneasy, not without finding a satisfaction in our unity like any young happily married couple faced by their first external crisis. One wakes from the daze of delight to find that unpleasant reality is not a wedge dividing, but an encirclement which compresses.

We went over the circumstantial evidence and had to admit that it was not limited to the two facts that Livetti's passport had been found close to the point where I ran out of petrol and that we had been in Pobeña on the night of the twenty-second before he was washed ashore. Besides this, they had (a) Arizmendi's report that I did not leave the Hostal on the night of the twenty-first, when they knew that I did; (b) information from the Deighton-Flagg woman that she had been anonymously warned to visit the hotel because some news might break there; (c) shoes, which both Gonzalez and I had left with a question mark.

Gonzalez must be well aware that my picture of Vigny as the jealous lover was pretty doubtful — questioning of the hotel staff would soon show him that Vigny had never even spoken to Olura — and that an examining magistrate would tie us into knots if he interrogated us separately. But if we had anything to do with the death of Livetti, Mgwana was in it up to the neck, and that could involve worldwide publicity. The confidential approach had to be tried before we were delivered into the crunch of the Law.

The following day we wished to heaven that we were over the frontier, but could not make up our minds to run. Wouldn't it be an admission of guilt? Olura thought not. She said indignantly that the natural reaction of innocent people tormented by questioning was to clear out. I remember gasping at the word *innocent*. Women so often seem unable to distinguish between absolute and relative truth. I suppose that the more intelligent are aware of the difference, but even for them words must conform to mood. They have no respect for language.

Personally I thought that we should not be allowed out of the country, and that when we drove up to the frontier either the car's papers or ours would be found to be out of order — all with the utmost regret and no mention at all of the Livetti inquiry. Olura did not agree. She had a limited view of police — all police — that they were cruel, corrupt and therefore incompetent. She could not believe that frontier posts would be warned to look out for us.

So we did nothing except drink rather more wine than usual — I fear that I had been debauching her prim opinion that two glasses were enough for a lady — and allow it to inspire us to transports of affection, as the Victorians called it. At least I think that was what they meant. I did not do my Leander act and go home before dawn. Such insistent respectability seemed even more futile than it was when I considered that we were both suspect criminals.

The next day showed that indeed we were. Elena, who had taken a motherly and adoring interest in Olura's affairs while under her roof, suddenly started to greet us with a face of such courage and agony that she reminded me of a seventeenth-century image of Our Lady of Sorrows. Likely enough, she imitated just that look; for all of us, especially Latins, need a model for the expression of our emotions. When I caught her weeping in the kitchen, she was pregnant with mystery and refused to explain. It was obvious that she had been ordered to report our every movement. Naturally enough, the manner in which I was treated by the smoothly trained management of the Hostal, on the rare occasions when I was in, revealed absolutely nothing.

I did not like the forty-eight hours' silence of the police. Gonzalez ought to have been along with apologies. I felt that a file was growing in Madrid or Bilbao, and had a presentiment of scruffy individuals who had shaved yesterday slipping reports and telegrams onto the desks of hard-faced officers shaved and powdered that very morning. Spanish justice is quite as fair as any other when the State is not involved. But wasn't it? There seemed to be nasty political undertones behind the death of Livetti.

At last we made up our minds to escape, abandoning the car and our baggage so that it would be assumed — with luck, until the evening — that we were only out for the day. Olura didn't mind. She said that Elena and her husband could not be dishonest if they tried and that she would get back all her things when we were cleared of suspicion. I have always understood that the rich were jealous of their possessions. She was not. She felt as strongly as any Bohemian that possessions were a nuisance and a tie.

Since the police did not know that trait of her character, there was a chance that our names and descriptions had been given only to the road posts, and not to Railway Control at Irún; in any case I hoped to find, once on the spot, a discreet way round the passport officers. What with the crowded tramway from Irún over the bridge to France, Basque porters and a sum of money as a favor from one gentleman to another, it should not be by any means hopeless.

Nobody interfered with our long mornings on the beaches and up the river, and we knew only too well three little paradises surrounded by high banks of sand where we could not be watched. One of them gave access, still in dead ground, to a low cliff on top of which was scrub and woodland. Once there, we could vanish into Vizcaya so long as we kept off the roads.

Our best bet was to reach Deva, where we would be inconspicuous among the assortment of foreign tourists and could safely take a taxi to Irún; but it meant a walk of some fifteen miles across country. We dared not use local buses or any of the local railway stations.

We set off at our regular time next morning, which was August 4, carrying nothing but towels, passports and money and appearing to be dressed as usual. For Olura that was easy, since the red cloak was familiar to everyone, and she could wear what she liked underneath it; for me, it was not; but I managed to conceal a heavy sweater under shirt and scarf.

The tide was very low. Two crossings of the sandy canyon of the river enabled us to reach the walls of a ruined cottage and its surrounding bramble bushes. There we buried the towels and the red cloak, over which — for I could not part with it so brutally — I conducted a short and romantic service.

Through the woods we easily reached the slope of the coastal range along which was cut the corniche road to Deva. The engineers had given it an easier passage than ours. We had to climb up and down the tangled ravines which the road crossed by bridges or a hairpin bend running far inland. I thought it too risky to sit by the roadside and thumb a lift. The traffic police on their motorcycles and the Civil Guard would give more than a casual glance at two carworthy and conspicuous English, if only to ask us whether we had had an accident.

Weary at last of scrambling along the side of the range, we toiled up to the watershed. There on the top were farms, farm tracks and men and their wives at work in the little fields, with whom we exchanged greetings, for there was no point in avoiding them. We were right off the beat of anyone likely to report our presence.

Olura, with a blister on her heel, was dead tired and disappointed with herself. When I had talked of fifteen miles across country, she was sure of her endurance, remembering that she could gaily outlast her drooping contemporaries on Aldermaston marches and other flat-footed protests — if you analyze them — against the normal working of democracy. She knew that our course would be up and down hill, following whatever paths there were, but she visualized turf or pine needles, not long stretches of eroded rock.

When at last we stopped by a spring on the edge of the southern slope, and ate such bits and pieces as we had managed to secrete from our overfilled plates at dinner the night before, I found it hard to persuade her to her feet again. Deva was only five or six more miles away, and we had to hurry if we were to be over the Bidasoa, the frontier river, by nightfall. But her thoughts were Lord knows where. Across the valley and over the rising ridges the pyramid of Mount Gorbea showed faintly green through the mists shimmering on its flanks. To the east the sullen, colorless line of the Pyrenees was producing its usual miracle play of the Wrath of Jehovah with cumulus cloud, streaked showers, lightning and sudden shafts of sunlight revealing the precipices.

It is my guess that whenever she felt that circumstance had utterly overcome her, she had acquired a habit of recalling and taking refuge in all those worthy causes which needed her and to which she was devoted. In such a mood a companion who could worry only about police and geography was far away from the point. She sat up with her arms round her knees and exclaimed that all this was lovely and marvelous, and what did men want to destroy it for?

The Bidasoa beckoned inexorably. I hope my tone was not one of impatience. I replied that it was not man who wanted to destroy the earth, but the earth which had to limit the pullulating mass of man, and would undoubtedly reduce us by half either through our overgrown intelligence and its nuclear physics or through our decreasing resistance to disease. For myself I was more alarmed by the efficiency of Spanish police, which I could do something about, than by nature's beta factor, which I couldn't.

"And that is what you see for our children? Ours?" she asked.

The devastating honesty of Olura! She made any mention of marriage wholly irrelevant, almost indecent. It was a statement of her intention.

I saw that she was nearly at the end of her strength and longing to be assured that she was loved. So easy. Far too easy. There is a kind of masochism in me — perhaps in all males of my type — which firmly suppresses all the responses which matter for the sake of immediate present effort. It should not have been beyond her understanding, for she herself was a masochist in a wider field of action and willing to drive herself slap into the grave for an ideal; but she could not be inspired to blind effort for the sake of her own personal safety.

So I gave way, and we dropped downhill over turf, smooth and easy as that of English downland, to a ribbon of road which was reflecting the late afternoon sun. Feminine gods were determined to prove her right. We had not been on the verge of the road more than a minute when a country bus came along, bound for Azpeitia. It was going in the wrong direction, southeast instead of north, but at least she could rest. Meanwhile we were miles from anywhere that the wildest guess of the police could place us. At Azpeitia was another bus about to start for Tolosa, and from Tolosa we took the last train to San Sebastián.

This remote and casual travel had wasted a lot of time. We were too late for expresses to Bordeaux or Paris and could only get over into France by local trams or trains in the small hours of the morning. Too risky, I thought. We would stand out as suspicious travelers among a horde of workmen.

In San Sebastián, however, we were just two of thousands of foreign tourists, and it was most unlikely that we would be spotted. We had a midnight dinner, and then — as we dared not register at a hotel — went on to a night club. In my scruffy state the management was doubtful about letting me in, but decided that Olura was rich and entitled to her pickups. After walking most of the day in a simple frock which, to my eyes, could have been bought off the peg anywhere for a couple of guineas, she still gave that impression. In spite of the heel she now wanted to dance. It was the first time that we had danced together.

The place closed at five and left us high and dry with nothing else open. The only safe course was to wander along the beach. A few impecunious students were sleeping there, not very privately. The bay of San Sebastián was so packed during daylight and left so full of sun shelters and other movable property during the night that it was patrolled by municipal watchmen. We were asked what we were doing, but left to sit or walk in peace when I explained that we had just come through from France, that our car was parked on the esplanade and that we were waiting for breakfast.

We got some eventually in a large café, where at nine o'clock there was already a safe sprinkling of businessmen and tourists. Next door a motor coach company was advertising a day return trip to Biarritz and Pau. It seemed a

safer and easier way out of Spain than hanging about railway stations, for it was inconceivable that the whole
coachload would have to show their passports at the frontier; it would be enough if they were shown to the clerk
when buying tickets. In that I was right; but either
through tiredness or plain ignorance I underestimated the
police. I never guessed that we were so important that
even in this wretched little office there would be a damned
agent behind the frosted glass alongside the ticket clerk.

After a minute's delay I was told that the coach was
full, and that there would be another in half an hour if we
didn't mind waiting. As I had bought the tickets, we
waited. An hour later I went from the café to the coach
office to see what was happening. The clerk said that the
second coach had unfortunately broken down and the
garage was rushing repairs. How well and smoothly they
play the mañana! I noticed that there was no indignant
crowd waiting for this second coach, but still I was not
suspicious. It was possible that everyone else knew what
was happening.

After another hour and a half, during which we drank
too many sherries and Olura lectured me on my wildly
idealistic view of Spanish efficiency, Gonzalez walked into
the café. He said — before we could say it ourselves —
that it was very natural for two distinguished foreigners
to want a night out in San Sebastián. If only we had let
him know beforehand, it could have been arranged. But
now he had to ask us to return to our respective hotels
where, he believed, we had kept on our rooms.

A car was waiting. With a gesture which quietly ensured compliance he placed himself between us on the back seat, but did not attempt to question us. The driver sat well into his corner with his right ear, as it were, extended backwards. Olura, like a desperate hostess, at least gave him something to listen to. She discussed with Gonzalez the cabaret we had visited and the number of English decanted from coaches into San Sebastián. I cleared my throat and tried to be comradely in Spanish. My remarks seemed to echo round the car before he replied to them.

When we dropped Olura at Maya, I started to accompany her into the inn. Gonzalez would have none of it. As I was about to protest, the driver left his seat and placed himself unobtrusively alongside me. There was no doubt what he was: a straight criminal detective without any of the airs and graces which fitted Gonzalez for his high-up security jobs. I waved to Olura as cheerfully as I could and got back into the car.

We drove up the valley and over the steel bridge at the top of the tidewater, then turned down a track used by builders' lorries loading sand. I felt a little anxious at this move, but it was easily explained. No police stations for me yet. I could be too influential. So, short of putting me through it in my own hotel room, a car parked among sandhills was a fair solution.

With Olura out of the way, Gonzalez at once and surprisingly returned to his usual manner.

"I am sorry, Don Felipe," he said, "but my instructions are that you are not permitted to speak to Miss Manoli."

"Which of us is supposed to be the guilty party?"

"Both of you."

"You don't really think that Miss Manoli killed this Livetti of yours?"

"Did you?"

I won't say I was not afraid of him; but the right game for the moment seemed to be to play on our liking for each other and to refuse to take any suspicions seriously.

"You had much better put your money on me," I said. "If you choose Miss Manoli, you'll only stir up the journalists. Think of the headlines! Franco's Police Arrest Red Heiress. And then that moving article by Mary Deighton-Flagg: Is No Holiday-Maker Safe In Spain?"

"It is not the time for wit, Don Felipe."

"Fact, not wit, my dear Teniente! Remember what a lot of foreign exchange was lost the last time police interfered with a British tourist!"

"If an uncivilized son of a whore walks down the main street of Barcelona with only a comic hat and a pair of bum bags on," replied Gonzalez with furious dignity, "we naturally arrest him whether he is a Trades Union official or not. You would do the same to any Spaniard in Piccadilly Circus."

"Of course we would. And if he was a socialist, Miss Manoli would probably pay his fine. But publicity is publicity!"

He was silent, and I began to feel that I might soon be let loose as an incorrigible and harmless rogue. His companion in the front seat, however, took out a notebook and began to scribble away in shorthand as a firm hint that we should get to the point. He had a general air of deadpan distrust. I don't suppose that the regular criminal investigation branch much cared for the intrusion of a secret agent into what was, on the face of it, a straight case of murder.

"What do you know about the señorita Flagg?" Gonzalez asked.

"Nothing — except that a colleague of yours in Madrid sticks her up against the office back door from time to time. So you can't pull her fingernails out. They are too short anyway. She paints them a dirty silver and then bites them."

"You know very well that we do not pull fingernails out!"

"It's true I haven't had the experience. But nothing would stop the Flagg saying that she had."

"What has she got to do with Livetti?"

"How should I know? I protest against all this just because a passport was found on a road which I among a hundred other drivers have used, and because you fish a damned photographer out of the sea on the same bit of coast where I happened to be a little ruthless in pursuit of Miss Manoli. If you find a corpse in San Sebastián tomorrow, am I guilty because I dined there last night? I have never set eyes on Livetti . . ."

"But Miss Manoli was acquainted with him."

He must have seen the utter astonishment on my face. By this time I had penetrated Gonzalez's character fairly well, both as an agent of government and a naturally friendly fellow. So I was sure he was not bluffing. He was stating a fact. And the whole foundation of our lies, always suspicious but difficult to break down, had collapsed.

I asked him how he knew. He replied dryly that there was a telephone line to Rome.

"It does not surprise me in the least that you are deeply attached to this lady," he went on in a tone of the utmost courtesy. "What a glory of a girl! I say it, believe me, with respect. But couldn't it be that she has deceived you? I do not mean in affairs of the heart, but, let's say, in that curious aversion to facts so common among women."

I agreed that it certainly could be, and probably was — but that it was preposterous to suppose Olura capable of violence.

"If you don't believe that I know her," I added, "ask your superiors to get a report on her from Scotland Yard."

"They have already."

"Well, what did it say?"

"That — with your permission — she is unreliable."

The bloody fools! But their answer was inevitable. Anyone who protested against the normal necessities of government was for Olura a hero and martyr. I can with an effort — needful since I mix with and endeavor to tutor the young — understand the solemnity of their faith that it is morally right to sit in the road and stick pins into police horses for the sake of certain political principles and morally wrong for the sake of other principles, though both sets of opinion are equally dubious and held with equal sincerity.

Some pattern, illogical but significant, might possibly

be discovered by a statistician. Hard-worked administrators, however, can only be expected to see hysteria. A police report on Olura would insist that she was of good character, but that anything became credible as soon as her conscience involved itself in politics.

"What did they say about me?" I asked.

"Nothing known."

A little unfair, perhaps. Still, the inquiry concerned criminal propensities, not academic distinction.

"You could hardly expect them to say anything else!"

Somehow I had to play for time and head him off Olura. But my sheer impudence in implying that I had indeed been secretly attached to Mgwana appalls me. So far as Gonzalez was concerned, it did some good; for he was compelled to interrogate me more or less as a colleague before deciding of exactly what I was guilty.

Meanwhile his impatient companion had to be allowed to get down to brass tacks.

"What about the wheelbarrow?" he asked.

"What wheelbarrow?"

Gonzalez raised his white, clerkly hand, suggesting that it was too soon to go into the subject of barrows, and shot a far more deadly question at me:

"You frequently wear rope-soled *alpargatas*, Don Felipe?"

"On the beach, yes."

"Were you wearing them on the night of July 22?"

"You know I wasn't."

"The señorita Flagg states that you entered the hotel next morning wearing rope-soled *alpargatas*."

"The señorita Flagg was so drunk she couldn't tell rope from rubber."

"You are known to wear them, Don Felipe. Why isn't there a pair in your cupboard?"

"That's simple. I always throw them away after I have mended the strings twice. They ought to be made stronger."

Their evidence smelt to high heaven, but was far from complete. I thanked the Lord that Mgwana had had the sense to pack our shoes, and that Olura's foot was small for her height and could be that of any local woman. The rope soles were more awkward, for nobody except a few middle-aged laborers — at any rate in Vizcaya — wears them any longer.

How much they had been able to deduce from the tracks of the barrow I could not guess. Evidently the groove of the wheel was still there in the dried mud along the edge of the old workings. A man in rope-soled shoes had pushed a wheelbarrow for three journeys; for two of them a woman had been hopping about behind or alongside. Farther afield, however, the tracks would be lost on bare rock, in the running puddles and through stiff, short heather and grass. No doubt one of Mgwana's less sophisticated countrymen with his eyes to the ground could have revealed all our movements, but I reckoned that the task would be too much for civilized police.

Gonzalez's next question was highly intelligent, for I had never revealed the state of my palms in his presence.

"May I see your hands?"

I opened and spread them out.

"How did you get those blisters?"

"Rowing."

"When?"

I'd got him there. Olura and I had taken a boat up river a week before, and I could quote the date, the time and the name of the owner. In fact it was Olura who did the rowing, since I could not bear to touch an oar. But who was to tell that?

The Lieutenant gave up the straight detective stuff, probably realizing that a police magistrate would do it much better, and returned to direct attack.

"If you didn't kill Livetti, who did?" he asked.

I said that I might be able to help him if I knew who was the other man in that black Seat.

"Piet Duyker. A South African."

"What's known about him?"

"Respectable and well-to-do. Frequent visits to Spain. Active in the affairs of the Protestant Church. Piety apparently sincere. Politically harmless. Believed to be treasurer and secretary of the Alliance des Blancs."

I refrained from showing absolute ignorance. Whatever kind of Commonwealth cloak-and-dagger operative I was supposed to be, I ought to know what the Alliance des Blancs was. Gonzalez's tone did not suggest that it was particularly sinister; on the other hand, if it was responsible for shoving Livetti through Olura's bathroom window, it could hardly be a charitable organization.

I ventured to ask why it was allowed to operate in Spain.

"Everyone is welcome in Spain so long as he does not break the law."

A patriotic myth! But Madrid certainly sheltered some odd characters with outdated sympathies — due partly to the old-boy network among ultraconservatives, partly to that tradition of political asylum which is even more a point of public honor in Latin America.

"Yours is the only government which doesn't mind annoying de Gaulle," I said.

"That is not what we are discussing, Don Felipe."

I could see that I had touched a nerve there. Gonzalez's overworked department probably cursed the right-wing activities of French exiles and former Nazis as heartily as Scotland Yard disliked those of Olura's woolly friends. I seemed to be on the right lines, so I tried again:

"Has des Aunes been long in Spain?"

"You know how long."

"Time passes so quickly."

"Yes, it doesn't seem two years since his trial," Gonzalez replied.

I tore into the dead news of forgotten front pages which still must be filed somewhere in the circuits of my brain, trying to extract and distinguish the sad careers of the more excitable military men in France. Sauche? Who had been Sauche? Now I could even recall the photographs of that embittered and disappointed leader of the O.A.S., condemned in absence to twenty years for plotting against de Gaulle and pretty lucky that he did not get the death penalty. Of course des Aunes was General Sauche. So much for the motor horns sounding Algérie Française!

Well, I could understand that Sauche would not approve of independence for Algerians; but it looked as if he hadn't stopped at that. Frustrated extremists are always inclined to exaggerate their importance by inventing some vast public conspiracy to account for their private defeat. The opinions which Vigny had expressed to me plus the activities of this South African of Boer descent — the sort of man to be a member of the secret Bruderbond — suggested that Sauche extended his resentment to all the emergent states of Africa. In one form or other this Alliance des Blancs probably held the dear old creed: that the Almighty had created Europeans to rule and that we shouldn't disappoint divinity by pandering to Africans. What's a European? What were Hitler's Aryans? What's an Arab when he has one leg and is black? Daddy, are Caucasians communists? Why not hold the Sabbath on Tuesday and be saved? Bah!

"And Vigny? How long has he been here?" I asked.

"He presented his request for asylum on July 11. We do not know how he crossed the frontier. Sauche expected him, and rented a villa at Zarauz for the pair.

"Then what were they doing at the Hostal de las Olas?"

"Waiting for the villa to be ready for them. You are aware that they left the hotel before Mr. Mgwana arrived, and you may as well know that their alibi after that is unbreakable. On the night of July 21 they were holding a small party at the villa."

I apologized for asking questions when I ought to be answering them and thanked him for his courtesy. He replied coolly that questions could be quite as revealing as

answers. However, I saw no harm in asking another:
"What had Vigny and Duyker to say for themselves?"

"They happened to be on the same road. They had no idea whom they passed. They stopped for a drink in Amorebieta. They well remembered that a taxi driver parked in front of them and had trouble with his hand brake, but what about it?"

"You believe that?"

"Until such time as you tell the truth. Why did you wish to avoid them?"

He would have none of my story that I was trying to ditch a jealous Vigny, and held me wriggling on the end of the hook. Finally I put the blame on Mgwana and said that it was he who had been worried. So I had left him under the Lieutenant's professional care and removed Olura.

"Why did Miss Manoli bring Mr. Mgwana here so secretly?"

"Because she is the sort of person who doesn't want to understand protocol."

"Yet the Alliance knew he was coming."

Obviously it did. I couldn't see where he was heading — in the direction, I hoped, of whom Livetti had offended and why.

"When did you notice that Miss Manoli had provided an opportunity for an attack on Mgwana?"

I gasped at the monstrosity of this implication. At the same time I could not help seeing that it was a possible reconstruction of the few solid facts, except for the vital misreading of Olura's character.

"But, Teniente, it is utterly inconceivable that Olura Manoli would connive at the assassination of Leopold Mgwana or anyone else! She is always campaigning for freedom, democracy, independence and keeping everybody out of prison except policemen!

"We know she is," he said. "And so we find it hard to believe that her friendship with a *caudillo* like Mr. Mgwana was sincere."

"Mgwana is an obvious exception."

"Why?"

"Because he is black."

"What has color to do with it? Don't come to me with baby talk!"

"But it's true!"

"Nonsense, Don Felipe! You might as well say she would approve the cruelties of Batista in Cuba because he was a sambo. Mr. Mgwana is a born leader, whom you or I would be proud to serve, but Miss Manoli, never! Now, tell me — who is Prebendary Flanders?"

"All I can tell you is that he organizes protests, and that, like Peter the Hermit, he has a considerable following among emotional youth. March, boys, march, and perhaps you'll reach Jerusalem! But without reference to the chaplain of my College or some similar authority I cannot say with any confidence exactly what a Prebendary is."

"This dignitary recommended the Hostal de las Olas to Miss Manoli?"

"Yes. I think he did."

"And he is the head of a left-wing and politically excitable movement?"

The threat to Olura was real. Unpleasant rather than dangerous, but there was no knowing. Spaniards take their politics seriously; what we dismiss as mere foam on the surface, to them is evidence of a wave. Prebendary Flanders, Olura, their committees and their civil disobedience were neither more nor less significant than the Alliance des Blancs, both appearing equally futile to the outsider and equally portentous to themselves.

It was this self-valuation which mattered to Gonzalez and his experienced department. No good Englishman would have been at all impressed if he had taken a beer with the early Hitler in Munich or a dismal tea with Karl Marx in London; but a Spaniard, well accustomed to *quijotismo* getting out of hand, would have made a note in his little black book and opened a file.

I told Gonzalez firmly that the first principle of Olura and her political friends was nonviolence.

"For many anarchists, too."

"But there is all the difference in the world!"

"Why? Why should you English be different?" he insisted. "Spaniards, Italians, Russians, Indians — their leaders often preached nonviolence at first, and then — waking up, let's say, upon a morning of sun with indigestion due to nuts and goat's milk — decided that the only effective route to nonviolence was by violence."

"But Miss Manoli's friends are NOT anarchists!" I shouted, my loud resentment at the accusation showing me that I was a little uncertain myself.

"Anarchists march with them, Don Felipe. At least *they*

understand that anyone who sets out to make government impossible is an anarchist whatever he calls himself."

The damned fellow must have been well educated by logical Jesuits. Given enough time and a decanter of port I could have tied him into knots; but one is not at one's best as a suspect, however unruly, under interrogation.

"If I follow you," he said, enjoying himself at my expense and, I think, deliberately shocking his stolid companion in the front seat, "neither Miss Manoli nor her chief, Prebendary Flanders, would attempt to assassinate our Generalissimo?"

"You can't call him her chief, and they most decidedly would not!"

"But if we caught, tried and shot an unsuccessful assassin, they would organize a march of protest and have questions asked in your parliament."

"They might. But it would be a protest against what they considered injustice, not a condonation of the attempt."

"It is injustice which excites them?"

"Yes! And why the devil not?"

"But now we have arrived, my dear Don Felipe! If Spanish justice offends them, what must they think of African? I do not, I fear, think it at all impossible that Miss Manoli used the Alliance des Blancs."

"And I tell you, much appreciated Teniente, that it's nonsense. After all, the one thing we know is that Vigny and this Duyker followed her."

"Yes, because the plot had failed."

"You might as well accuse Leopold Mgwana!"

"A prime minister? Of a friendly state? We are not Albanians, Don Felipe! But he has of course been asked unofficially through diplomatic channels to make any statement he pleases."

"Good God! And did he?"

"Naturally I have not seen the text of his reply. But my superiors have given me to understand that he says he killed Livetti in self-defense on the night of July 21, that he claims diplomatic immunity and that he has requested our Minister of Justice to close the case discreetly. He has also stated that neither you nor Miss Manoli had any part in it."

I stared at him, not daring to open my mouth. So Mgwana's talk of chivalry had not been merely allusive. His word of honor that he would not involve me had also been nobly kept. But this superbly medieval attempt to squash all publicity was deadly. Since Olura had some mysterious connection with Livetti, she was in trouble whatever Mgwana said.

No doubt the Spanish Foreign Office had replied to Mgwana thanking him very much, regretting that he should have been molested on Spanish soil and assuring him that the case was closed. But no government could let it go at that. Attempts at assassination are too serious. The question of who employed Livetti became more serious than who killed him. Mgwana quite unintentionally had removed himself from the case, leaving us two hopelessly stuck in it.

"Why don't you accept his statement?" I asked.

The cop in the front seat looked round like a dog asking to be let off the leash. My question had, I suppose, implied that I did not accept Mgwana's statement either.

"Although Mr. Mgwana and I did not speak a common language," Gonzalez went on, "I had great respect for him. He was very much a gentleman. I observed that he treated and loved Miss Manoli as a sister. It could be that he is protecting her."

"Where did he kill Livetti?"

"On the beach, where he was taking a stroll after nightfall. Then he waded out to sea with the body."

"It sounds like the truth."

"Truth? When the hotel porters and that fellow Arizmendi swear that he never left the hotel? But say they are mistaken! We must then assume that Livetti was provided with sail or propeller, for only so could he have traveled round Cape Machichaco and Cape Ormenza against the set of wind and tide. And then into Pobeña! Perhaps to take on a cargo of iron ore, of which some pieces were found in his pockets? You dropped Livetti into the bay of Pobeña on the twenty-second. When and where you killed him I do not know, but I advise you to tell me. If I had been there at the time, it might have been my duty to do the same."

I was strongly tempted to accept the invitation. Given the faintest notion how, when and where Livetti had in fact been killed, I might have confessed to dealing with him in defense of Mgwana. But, as it was, I had no facts on which to base invention. Medical and scientific evidence would soon show that I was lying. And whatever I said must increase their prejudice towards assassination and strengthen the absurd suspicion of Olura.

A still easier way out was to admit that I had got rid of the body for Mgwana, and that I did not know why he had been compelled to kill. Well, but was it likely? Was it even conceivable that after meeting him only twenty-four hours earlier I would take such a risk? Together Mgwana and I might have cooked up some fairly credible story, but I had no means of getting in touch with him.

The third alternative before me was to tell the truth. That I could not bear, for it would leave Olura all alone in Maya, carrying the can for everybody and defenseless against the accusation that Livetti was a friend of hers. The scandal I no longer gave a damn about; nor, I expect, did she. The Law had become far more dangerous than the Press. She had no proof whatever that Livetti was dead when he appeared in her bathroom window — indeed, no proof that he had ever been there at all.

So I persisted in my denials and was pressed with question after question until I found myself denying what I had already admitted, and Gonzalez's face became grimmer and grimmer, though always with a shade of contemptuous pity.

"Listen," he said at last, "you are not any sort of agent! You are just a poor devil of a professor in love with Miss Manoli."

Then with the gesture of an inquisitor handing over a relapsed heretic to the secular arm he permitted his companion to arrest me on a charge of murder.

My Intervention

O LURA makes sufficient mention of my arrival in the village to which her movements were confined. As a prison without bars, it was at least picturesque; as a setting for Olura, it appeared to me inadequate and at first inexplicable.

The mannerisms of my dear ward were pitiably unfamiliar. She ignored her primitive living conditions — though I should not apply that adjective either to the kindness or the culinary skill of her hosts — and was inclined to spend her time staring out of her bedroom window at a dull waste of sand upon which it was generally raining.

I did not recognize her in the part of poor little rich girl, nor in her mood of bewildered resignation. Perhaps I had always ascribed to her a self-confidence more aggressive than it really was. Yet I had long since observed that the true motive of her Prebendary and his friends in persuading her that she had political influence was to obtain the maximum publicity for their antisocial activities by ensuring that it was always Olura who should appear before the Bench.

Of her social function, so far as it could be disentangled from the political, I have always been secretly proud. Some fellow writing in a gossip column for his bread — a low and abject condition as John Cleland called it — described her as the uncrowned queen of Africa. If we reduce that statement to something nearer Truth than News, the correct title would be unpaid tea-provider for African students.

There, however, reacting against exaggeration, I may err by underestimating her value. When some poor devil has spent a humiliating day searching for lodgings in a district where it is extremely unlikely that he will find any, it is something to be treated like a prince in a Belgravia drawing room and to meet — an improbable encounter under the palm leaves of his parents' hut — the Prime Minister of his country.

After listening to Olura's incoherencies I naturally visualized Dr. Ardower as belonging to the academic fringe of her ungroomed and arrogantly emotional Group, but sufficiently in touch with reality to be after her money. Against this picture, however, was the fact that Leopold Mgwana had obviously liked and trusted him. Mgwana, whom I had several times met — not unprofitably — at Olura's house, impressed me as an admirable judge of men, appreciating energy whether in a missionary or one of his own unprincipled and dynamic young administrators.

I wondered if Ardower himself might not possess these qualities, and with them the morality of an able gangster. That he was Fellow and Tutor of a reputable Oxford College meant nothing. The virtue which these worthy and doubtless indispensable citizens value most highly is meticulous scholarship. Who has more of it than the planner of an ingenious, successful and bloodless raid upon a bank?

When I had spent a couple of days assuring Olura that she had little to fear — an occupation which I myself found more pleasant than plausible — I left for Madrid, recommending that during my short absence she should put down on paper a concise account of what had happened. I obtained little satisfaction from the Ministry of Justice in spite of my influence and my introductions. I was not surprised, for I did not know myself what or how much to believe. The Minister put off my inquiries by begging me to consider whether I might not be inconveniencing myself for the sake of a vulgar crime of passion. The only concession I could extract from him was permission to remain with Olura.

On my return to Maya the following narrative awaited me. I saw at once that there was no action I could usefully take — a position which, I have observed, exasperates most of my fellows into excitable follies. To accept impotence with equanimity one must be confident of the speed and unexpectedness of one's attack whenever the opposing force is at last free of obfuscation.

Meanwhile I hired a villa for the pair of us — at ridiculous expense since there was none readily available — and rewarded Olura's kind hosts by eating in their establishment at least once a day. I noticed that Dr. Ardower, whatever his faults, had aroused in my dear goddaughter a latent sensuality — I refer of course only to the pleasures of the table — which had hitherto been sadly lacking.

For the rest, police surveillance was tactful. I had no more reason to object to it than to the temporary prohibition of all correspondence, for I had already warned my young partners in the firm that I did not desire for the time being to be bothered either with my own affairs or what they considered to be theirs.

Narrative of Olura Manoli

I T cannot be as bad as you say. Philip's story and Leopold's and mine must all agree. These horrible police
who will not let us see each other or write to each other
know that we couldn't all have invented it. But they will
not tell me what either of them said. I do not even know
what I am accused of. They never tell me anything outright. They treat me as if I were something very precious
and very guilty.

I can hear you say: my dear Olura, I have not the least
interest in your personal affairs. Which is what you always say when you really are interested but disapprove.
You have the caution of a wise, old eunuch in a harem.
You would have liked to marry me off at nineteen to some
grave young man sure to succeed his father as Lord Lieutenant of the County or confine me in an ivory cage on a
fairy-story glass mountain. But you haven't had so much
to throw stones at as you think.

Philip says I am like what he calls the three bloody
monkeys. When you meet him . . . Oh, that *when!*
Where shall we be? What will have happened? How old
shall we be? . . . But when you meet him, you will love

his dry voice with the ripple of laughter always underneath it. It's not true that I don't hear or see or speak any evil. I feel more than anyone the cowardice of humanity, which won't act until somebody is sacrificed to show the way. I wish I had more than money with which to serve my generation.

I think Philip meant that I have stood too apart from life in spite of all I have done. It may be true. I knew what everyone would say when I took that genius, Hilaire Bomumba, to Rome. But I was right not to care. Let them say! I am to be judged by what I am seen to give. Why must they all assume that I give my body too?

It is not as if I had been without normal desires, but when one hears one's friends continually talking about the unimportance of the sexual act, is it surprising that one believes them? And if the act is so unimportant, why allow it to complicate one's life and work? They can't have it both ways.

I have a feeling that this will not seem to your old-fashioned morality as crazy as it did to Philip. I tried to explain it to him, but he would not let me talk. He said that it was a crime against nature, and I could taste the salt of his tears. I suppose, traditionally, they ought to have been mine.

But I am always and only in love with *him*. He loves both me and something else that I represent for him. The beauty and fecundity of the earth. The tragedy and ecstasy of being alive. I, too, know that our love extends in space, but I want only to feel it, not to exclaim poetry about it.

I have to tell you about my emotional life, though I know that isn't what you want me to write. Where was Olura on the night of July 22 isn't so important a question as why was she and what was she thinking, because those may explain things that we do not even know need explaining. The old me and the new me matter. The first was in the sort of muddle which only a psychiatrist could have straightened out. The second is very humble and very unhappy, but she doesn't want to be changed at all.

If this holiday had not started as it did, I could have resisted Philip's attraction. I might have denied it, or never realized it at all. It was a mixture of fascination and repulsion anyway. I do not think it would have been difficult to emphasize for myself his self-indulgence and conceit.

Philip, darling, that is what I am calling your vitality and your blessed self-confidence! How cruel that it is not to you I am writing in front of our window, instead of trying to explain why it *is* our window!

The facts. All right, you shall have them brutally. When the holiday started, I was prepared for whatever might happen. If Leopold wanted me, he could have me. I admired him greatly, and it was to be the final gesture of my trust. You are not to comment. The only person who has a right to, and to laugh, is Philip.

Those two long conferences with the Commonwealth Relations Office, keeping Leopold in London when he should have been at home leading his people to social democracy, had worn him out. I remember his saying that the real choice before a new country was whether to shoot all its lawyers or all its economists, and that neither of them was worth the trouble. Cyril Flanders was grieved by his bitterness.

It was that sort of cynicism which made Cyril feel that Leopold Mgwana had more in common with the Establishment than with us. Personally I did not think he had changed in anything essential. It stands to reason that prime ministers enjoy the society of prime ministers; or, if they don't, at least they must have enough unspoken thoughts in common to be at ease. But I did notice that his interests had widened. And I saw more than anyone of the little leisure he had. Often he would telephone me when some official dinner was over and ask if he might come round for an hour.

There is always truth in what Cyril says, and he is so appreciative of all I do. He explained that the reason why Leopold gave less importance to our advice and guidance was that we allowed him to feel that we had less admiration for him. Above all he needed rest, and to be persuaded all over again that what mattered was not authority, but our ideals of brotherhood and democracy. It was my duty, Cyril thought, to take him away from London and try to break down his growing reserve.

I thought at first of Italy or France, but the hotels are so alike — all with the same routine and little hope of privacy. Cyril suggested the Hostal de las Olas where he stayed last year. He was sure we should not be bothered by any publicity.

So it was I who invited Leopold. He was at first uncertain, and said that for my sake he did not think we should leave together. I told him that was ridiculous: that no intelligent person paid any attention to such nonsense. But if he preferred it, I would drive down some days beforehand and arrange his holiday like any private secretary. That would not arouse any comment, and if it did I didn't care.

When I arrived and booked our rooms, I did not mention the name of Mgwana to the desk. Cyril might think the hotel too remote for publicity, but I knew from experience that we should have the news hawks round at once. So I simply told the management that a friend of mine would shortly join me, and let them believe that he was some distinguished American of color.

While I waited for him I was lonely. I felt that people thought I had no right to be there. There were Frenchmen who looked away from me, and people who could not understand why I was there alone, why I had chosen that hotel instead of some international palace for the rich. I couldn't help feeling that I was offering myself like the beautiful spies of fiction. And then I would ask myself *Why not?* They too, if they actually exist, serve something bigger than themselves.

Once away from the Group, this whole thing seemed to me artificial. It was real enough in one sense, for I knew very well that Leopold was physically attracted by me; but in another sense it was not real at all. He had a curious, fierce sentimentalism which was too purely African to understand. Our deep and affectionate friendship was poten-

tially critical — a silly word which I use in the sense of
the heat and silence of an atomic plant — but never
looked like getting out of control.

So there I was, alone, forced to introspection, persuading myself that I hadn't any exaggerated worth and that
anyway what Leopold needed from me was work and time
and sympathy. But I couldn't be calm about it. It was I
who had gone critical. That ought to be a humiliating confession and yet I am not in the least ashamed of it.

When I first noticed Philip he aroused my curiosity. He
was very English — tall and sandy-haired with a face
which was bumpy rather than craggy and an eagerness to
go forward which made him look as if his shoulders
stooped, though they didn't. He too seemed out of place in
the hotel. Very subtly. One would never have guessed it by
watching him, for he was always swinging about the bar
and the dining room, chatting to everybody with an un-
usual command of foreign languages.

He made no special effort to talk to me. That annoyed
me. I knew I had made an impression on him, but he
didn't take the trouble to follow it up. He was behaving
just as if he had been snubbed and decided that I was too
difficult. One might have thought he was interested only
in his Basque peasant girls.

It was July 20 at 11:45 precisely — there's a time and a
date for you, and does it matter to anyone but me? — and
I was coming back from a long, weary walk, during most
of which I had been worrying and worrying about Cyril's
extraordinary innocence. I had never confided anything
about my private life to him; he probably thought that I

was discreetly promiscuous. Perhaps it was not fair to expect him to understand the relationship between Leopold and me. But didn't he have a dirty mind? I mean by that a conventional mind, not clean thinking, prejudiced. Did he, could he, believe that Africans were so strongly sexed that they behaved like animals? No more true of them than of healthy men anywhere! Didn't all this talking round the point of love and admiration imply that he thought, like some wretched, poor white in the southern states, that Leopold would jump at an affair with any moderately attractive white woman? Cyril is a saint, of course, but I saw it as revolting. If there was one thing certain about Leopold it was that he had complete command over his own actions and emotions.

We were the only two people — Philip and I, I mean — on miles of windswept beach. The wind was tearing at my cloak and the seas were like green and white dinosaurs, hungry after their long journey and leaping at me because I was the first vulnerable, lonely thing to be tortured. And this man was going to pass me without a word.

I made him cross the river with me to this inn. He had absurd false modesty and did not like the precious Basque villagers to see him without his trousers. So I lent him my red cloak. I thought that would embarrass him even more, but it didn't. He is quite uninhibited whenever he sees a richness of humor.

Since the curiosity of each had been at work on the other, we reached at once a strange, challenging sort of intimacy. My impression was that he had had little experience of women of character — leaving out philolo-

gists, of course, as I think it is fair to do. Philip would say
that I am generalizing on insufficient evidence. But it
stands to reason.

I had not forgiven him for ignoring me, and I thought
him too self-satisfied to be really likable. He sat there
stuffing grilled prawns and swilling white wine as if he
were wholeheartedly content with the world as he found
it. His eyes were intolerable. I felt that if he made love to
me I should be enjoyed rather like the prawns. No more
and no less. And yet when he paid some attention to what
I was saying instead of the way I was made, he showed an
amused tenderness as if he were trying to tell me that philologists didn't do that kind of thing to little girls. I said to
myself that he was academic and limited and patronizing,
but now and then he reminded me of my father. The same
sort of dry, outrageous humor. He did not fit into any of
the monotonous pigeonholes where I kept my admirers.

Leopold arrived that evening. I introduced Philip and
noticed that his manners were perfect — natural, but
with just the right tone of respect. Both of them seemed to
appreciate something in the other which I could not altogether understand. I had that maddening impression that
after ten minutes they had formed a club to which women
were not admitted, and later on I mentioned it to Philip.

"Oh, we were just glorying in you!" he said.

I replied that I did not like being treated as a museum
exhibit, and that of course started him off on lovely, obscure nonsense about Aphrodite rising innocently from
the sea and puzzled by the goings-on of ordinary human

beings. Period: Late Hellenistic, he added — just to make it all safely impersonal.

The next morning I thought Leopold looked tired after his journey, and persuaded him to stay in bed. The sun was hot, and the beach opposite the hotel was crowded. So I walked along the sands towards the rocks near the mouth of the estuary where I had met Philip the day before. He was there, with a blue, sheltered pool rising and falling at his feet, as the surf crashed against the other side of the promontory.

I discovered that he knew very little about me, but at least had heard of my father. It was rather a tense morning. I did not want to lecture him about my interests; on the other hand I was not going to let him shrug me off as a wealthy society girl whose intelligence was not worth bothering with. And on the top of that he made me self-conscious about my apple-green and white. Anyway he deserved it, and I meant him to remember me in future.

In the afternoon I drove Leopold along the coast nearly as far as Santander. He was rested, and fascinated by country so different from anything he had ever seen. Cyril had at least been right in his choice of a place for us. When we came back very late I went up to my room, feeling rewarded for doing my duty by such a sense of joy and flowering.

It was a hot, humid night after the storm. In the late evening we had seen the flanks of those huge, round hills steaming like horses. When Leopold came up about midnight, he looked as if he expected me to be dressed for

winter. One would have thought that he at any rate would
be accustomed to women wearing as little as they please.
But I suppose there are conventions as illogical as our
own. A girl is probably considered an abandoned hussy if
she doesn't have the proper little pattern of scars or something on her right breast.

Leopold had brought with him a draft of the proposed
agenda for the Addis Ababa meeting. He wanted me to
read through it all and tell him what would be the attitude
of my Group if the resolutions of the conference recommended direct action in states where Africans were not
yet free and equal citizens. I said that I thought it would
depend on the wording and the circumstances. For me
and my friends violence was always wrong. But, so long
as it was recognized to be wrong, it might sometimes be
justifiable without being condoned. He was afraid that
point might be too subtle for inexperienced politicians.

I worked on the papers till it was nearly half past one,
trying to suggest phrasing which Cyril would approve.
Then I went into the bathroom. There was half a man
hanging down from the little window with a camera
round his neck.

Can you imagine the shock and the vileness of it? He
looked dead. At first it was not so much that which appalled me as what he believed, what he intended. Obviously he had hoped to get a shot of my bed through the
open bathroom door.

But nothing quite fitted. He could never have done it
secretly because of the flash. Perhaps he thought he would
have time to escape. Perhaps he meant to try and black-

mail me on the spot. Another funny thing was that the bathroom door was shut. I am almost sure that I left it a little open — which would be much more convenient if somebody wanted first to listen and then to throw it wide open suddenly.

I didn't scream. I couldn't. I was like someone killed instantaneously. I told Leopold to look. The effect on him was to make him savagely angry. Against me, it almost seemed. There was a yellow light in his eyes. Then he stood very still, looking at that limp thing. He said that the man must have been pushed through the window already dead, and that we were not only compromised but would be accused of murder.

I could not believe that. I told myself that it was I who must do something. This was my civilization, not his. Spain or not, instinctively I must be nearer to it than he. And Philip nearer still. I asked him if I should fetch Philip.

He was doubtful. In spite of their mutual admiration society he did not know what kind of person Philip was. I did. He was not committed to anything at all except scholarship, but he had kindness and absolute integrity. I did not understand — then — how anyone could have moral courage without a set of firm beliefs, but I was sure he would help me, because he would be outraged at what had been done, not because he was attracted by me.

Leopold considered that neither of us should open the door to go out, since we did not know who might be waiting in the passage nor what sort of trap had been set. I wasn't going to open the door anyway. I knew very well

how Philip could get to my room. It was two balconies
away from his, and I had often seen him leaning on the
railings.

When we had turned out the light, everything outside
was dark. So I risked it. Philip was asleep. He did not
make any remark or want to know what it was all about.
He just came. And when he had looked into my bathroom,
he believed at once in our innocence. Only afterwards I
saw how wonderful it was that he should be so confident.

He did what we ought to have done — feeling the man
and making certain that he was really dead. He treated
the body as if it had never been alive at all, calling it
Punch or the Puppet or something. It was heartless — like
those horrible, falsely humorous expressions of soldiers by
which they prevent themselves feeling what they know
they ought to be feeling. It only breeds more killing if you
shrug your shoulders and say a man "has had it" when he
is dead.

Under Philip's influence Leopold showed that he was
not either as resigned or as sensitive as I had thought. Together they pulled the body into the bathroom and laid it
face upwards on the floor.

I recognized him. It was Alberto Livetti. He was notorious for his lack of scruples and his enterprise. He was
just the man to make his way into a hotel and try to get
pictures of a prime minister and his girl friend. I couldn't
speak. There was a stupid inhibition which any woman
would understand and, besides that, a second shock, for I
never thought he would try to degrade me all over again
after what had passed between us.

Three years ago when I was in Rome with Hilaire Bomumba I employed Livetti to take the publicity stills. All that I knew about him then was that he was a superb artist with an extraordinary gift for catching the glow and vigor of the human body. He worked for the Press, of course, like the rest of them, but he was much more important than the loathsome little men who were always trying to get intimate shots of celebrities and pestered us. Every picture they made was an innuendo.

Hilaire was temperamental, never still. He would not have had the patience to endure sittings if I hadn't accompanied him to the studio and held his hand — sometimes literally — while Livetti experimented and experimented with his animal, elemental quality. Some of the poses were more candid than were really necessary. Livetti was as fascinated by anatomy as any sculptor. I think that is what he ought to have been, not a photographer at all.

He tried to catch my interest, and he did. He pretended to share my opinions, which was easy; for, if he had any sincere politics at all, he was a left-wing socialist. He told me that I was the most beautiful woman he had ever seen. Though I knew very well that from an Italian to any girl with money that meant no more than tenderly wishing her good afternoon, I could not help being impressed since he never attempted to make love to me. He treated me with a sort of neutrality, like a judge in the show ring awarding a Highly Commended.

When he asked me if I would sit for him I hesitated, because his cynicism and his comments were unpleasant. But he was a genius in his own way, and his pictures of

Hilaire were quite marvelous. I felt that I would be untrue to myself if I refused, for what he needed was not mine any more than my money. I hate possessions except when they make it possible for me to give.

So I sat for Livetti because it was my duty, and I could not allow personal, prudish feelings to interfere with duty. What a muddle! As if I could have had the detachment of a professional model! As if I could separate myself from what I live in!

After he had taken a few of the simpler shots, he started to paw me under the pretense of arranging shadows, but so delicately that I was not quite sure. The delicacy was the appalling thing, even worse than his disgusting candor. He told me that Hilaire was being unfaithful to me with a senator and his daughter at the same time and wanted to know what sort of sexual intercourse I enjoyed myself.

The situation was more unmanageable than if he had attacked me violently. I was lost and did not know what to do. I couldn't reach my clothes and I was completely defenseless. I felt like a schoolgirl and wanted to cry like one. But I couldn't do that either. So I just stood still and met his eyes and told him what I was.

The change in him was devastatingly unexpected. Of course he made it twice as dramatic as was necessary. He begged my forgiveness. He kept on exclaiming that how could they know. For him, he said, I had been simply a girl with too much money entertaining a brutally amoral dancer whose behavior made us both fair game for anyone.

While I dressed, he defended himself. The words streamed out of him. He boasted that he was a man of the renaissance, that he had no religion, no principles, and that his only duty was to the truth. He despised the rotten, corrupt society which paid him, and laughed at it and humiliated it. He spat at the film stars who paid for publicity and screeched when he gave them too much of it. He confessed to the vilest things — photographing poor old American nymphomaniacs without their makeup on and selling the negatives back to them. He claimed to be a specialist in bad taste who exaggerated the bad taste of others until it recoiled on them. He said that he used his camera like a dagger between the shoulders of the despicable and dishonored.

I could hardly bear to speak to him, but I asked him what all this had to do with his attempt to excite me. He said that "they" wanted to find out what I liked. "They" were all prepared to give such a woman whatever she wanted of either sex. It was only afterwards that I began to imagine that "they" had been watching.

I left Rome and Hilaire at once. I knew the whole thing ought to have no effect on me at all, but I felt humiliated and degraded. The only comfort was that I believed Livetti's remorse to be sincere, and that so far as he was capable of recognizing simplicity, he had. Even there I was wrong. Evidently I had not impressed him at all. He still put me in the class of rich girls who he thought deserved his camera.

All through that horrible night of his death I tried to believe some good of him. Livetti's mind was full of patterns instead of worries and scruples like the rest of us; he used to deny that they had any relationship to life or morals or beauty or anything. But I was never allowed to agree with him. If I said that Form had no meaning, he would get very excited and shout that it did, that of course it had a human value, that of course Form was a shadow of reality. So he must have had a sort of religion — something he believed in, something for which he would fight.

Philip and Leopold removed the body down the ladder which Livetti had put up against my bathroom window. I could not help or watch or do any more. I was on my bed, shaking without being able to control myself. They took him out to the garage through the central shaft. They must have done it very carefully, for the police never suspected that Livetti had been inside the hotel at all.

Philip drove away with him in the boot of my car and ran out of petrol before he had a chance to get rid of him. He had to hide Livetti in a field in case the Civil Guard searched the car — which they did. When he recovered the body, Livetti's passport fell out of his pocket and was found in the road. That was the first bit of evidence which pointed at us.

He returned to the hotel, still with Livetti, and never blamed me for not telling him that Leopold and I had finished our afternoon's tour on the reserve tank. He was gentle and patronizing as if it were quite natural for me to forget. It was infuriating to be treated as a hysterical, irresponsible child when I couldn't forgive myself and never shall.

Leopold and I kept an eye on the car while poor Philip

got some sleep. When it was my turn to go down to lunch
— I didn't want any but I had to try to behave naturally
— I was appalled to see Mary Deighton-Flagg in the restaurant. There was no way of avoiding her. She had been
at school with me, and was a monitor when I was a little,
long-legged thing in the junior. Always there was something unhealthy about her. I think she had been overwhelmed by trying to keep up with too many brothers; at
that age the effort made her coarse and unfeminine. Under her influence — and in the comparative privacy of
their own room — the monitors used to compete who
could break wind the loudest. I suppose it was a revolt
against the over-ladylike manners upon which the school
insisted. Decorum would have been easier to observe if the
food had contained fewer starches.

I mention this because it holds the key to Mary's character. She was so determined to be the leader who formed
public taste that she did not care if it was tastelessness.
That must have been a great help to her when she went in
for journalism. She could write, too.

Her specialty was castigating vice in high places. Her
stuff was thin after the paper's legal staff had removed all
the possible libels, but she used to dine out on the bits that
her editor wouldn't touch. One of these startling revela-
tions of hers was every word of it true, and could not be
ignored. Fortunately she got out of the country a few
hours before she would have been arrested on a charge of
criminal slander.

I couldn't prevent her taking the rest of her lunch at my
table. She asked me if I had been ill; I was looking so

lovely and so tired. I said that I had been a little over-worked in London, to which she replied that she had noticed Mr. Mgwana in the hotel. I let the innuendo pass. I wasn't equal to the effort.

Then she wanted to know who Philip was. I gathered that he had been down already to the bar, that she had spoken to him and that she knew he was in some way close to Leopold and me. It occurred to me that I really did not know Philip well. Her dark hair and large, sad eyes were beautiful. But I felt he was not the sort of man to be taken in by foam rubber at one end and a too slithery skirt at the other.

I told her that Philip was just a friend, and remembered too late that the phrase is a cliché in her profession. She promptly asked — as an old schoolfriend and off the record — if the two weren't jealous of each other and how did I manage so cleverly.

I tried to understand her and be charitable. I reminded myself that after all this time she probably could not help believing what she wrote. She was such a pitiable creature, and her life must have been desolate — living in Madrid on men, cadging stories from the police and the café journalists and the movie extras.

So I did my best to explain to her what my relations with Leopold Mgwana really were, and that I had accompanied him as cicerone and secretary because Cyril Flanders and the Group thought it important that I should. I think now that when the police questioned her she passed on all I said, naturally making it sound an exclusive, mysterious spy story. At the time I just kept on talking about Leopold to head her off Philip. I felt that Philip might be already afraid that I was an embarrassing person to know, and that one of Mary's little paragraphs suggesting that Olura Manoli was now taking an interest in the older universities would just about finish him.

From time to time I shivered with nervousness. I had to say that the dining room was icy. The wind was getting up again, so perhaps it was. She couldn't help seeing that there was something badly wrong. She told me that now she had met me she would stay another night.

I went up to Leopold's room and found Philip there. Mary had made a bad impression on him. In fact he was so disgustingly rude about her that I had to tell him she had been at school with me and that it wasn't her fault if she had to fight to get enough to live on.

That afternoon Pedro Gonzalez turned up, so detestably obliging and polite and unavoidable that he haunted us like the ghost of an income tax inspector. I am sure he has exactly the same expression whether he is torturing a suspect or accepting a drink. The Government had attached him to Leopold as a security guard. The last thing Cyril and I wanted was that he should be bothered by Franco's police. And if Gonzalez had to come and protect us he might have started it earlier!

As it was, his arrival meant that Leopold could not help with the body. Philip insisted on going alone. I would not allow it. He had sacrificed enough already for a helpless, notorious society girl who couldn't even remember that there was no petrol in her car. I was determined to show him that I didn't use either tears or tranquillizers and that

I could face for his sake just as much as he could for mine.

I think he was the more nervous of the two. For no reason at all he objected to my red cloak. I could not see why, for it didn't matter if it was ruined; and I knew very well how conventional he was and that he thought it affected. But then suddenly I did understand. The cloak had become my trademark and dear to him. I could have thrown it over him and kissed him. It would have shocked his masculine sense of propriety if I had told him that, however much I shrank from what we had to do, I did not intend to lose a moment of his society by fainting when the boot was opened.

We were about to set off when Leopold stormed into my room. It was the second time that I had seen him angry. There must be a side of him which he has never shown to me. He had just received a telephone call in his native language from someone who knew that we were hiding the body. This terrified me, though it stood to reason all the time that the murderer must guess what had happened. Up to then I was just living a piece of theater — fast and unreal and on a dream stage where we three were the only players. I had no picture at all of the other members of the cast waiting in the wings. I should have realized — Philip and Leopold did — that Mary would not have come up from Madrid for nothing.

Philip would have made as painstaking a criminal as a philologist. He pointed out that whoever had killed Livetti knew nothing as yet about Gonzalez and himself and would not dare to attack us or blackmail us when they saw that Leopold and I were accompanied by two strange men. He was right — though all I saw at the time was a black car on my tail, which passed, slowed down and then ran away.

We stopped at a little town called Amorebieta, where Philip ordered dinner for us and vanished. He didn't come back for hours, and had no right whatever to look so pleased with himself after leaving me to chatter French with that tiresome Gonzalez and appear quite unconcerned, when I could not guess whether he had been kidnaped or assassinated or was merely showing off his Basque to complete strangers.

He told Gonzalez that he was going off in my car, and that he had ordered a taxi to take the three of us back to the hotel because I was tired. I was having none of that. When he suddenly jumped up to go, I went straight out with him and started the car.

He did not even bother to explain himself. He just told me in a superior way that he had got a taxi driver to block the car which had followed us, and that I shouldn't amble. We spent the next hour and a half bumping over the potholes of mountain roads while I listened to him pretending that he wasn't lost. He did not know his beloved Vizcaya as well as he thought he did, and he was. And all the while the Atlantic was hurling wind and rain at us.

At last we saw the lights and filling stations of a main road below us. When we had crossed it, quickly from one darkness to another, I felt that we were committed. From then on what we had to do was far too serious for me to be petty or Philip to be patronizing. His plan was to dump the body in a pool at the bottom of a disused iron mine. He left me alone in the car while he explored the place, and at last came back with an old wheelbarrow. Again it was he who was the more upset of the pair of us. Why cannot sensitive men face a necessity without making fun of it? Naturally I loathed the job, but humor made it no better.

Philip wheeled the body along a rough path which ran between the edge of the old quarry and the fence round the new workings. We were very close to men stoking the furnaces, but on so rackety a night we should never have been noticed if Philip had not been very nearly killed by a landslide. The men heard the stones crashing on the floor of the quarry and heard me scream and came, as they thought, to help. We were very lucky to get clear away with Livetti and the barrow.

So we still had him; and there was nothing we could do except drive off quickly before police and officials came out to investigate the cause of the disturbance. Philip absolutely refused to put the body back in the boot. All the time he was thinking of me and of the horror and disgust which I ought to have been feeling and was by now too desperate to feel.

He sent me into Pobeña to wait for him while he wheeled Livetti over the hill which lay between us and the sea and dropped him down the chute which the iron company used for loading ore into ships. When he came back to me, I was tortured by conscience and pity. His hands were raw and bleeding, and he was plastered with dripping mud. And still it was only me he thought of, horrified because my clothes were in rags and I had a cut or two from stones and old iron. I had been tangled up in a rubbish tip when I tried to lead the quarrymen away from us.

It was over. I felt as if I had recovered from high fever — weak, frightened, thankful, passionately looking forward to resuming normal life, especially since I didn't want it to be normal. All the same, I did remember how I had always thought that rescued damsels in the nursery stories tended to fall in love rather easily. Are we so primitive that we have to believe that the rescuer has charm and character as well as courage? But then Philip had.

I persuaded him that we should attract less notice if we returned to the Hostal de las Olas at an hour when people were freely going in and out. Meanwhile we drove slowly through the great hills, where first the turf and then the trees turned from gray to green. When the sun rose into a great gap in the Pyrenees, like a huge, warm ruby deep in the V of black velvet, we got out of the car — the heater and our drying clothes had made it as fuggy as a linen cupboard — and reveled in the air and the coming day. Philip, who had walked all over that country when he was staying at Eibar, said that we were near to a spectacular spring where we could clean ourselves and the car.

Iturrioz was an exquisite, lonely place, approached by a deep cart track just wide enough for the car. The water trickled down from one rock pool to another through a miniature grove of tall, white heather. Below the pools was a natural ford with a hard rock bottom, and there Philip cleaned out the car — purified was the word I felt — while I went upstream to the pools.

The cool water resurrected me. Blood and mud and the brown stains of iron vanished in the effervescence of the little falls, taking a part of myself with them and leaving only my longing for Philip. I could not be as open and sincere as I wished, for I was still not sure what picture he really had of me. Yet I had to sweep him off his feet. Philip being Philip, he would chivalrously decide that after such a night I could bear to be made love to.

I ought to be ashamed of calculating — far from coldly — what his reactions were likely to be. But he was sensitive to what he chose to consider immodesty. So I created for him a shy and radiant nymph of Iturrioz, inadequately held together by safety pins. Why not? I cannot see that composing the stuff which poetry is made of is any different from writing it. And I couldn't help being aware as I parted the long, soft spires and came towards him that I had an affinity to white heather.

I tell you all this because I want you to understand Philip and me together as one person made of two utterly different halves. You must not ever think that I was seduced by him in typically masculine triumph, though I would rather you believed that than what you used to suspect about me.

And anyway it wasn't then and there. Olura — that old Olura — was disintegrated, weeping with joy and astonishment at herself and at being overfastidious at the same time. The rocks were so cold and damp, and the car was vulgar. But I knew that it didn't matter, that I belonged to Philip for as long as he should ever want me and that if my "not now" sounded as alarmed as he tells me it did, it was because I longed to give myself to him in my own time and my own way — not clumsily, but free, free, free.

It was strange that he did not know that as confidently as I did. But he still did not understand me. When I had to pretend to be leaving Spain next day with Leopold, he believed every word of it, the poor darling!

But I must explain what happened. We returned to the hotel about breakfast time and cheered up Leopold, who had worked himself into such a state of anxiety that he had been on the point of asking Gonzalez to call in the police and the army to look for us. Then we got our first real sleep for forty-eight hours.

In the evening I could see that the holiday had been too exhausting for Leopold and that he was ready to return to London and on to Africa at the end of the week. I did not think I had any right to persuade him to stay, so I arranged to drive him and Gonzalez to the airport and gave them the impression that I intended to go home by road.

I could not admit to Philip that I would drive straight back to him, in case he started to look happy and mysterious; also I felt it would be slightly discourteous to Leopold if I let him know that I meant to stay on after he had left. There was no question of deceiving either of them; it was just that tact prevented me being completely frank. So not until the very last moment did I tell Philip that I would be back and that he was to order lunch for me here.

I took the room where you found me. You were surprised at its simplicity. But what else could I want? It is Philip, not I, who cares for comfort and wouldn't be content long with Love in a Cottage. Bread and cheese and

sleeping in the open — all that he would accept unhesitatingly (so long as he had some wine) for the sake of
knowledge, but not for me — I mean, not naturally.

My only rival is Comparative Philology. That, next to
me, will always be the most important thing in his life. I
don't accept it, but I cannot argue. I once told him that our
duty is not to learn but to serve. He replied that service
without knowledge was no bloody use at all.

That obsession of his makes him impatient with such
altruists as Cyril who do good instinctively and at any cost
and have no need of a lot of facts. The only quarrel we
ever had was over Cyril. I didn't know I could be so angry.
Olura wrecked the bedroom door just like a wife in a farce
who finds her husband unfaithful. And then both of us
were in fits of laughter. I cannot bear it. Remembered
laughter brings tears far more helpless than those of remembered misery.

Whatever happens, I must thank God for a week of
such unimaginable sweetness. I see it as a unity of sun
and passion and joy, yet I can sit here and count on fingers every separate hour and recall what we did with it
and where. I could give you those times and dates so exactly, but they are not what you want.

What have I written? I have just read it all through,
and it seems to me — except when I draw Philip to me
by describing him — just a story of mistakes, of follies
which can never happen again. I might merely be saying
like you *A fine mess you've got yourself into now!* but
without the tenderness in your voice. My dear, no mess, as

you call it, would be enough to make me choke with misery. I told you why, and you said all the things you thought you ought to say. Now I tell you again, because once and for all you must understand. I love Philip. I love him so much that far more than my own private world is changed. Even such tiny universes must radiate when they collide and become one.

I know so little of your youth. But you must have loved as you have lived, eagerly and with all your heart. Remember it! Remember it for my sake! A woman's love is as impetuous as your own. I did not know it. All I read and heard made me feel it was a tender, consenting sort of thing, however jealous, however sensual. I thought that men must love more desperately, more passionately, more blindly, though perhaps not so long. That is not true. I know that my love for Philip is as whole and luminous as his for me. In that alone he is not my superior. I love like a man. I love like a woman. My breasts ache for him as if a newborn child had been torn from me. My body is hungry for him. I am in darkness without the only companionship which can ever matter to me. I love.

I had to write that. Forgive me! It is just a woman crying on your shoulder, and soon over. I will go back to dates and times.

All this cruelty began on the first of August. I was sitting on the little wall in front of the terrace — I could see from there a corner of the Hostal de las Olas — and swinging my legs like a child and eating my breakfast. A car with two men drove up, and I was very surprised to see

Lieutenant Gonzalez get out of it. He asked me if there were some quiet place where we could talk. For a moment I thought I must have made an unexpected conquest.

I took him into the bar, which was always smelly and empty at that time of day. With hardly any preliminaries he asked me what Philip had been doing in my car on the night of July twenty-first. Everything which had happened in my other lonely life seemed so remote and unreal that my apprehension of danger was not sharp at all. I assumed that his inquiry had something to do with tourist regulations and that Philip should not have been driving a car which did not belong to him. That stupidity was lucky, for I must have looked completely innocent. A second later, when I had realized that they might be on the trail of Livetti, I was halfway through my reply and my expression just carried on. I said that I had given Philip leave to drive it whenever he liked, and that I didn't know where he had gone.

Gonzalez thanked me and let it go at that, but kept on talking and talking about our Group and Cyril and Civil Disobedience, and seemed to know something about our ideals. Were we really prepared, he asked, to go to prison for what we believed? I left him in no doubt at all that we were.

He was so enthusiastic that I thought I had made a convert. But he did not think our methods would work in Spain, because the people would just laugh at nonviolence when they had such a tradition of rising in arms. While he was only Leopold's shadow, I had not realized that he had a mind of his own. One wouldn't expect to find an intellectual in Franco's secret police.

Then he told me that he needed a few details to round off his report on the Prime Minister's short stay. Who had recommended the Hostal de las Olas, and was it widely known that the visit was planned? I replied that Prebendary Flanders had arranged it, and that I personally had not talked about it but that the Prebendary might have. He probably did. Much as I admire him and although I know that I am wrong, he sometimes seems to me too boastful. He might very well have been eloquent about our influence over Leopold and held me up as an example of devotion and liberal-mindedness.

When Gonzalez had gone, I ran up to my room to change for Philip and the beach, and got the impression that my shoes had been moved. There was nowhere convenient to keep them, so I had distributed them between a suitcase and the bedside cupboard. I couldn't be sure. I thought that Leopold might have put the idea into my head. He was uneasy about our footprints in the mud of the quarry, and had packed the shoes which we were wearing. It was possible for the driver to have searched my room while I was engaged with Gonzalez downstairs, and the chambermaid was looking uncomfortable and would not meet my eyes. It must be very difficult for a criminal to know whether he is panicking or is really under suspicion.

When I met Philip on the sands of our private river, he was less worried than I. He told me that he had been questioned at the same time and given more or less the same answers. I did not bother to let him know of my success in making the Lieutenant a bit ashamed of his disreputable profession, for I knew what he would say — that if I wanted to hold prayer meetings I had better start with the Pentagon, or something Philipish of that sort.

In the evening Gonzalez picked us both up and questioned us. Because of my suspicion that my shoes had been examined I was not so startled as Philip when Gonzalez suddenly asked us what we had been doing at Pobeña, and I invented a story that Philip had abducted me from Amorebieta with intent to ravish. He backed me up with a lot of detail which was far too convincing and must have been drawn from some sordid personal experience.

That we had been in Pobeña was all Gonzalez knew, and he only knew so much because some wretched little official wandered about taking the numbers of cars. It must be disgusting to live in a police state where one's private movements are recorded. Philip annoyed me by refusing to take my indignation seriously. He pronounced with his best Senior Common Room irony that we had been copped by the correlation of useless statistics, and he only hoped British police were equally efficient.

For two last days, madly happy in spite of our uneasiness, the police left us alone. Philip disliked this silence; it meant, he said, that inquiries were continuing and that the next time we were interrogated we would be in serious trouble — especially if a magistrate took us separately. It was curious that I should be conscious only of innocence and helplessness, while he felt guilty and determined. He piled up all the evidence against us which might come out, using sheets of paper and headings and subheadings.

It all led him to the conclusion that we must try to reach France, and that we had no chance of being allowed to cross the frontier legally. I didn't believe this until I saw how oddly and sadly dear Elena was behaving. We had only bits of a common language, but she once seized my hands and cried that they all knew I was innocent. I guessed that she was being pestered by the police and had orders to telephone them if I looked like packing and leaving.

We decided to disappear, leaving car and baggage behind. Sometimes we did not come back from our own beaches up the estuary till even the Spaniards had nearly finished lunch, so neither Elena nor anyone else would think it worthwhile to report our absence before the late afternoon. By that time we hoped to be at Deva where we could mix with tourists and take a taxi to the frontier.

The plan might have worked if only we had known each other better. The more Philip worried about whether I could walk fifteen miles across country, the more I insisted that I could. But I couldn't. I did not ever imagine what he meant by "across country." It turned out to be practically mountaineering through virgin forest.

When we did at last reach the top of the hills where it was possible to walk, I still tried to play up to the gallant leadership of the sergeant major. That was what he was like — brutal and noble and full of obvious jokes. At last I didn't see why I should stand any more of it; we were just as likely or unlikely to be stopped by police whatever we did. I knew he was disappointed, and I felt lost and inadequate. And then, for no reason at all, when I was expecting still another exhortation, he was comforting me and caressing me and swearing that the whole thing was futile and that we would do anything I wanted.

After that I cannot remember much of our roundabout journey. Philip led me, half asleep, from bus to bus, and bus to train, until we ended up in San Sebastián just before midnight.

It was too late to cross the frontier, but I felt positive that we could get out next day. In all that drifting crowd of French and Germans and English we were so much less noticeable than in our dear, remote Maya. Quite illogically, I loved to be with Philip in the gaiety of a civilized town. I have never been fond of the vulgarities of night-clubs, but that night I adored the cabaret to which he took me — or rather to which I took him, for he was so deliciously disreputable that at first they wouldn't let him in.

To be wanted by the police, and yet to feel more free than ever in my life! What a contradiction and how typical of a woman in love! But every day I spent with Philip took off me a whole weight of duties and the still heavier weight of wondering what my duty was. There was so much laughter. If ever we have a life together, I hope that Philip does not teach me that nothing — except scholarship, of course! — should be taken too seriously. He does not care enough for the future of humanity. But I must admit I can easily forgive it so long as he cares enough for me.

And then the sun of that terrible day came up over the

Bidasoa which I had stopped us reaching. We thought we should be safe if we booked on a round tour to Biarritz. But even that dingy little tourist agency must have been warned to look out for us. While we were waiting in a café for our coach, Gonzalez arrested us without charging us with anything at all and took me back here and drove away with Philip without even letting us say good-bye.

I was forbidden to leave the village, and told that if I tried I would instantly be escorted back. To be confined to a little inn, always under the eyes of fellow guests who glance and look away — can you imagine it? I lived like a ghost, flitting from my room at set times. I saw human beings on holiday and pretended I was alive. They saw me and talked to me and found me harmless. They thought that after a fearful row I had been deserted by my lover. Elena probably started that rumor as being less embarrassing to all of us than the truth. She had already found out for me that Philip had been taken to Madrid.

After two days of this agony Lieutenant Gonzalez called on me. I had him shown up to my room. I loathed him, but anyone who could tell me about Philip was a friend. So I controlled myself and tried to treat him as if he had come with an unwanted bunch of flowers. I asked him to explain my position to me. Was I under arrest or wasn't I?

"At present, Mademoiselle, you are not being detained as a suspect, but as a key witness," he replied.

"To what?"

"To the attempted assassination of Mr. Leopold Mgwana."

I simply stared at him and said that it was nonsense, that I knew of no attempt to assassinate Leopold.

"Then will you tell me why M. Ardower killed Livetti?"

The sincerity of my cry that Philip did not kill him must have impressed Gonzalez. He gave me a thin smile from that nasty, mobile slit of a mouth of his, and said that it was curious how each of us told him in unmistakable good faith that the other did not kill Livetti. Both of us, therefore, knew who did.

"But we don't!" I exclaimed.

"Could it be," he asked, still smiling, "that it was Mr. Mgwana? Before you answer, let me tell you that he has confessed."

That kind of cheap police trickery made me really angry. I told Gonzalez that I realized that I had to submit to being questioned, but that I was not going to have straight lies thrown at me.

"Then of you three, the only suspect left is you, Mademoiselle," he said, still with his offensive smile.

I asked him if he would do me the honor to provide me with a motive.

"Certainly!" he replied. "It is typical of the uniformed branch and somewhat crude; but I invite your comments. You are reported to have been on intimate terms with Alberto Livetti in Rome. When he appeared here, perhaps wishing to revive an old friendship which now repelled you, there was a quarrel and — shall we say? — an accident. And then, owing to the exaggerated chivalry which Mademoiselle is able to inspire, you were assisted by your two devoted friends to dispose of the body."

I could feel myself flushing all over. I could have killed myself. I don't know whether he took it as proof of guilt or not. I suppose a man as accustomed as Gonzalez to torturing suspects with words or worse would be a good enough psychologist to know that he had poked his fingers into shame, not necessarily guilt.

"And the car which followed us?" I asked.

"They could have known."

"If they did and said nothing to the police, wouldn't it be a crime?"

"It would indeed, Mademoiselle," he said, "and when my superiors have been able to settle the first question of how Livetti died, we can all proceed to the second of who else knew and why."

I asked him what had happened to Philip, for I had no more fight left in me. He had been waiting for that question, and complacently drove the knife of his answer straight into me.

"M. Ardower is in jail on suspicion of murder. He has already undergone preliminary interrogation."

I forgot everything but Philip. I forgot what Philip and Leopold knew very well: that we had no proof at all that we hadn't killed Livetti, and that if ever we confessed to getting rid of his body there was bound to be a strong presumption that we did kill him. I told the Lieutenant the whole story exactly as it happened, every detail of it. He took a few notes, and let me talk. I could tell from his face that some of it he did not believe. He merely said that he would ask his colleagues of the criminal investigation department to see how much of my story they could confirm.

Then he very formally pronounced that if I wished to communicate with our embassy or with the Consul at Bilbao, I might do so immediately. I did not want to. First Secretaries and Consuls — what would they understand? I would be considered, as always, a nuisance to government servants. I could not bear to think of the smooth, wearied politeness with which they would treat me, and what they would say as soon as I was out of the room about my gift for getting into trouble.

So I answered Gonzalez with just the remnants of pride which remained to me that it was the duty of the Spanish Police to prove my story true, not of diplomatists; and that all I asked was permission for a member of my family to stay with me.

"I am not some girl you have run in from a cabaret, Lieutenant," I said. "I am without reproach, alone, and at the mercy of the police. I have a right to demand that my honor be protected."

It worked; and if I had been capable of being amused by anything, I would have smiled at the utter ridiculousness of convention. There was I, suspected of being Livetti's mistress and possibly Mgwana's too and proud to be known quite certainly as Philip's, but still able to make a fuss about My Honor as if I never went down the street without a duenna. I suppose it is just a matter of words. Society — at any rate Latin society — grants women a right to Our Taste and agrees that we may call it Our Honor.

Gonzalez felt sure that his superiors would agree. Oh, those superiors! I imagine them sitting round a table on high leather chairs dressed like the councillors of Philip II and each with a typist on his knee. He allowed me to write out that urgent telegram to you. Even so it was altered, but it brought you.

Two more days went by without a word, and then Gonzalez came again. No magistrate. No detectives. Now do you see why I said they treated me as something very precious and very guilty? As always he was polite and deadly. He said that I was not to think he was trying to trap me, that he would share with me the evidence exactly as a prosecuting judge would do and encourage me to explain it.

He thanked me for informing the authorities that the murder took place in the Hostal de las Olas. I protested at once that I had said nothing of the kind, and I did not know where it took place. He waved that aside, and told me that my story had to some extent been confirmed. The screws on my bathroom window and Philip's had indeed been taken out and replaced; there were prints of gloved fingers on both sills; the rough wood of the ladder had caught a few threads of Livetti's jacket; at the iron ore chute the tracks of the barrow had been found.

"Our only difficulty, Mademoiselle, is that you expect us to believe that Alberto Livetti climbed up the ladder when he was dead," he said.

I repeated that he had been put through my window dead, and explained the motive.

"It is incredible," he insisted. "Nobody would risk murder simply to create a scandal."

That was an echo. I remember Leopold saying the same

thing. We were worse off than ever. Why did I dash into trying to save Philip by telling the truth?

"You also ask me to believe, Mademoiselle, that it is mere coincidence that Livetti happened to know you."

I tried to explain that it was not a coincidence at all, that Livetti was a natural choice for anyone trying to create a damaging news story. He couldn't be kept out of anywhere. He had been lowered on a rope to take photographs of newly married celebrities through their bedroom window.

Gonzalez was shocked and incredulous. He knew of the beastliness of Italian press photographers from hearsay, but thought it exaggerated. In Spain, he said, there was police control on the behavior of photographers and censorship control on what they could publish. For the first time in my life I wondered if Freedom of the Press was so essential a part of democracy as I believed.

He returned to his crazy theory of assassination, question after question leading nowhere. Why had the Prebendary and I not given notice to the police of Leopold's arrival? Why was it known to other interested parties? What were my politics? Hadn't I been disillusioned after Mr. Mgwana came to power?

When I had denied and denied that Cyril Flanders knew Livetti and that I had employed him, Gonzalez dropped his obsession with politics and went back to the facts.

"This telephone call to Mr. Mgwana by some person who knew you were concealing Livetti's body — did you actually hear the conversation?"

I replied that from Leopold's appearance and anxiety I had no doubt at all that it took place, and surely the call alone should be sufficient proof of Philip's innocence.

"The degree of homicide of which he is guilty will eventually be decided by the Law," he replied very coldly.

Then there was nothing else left for me to do. I confessed that I had hit Livetti hard with a bottle when I found him climbing in through my bathroom window.

I thought that must be the end of it, that they would take me away and let Philip go. But Gonzalez was simply vague and melancholy.

"You did not believe me, Mademoiselle," he said, "when I told you that Mr. Mgwana had admitted he killed Livetti in self-defense. But it was true. And now you also confess. It is a pleasure for us all to observe nobility, but I fear we cannot allow it to distract us from our duty."

That is all. A day later you arrived, and I bless you for your love and trust.

My Comments

THAT was the story as I first read it; what I ought to read into it was beyond conjecture. I was certain of only two facts: that Olura, though she might omit and exaggerate, was not a liar, and that Mr. Mgwana was to blame.

The discovery of Livetti's corpse plainly threw him off balance; he was always well aware of his cherished Olura's indiscretions and his first reaction might indeed have been one of wild alarm. To some extent it was justifiable. The Spanish censorship could not have acted in time to prevent Miss Deighton-Flagg and her like from telephoning such highly profitable news. I am sure, however, that any responsible editor would have demanded the fullest confirmation before publishing the story, and thus given the Government time to suppress it.

When Mgwana should have gone straight to the Ministry of Foreign Affairs or the Generalissimo and had the whole scandal stamped into oblivion, he did not; and when he should have been flexible and invited someone like this Gonzalez to fly out immediately to Africa, he was offhand, on his dignity and expecting his say-so to be accepted without investigation.

In effect he prohibited further inquiry; for an ambassador, while perfectly capable of suggesting to a prime minister, where affairs of state are concerned, that he is a liar and a bad one at that, cannot do so when the statement is private, personal, voluntary and manifestly chivalrous.

My poor Olura was, as she writes, helpless as a ghost. I managed to comfort her by my certainty that the Government, out of respect for Mgwana, would never push the inquiry as far as a trial; but in fact I felt no absolute certainty. Such a trial might be convenient for some overriding reasons of state. Apparently there really was a political angle, though I could not imagine how the devil it was possible. It seemed highly unlikely that Prebendary Flanders was as symbolic of evil to General Franco as General Franco was to Prebendary Flanders.

I was of course interviewed by Lieutenant Pedro Gonzalez, whom I found to be hurt by Olura's treatment of him. I could appreciate his point of view, though I do not know what else he could have expected. I had to explain to him that Olura and the secret policemen of a dictatorship were irreconcilable. I also endeavored tactfully to point out the blazing idiocy of suggesting that she and her Group would be privy to an attempt on Mgwana.

Yes, he said, he thought so too. But it was difficult to convince his superiors. I dare say it was. Communists and trigger-happy Africans had tried in vain to assassinate Mgwana, and it was believable enough that anarchists —

whom any Spanish Government finds far from merely comic — would not wish to be omitted from the list.

I remember my telling Mgwana that I could raise a hundred million for his country if the City thought it odds-on that he would live for ten years. He replied very simply that he trusted in God and his Chief of Police. I refrained from remarking that it was a pity neither of them was in a position to underwrite the issue.

Gonzalez was eager to impress it on me that interrogation of suspects was not his normal duty. The last thing the Government wanted at this stage was to commit Olura to jail or even to allow her to appear formally before a police magistrate; it did not wish to provoke headlines on the subject of imprisoning prominent British citizens; it was well aware of our excitable and superstitious respect for Habeas Corpus.

So Gonzalez was left holding the baby, as I believe the expression is. He sometimes felt, he admitted after his sixth sherry-and-bitters — a custom of my Edwardian youth to which I had introduced him — as if he were torturing a Christian saint. I fear he was not proof against my goddaughter's physical attractions and her devastating ability to act out, unconsciously and to perfection, whatever high-minded part she had conceived for herself. I was relieved to notice in her narrative that she was also capable of self-dramatization in less moral but possibly healthier causes. The affinity to tall white heather was more marked at sixteen than twenty-four, but is still undeniable.

I emphasized for Gonzalez the ambiguity of the two

men in the black car, one of whom seemed to be a Frenchman called Vigny. He was not so sure of their importance. Vigny had a perfect alibi and could be the reddest of red herrings. Sauche and his Alliance des Blancs, he said, might welcome an accident to Mgwana — the first indication I had that they were involved, for I had not then heard Ardower's story — but it was inconceivable that the former General would plot assassination on Spanish soil, well knowing that he would be returned to France and his sentence on the slightest suspicion of anything of the sort. I was not impressed by this argument. Organizations which use plastic bombs to blow up children are unlikely to shrink from blowing up adults by means of a corpse.

I tried to lead him on into further disclosures, but he realized that he had already said too much. His candor was not, I think, due so much to my finesse as to his admiration for Olura. In face of her guardian he permitted himself indiscretions. To be allowed to worship at a distance is one of the rights of man; but, like so many of them, it is incompatible with security.

When I asked him where Ardower was, he was thoroughly evasive. Doubtless Madrid would know, he said. It was out of his province, he said. I detected a love-hate relationship with Ardower which was not wholly due to jealousy. He both resented and admired a quality in that then unknown character which came through to me as a sort of impenetrable cheerfulness.

I shall now append the second half of Ardower's narrative, having, as I say, somewhat arbitrarily divided it into two in order to clarify facts and motives should this case ever be reopened, and my actions as well as those of other interested parties be submitted to political scrutiny which, I am satisfied, will be as peevish as it must be futile.

Continuation of Dr. Ardower's Narrative

I WAS taken down to Madrid by Gonzalez's companion, a sulky and self-important fellow who gave me little information except that his name was Captain Feria. Everybody in this affair seemed to have officer status. The cell in which I was duly and perhaps deservedly incarcerated was clean, and the food more to my taste than in, let us say, an English boardinghouse. A diet of beans and chick-peas was evidently considered to be punitive, but they were extremely well cooked.

In the usual Spanish way I was at first left to meditate upon my crimes without any person in authority adding insult to injury by saying exactly what they were. I comforted myself between mealtimes by remembering that the Clerk in Holy Orders who had occupied my college rooms some five centuries ago would have been amply content with such simplicity as his successor now enjoyed.

Until they gave me something to read — a matter which Spanish criminals are not expected to consider urgent — I tried to channel my longing for Olura into fantasies more constructive than those which are inevitable in solitary confinement. What future could there ever be for us and how?

Her voice, which I succeeded in analyzing, vowel sound by vowel sound and intonation by intonation, until I had recreated its soft impetuosity, became so vivid that I heard it. Easier still to summon up was a mental tape recording of the Master of my College, harsh and intensely friendly, like the cawing of the rooks behind his lodgings, as he broke to me my lack of any future.

"I do not mind your involvement in a political scandal, dear boy," he would say. "I am prepared to overlook murder on the assumption that a Fellow of this College would not permit the ephemeral to interfere with his research. Fornication I should never describe as deadly sin, though I personally have not felt it a frequent necessity. But you must realize, as I am sure you do, that in these days when we can no longer afford openly to ridicule so-called public opinion, the College cannot be expected to condone scandal, murder and fornication simultaneously."

To this I could only reply (I am sorry to give you these dreams of a criminal, but they did have a definite bearing on my problem of whether I should hope for a future or renounce it) that I was guiltless of murder, that a gentleman must deny fornication in the particular while he may confess to it in general and that scandal, like debt, was unavoidable in our witless flight across the hall from dark to dark.

My duty to resign would, however, be plain. Marriage to Olura, difficult in any case since I had only my professional achievement to set against her money, became absolutely impossible. There would be nothing for it, after serving my sentence, but to hunt for the compound nouns of primitive man among Mgwana's mangrove swamps.

After a couple of unpleasant weeks — which I could not resent, for I was caged and nourished as good-naturedly as some rare acquisition in a zoo — I came up before the police magistrate for my third interrogation. It was at once clear that the worst had happened. So long as Livetti was believed to have been killed on the road or the beach and so long as there was no conclusive proof that Olura and I had disposed of the body, I was only No. 1 suspect and far from convicted. But now they knew that Livetti, dead or alive, had been in the Hostal de las Olas. Obviously the police had hammered away at Olura's relations with him, whatever the devil they were, and got a full confession out of her.

In the light of the new evidence the magistrate questioned me for half an hour on London anarchists, Prebendary Flanders and assassination theory. Had I met Mr. Mgwana and Miss Manoli before this holiday? No, I hadn't. Had I been employed by Mgwana or by any public or private security agency? No, I hadn't. Then why did I interfere? Because a fellow countrywoman in trouble appealed to me. If I did not kill Alberto Livetti, why did I get rid of his body? To oblige Mr. Mgwana. At least I could answer that one without involving Olura. I pleaded a mistaken and irresponsible sense of public duty.

My interrogator nodded to the guard who stood at the door. A tawny little Spaniard with Arab features and lank, black hair was led in and made to sit down opposite me.

Asked if I knew him, I replied that I had a vague impression I had seen his face before but could not remember where or when; he might, for example, be a waiter or a hairdresser's assistant.

I felt sorry for him. Much as I love Spain I cannot deny that the treatment an offender receives from the police depends on his education and social class. This one looked helpless and guilty and the worse for wear. I could not distinguish any weals or bruises, but he faintly reminded me of a boxer efficiently patched up by his seconds. Also he walked clumsily, with his legs far apart.

When he had mumbled sulkily that he recognized me, that I was someone they all called Don Felipe who spoke Basque and stayed in the Hostal, the magistrate told me that his name was Araña and asked what I knew of him.

At last I could answer with relish. I explained how the Deighton-Flagg woman had been warned by an anonymous telephone call that news was likely to break in the Hostal, and that she should talk to Araña if she wanted inside information; and how I had thought that Arizmendi, the sympathetic old waiter employed on temporary security duties, might be Araña. Then Arizmendi had told me that he was a gardener and odd-job man.

The magistrate looked through the file of depositions on his desk and nodded approvingly. I should think it was about the first time that somebody's story had exactly confirmed somebody else's. He turned ferociously on this poor little bastard who had unwittingly landed himself in a case of sinister importance by taking a bribe of a few hundred pesetas.

"Araña, who paid you to unlock the shaft and put a ladder in it?"

"I have told you," Araña whined. "A man in a café."

It was a professional whine which destroyed all confidence in his word. I should think he was at least half gypsy.

"What excuse did he give you?"

"The English lady's lover wanted to visit her — the English lady who was staying with a black man."

"You said on another occasion that it was the English lady who gave you the money."

"What language did you speak?" I interrupted.

My impertinence seemed to be taken as fair comment. I remembered later that when witnesses are confronted with each other, the police magistrate is only too satisfied if they start a row.

"Christian! Christian!" he exclaimed.

"The lady does not speak a word of what you call Christian," the magistrate said coldly.

"I do not know what you want from me," Araña complained. "I will say whatever you like."

A man in a café. It is such an unsatisfactory answer from a policeman's point of view. Every thief, crook and receiver must try it. Guv, it was a man in a café who gave me the crown jewels. I swear I'd never seen him before! Yet I suspected that this time it could well be the truth. If Vigny was the man who had brought Livetti and the ladder together, he certainly would not have approached Araña in person. He didn't speak Christian either. And thought it a damned sight less!

When Araña had been removed, the magistrate asked me in a much more friendly tone:

"What is your own explanation of this murder?"

"I am sure that Livetti came to the Hostal because he had been paid to blackmail or compromise Miss Manoli and Mr. Mgwana, but by whom he was killed or why I do not know."

"Miss Manoli states that he had a camera slung round his neck. If he did, where is it?"

"Under a stone to the right of the ford a hundred meters below the spring of Iturrioz. The Civil Guard at Marquiña will tell you where Iturrioz is."

So direct an answer seemed to take him aback. He was human enough to smile and then returned to business.

"Miss Manoli never told you that she knew Livetti?"

I admitted that she had not. I thought it wise not to lie, even if I deepened for a moment the cloud of suspicion around Olura. From my experience of her, I knew that once she had decided to tell the truth she would tell all of it.

"Did she show any sign of recognition?"

I said that we were all so revolted that I wouldn't have noticed it if she had.

"If you do not believe that Miss Manoli invited Livetti to the Hostal," he said, "you must admit that the fact that they knew each other is a most improbable coincidence."

"She did not invite him. She was not in any way responsible for his arrival," I answered. "I saw her surprise and horror, and it was genuine. I also reject coincidence. A possible theory is that Livetti's death was directly due to the fact that the persons who tried to compromise Mr. Mgwana found out too late that she would recognize him."

He did not reply to that, and changed the course of questioning to suspicions which I found far more satisfactory.

"You knew two Frenchmen, named Vigny and des Aunes?"

"As hotel acquaintances, yes."

"They left the Hostal the morning before Mr. Mgwana arrived. Did they appear to you afraid?"

They did not. But the more difficulties I could create for them, the better. So, remembering Vigny's impatience about the lunch hour, I said that they seemed nervous and on edge.

"The rooms occupied by these two gentlemen also had bathroom windows opening on the central shaft?"

I replied that I did not know the layout of the hotel well enough. They had two cheaper rooms which did not face the sea, but it was probable that the bathrooms were on the shaft.

"Do you know anything of the past of M. des Aunes?"

I saw no reason to give away Gonzalez, who might well be censured for telling me as much as he did while he was still playing with the idea that I might be Mgwana's bodyguard. So I said I knew nothing.

"He is General Sauche."

"How lamentable!" I exclaimed — which didn't commit me to anything.

"When you and Miss Manoli left the Hostal on July 22 with Mr. Mgwana and Lieutenant Gonzalez, you believed that Vigny and another man deliberately followed you?"

"I am sure they did. One of them had already telephoned Mr. Mgwana to say he knew we had the body."

"That cannot be proved. If you are suggesting that these Frenchmen killed Livetti, what motive do you ascribe to them?"

"I have told you. To compromise Mr. Mgwana."

"But a dead man cannot take photographs."

It was no good saying that a corpse would be more compromising still. At once we came up against the good old argument that no one would risk murder for such a doubtful object.

"You have stated," he went on, "that the admiration of Miss Manoli and her Group for Mr. Mgwana was quite genuine."

I repeated that of course it was, and begged him not to bother Scotland Yard, which was obviously prejudiced against such damned nuisances, but to ask anyone in the London Embassy who understood British politics.

"Would you agree that General Sauche and any organization of his would be bitterly opposed to the ideals of this Group?"

"Yes, they would," I replied much too eagerly.

"Then suppose we consider General Sauche, not Mr. Mgwana, as Livetti's objective?"

"Sauche was no longer there."

"No. Because he had news of the plot and left in a hurry."

This was a nightmare. In my effort to head him off the

supposed attempt on Mgwana I had nearly agreed that Mgwana might have been plotting the assassination of General Sauche, presumably with Olura's complicity; and I could not help seeing that Sauche was a far more convincing objective.

"Your Worship is pleased to ask my opinion," I said, "but in your trade as well as mine an opinion without evidence is worthless. What were Livetti's movements? Who paid him to visit Spain? What was he doing here?"

The police magistrate was easily frank about that. No mystery at all! Livetti had been shadowing — like Lieutenant Gonzalez — that newsworthy Teutonic princeling whose dubious divorces from equally newsworthy wives had confused the entries in the studbook. Who had kidnaped whose babies from which was more than I could sort out, though doubtless clear to every female reader of the popular press, avid for still more photographs of bikinis wet with maternal tears. No wonder Livetti was on the spot! And all this at Zarauz where Sauche had rented a villa and acquired enough friends for a party!

"But the General could have known Livetti!" I exclaimed.

"He did, and was pleased to be recognized. The camera of even a Livetti is proof that one is not forgotten by the public."

"But then that is the end of it!"

"Is it, Don Felipe? You think so?" he replied, for the first time using the polite form of address. "I suggest to you that if Mr. Mgwana wished to rid the French and himself of General Sauche, he would choose an assassin who was known to the General and had access to him at any time."

What I could do to retrieve the situation I did. I said that assuming Mgwana had killed Livetti because he knew too much I couldn't see why he should put the body through Miss Manoli's window. As for the complicity of her precious Group, I doubted if they had ever heard of the Alliance des Blancs, or the Alliance of them.

That was not true, since I knew very well that at least Vigny did consider Olura and her influence important. It looked as if he and Sauche had been clever enough to drop a hint to their protectors in high quarters that it was alarm which made them leave the hotel when they did.

"I have another suggestion for you," said the police magistrate. "Livetti was Miss Manoli's lover. He climbed in through the bathroom window and in a fit of jealousy you killed him."

By this time I was exasperated. I retorted that if I killed Livetti it was not likely that Mr. Mgwana would be my accomplice and swear he had done it himself, and I added that I was perfectly willing to confess to a crime of passion if that was what he wanted, since it would carry a shorter sentence than whatever the hell I was supposed to have done.

To my utter astonishment he stood up, smiled, shook my hand and told me I would be released that evening on condition I left Spain immediately.

I could only murmur idiotically that I hadn't had a chance to pay my hotel bill.

"That will be done for you. And you will be escorted to the North Express tonight."

He read me a lecture on the disastrous results of impulsive action, saying that I should not allow the Spanish ardor which I had so graciously assimilated to overcome my British phlegm. Since, however, I had in fact assisted in averting a scandal of unknown proportions, the authorities were not ungrateful. He hoped that my affection and respect for his country would be in no way affected by this unfortunate incident, and that I would for the time being preserve discretion.

Discreetly, by a plainclothes agent who looked like a high civil servant's valet, I was put into a first-class sleeper on the North Express. Discreetly, next morning, August 19, I got out at Bayonne. I do not consider my action chivalrous, praiseworthy or even impetuous. It was obviously Olura's confession which had released me, and the Lord only knew what else she had said or how deeply she had incriminated herself. In England I could do nothing whatever for her; but on my own familiar ground of Vizcaya I could at least hover between sea and mountain, inhibited as a guardian angel, yet ready to influence events, possibly able to collect evidence.

I could not know that you had flown out from London to be with her. Even if I had known, it would have made no difference. You were only a name implanted in Olura's conversation. Her affection was clear; you as its object were not. Perhaps you should have been. But lovers are impatient when one or the other describes beings essential to a past which is not shared. The present is so much more important. If we are immortal, how bored we shall all be with each other's reminiscences for the first few hundred years of eternity!

I changed what remained of my traveler's checks and bought pesetas. I had also a reserve of cash which would be enough for weeks of simple living. I had wired for it as soon as Olura moved to Maya and I saw that of all times in my life this was the one when I would least repent extravagance. Fortunately the money arrived just before our attempted escape and my arrest.

I bought a bottle of black hair dye, a cheap coat, a gaudy pullover and sturdy blue cotton trousers. My outfit was all too new and needed to be walked in and slept in for several days; but then I would look like any Basque peasant or workingman on his way from one village to another. When I had changed, I left my baggage at Bayonne station and went off into my world — for, within reason, mine it was — with nothing but comb, razor, toothbrush, money and passport.

Language offered no difficulty. I could pass as a Basque who had taken some trouble with the purity of his speech. Imperfections in my French and Spanish could be explained, when I had to speak either language, by saying that I had come from the other side of the frontier.

I took a train to St. Jean Pied-de-Port, hoping that there I could get a line on how to cross the frontier illegally. I knew that the regular routes were farther east, over the main massif of the Pyrenees and down into Navarra or Aragon. But since I would have to walk — the Spanish habit of checking travelers' papers made public transport dangerous — I did not want to hit Spain at a point so far from Vizcaya.

I sat around in the cheap bistros and cafés, watching and waiting. A start had to be made somewhere, but I was fearful of approaching the wrong man. St. Jean was a bad choice, too full of tourists and cars, too empty of the simple dishonesties. I wanted a village, yet not a village which was so close to the frontier that my presence could arouse suspicion.

I walked out along the road to Lecumberry, attracted by a bridle path shown on my map; but I felt a fool. Where was a Spanish Basque walking to and why? And that I gave the impression of a Spanish Basque was far too certain. My *boina* — an old possession — was much more luxuriant than the French *béret,* and my clothes, as I began to realize, were more like those of a Vizcayan fisherman on his day off than of the evenly dressed bourgeois on the French side of the frontier.

Giving up that bridle path and all sense of being a competent adventurer, I turned back towards St. Jean. Obviously morale had to be restored, so I dropped into a dark roadside café for half a liter of whatever red poison they sold. Luck at last was with me. Arguing away in a corner — about the iniquity of mixing Algerian wine with good Béarn — were two middle-aged French Basques speaking Euzkadi. They seemed honest chaps, so I joined them. After confidence had been established, I told my story. I came from Eibar and had lost my passport. My mother was critically ill and I had to get home without delays and consuls and red tape.

A lot of good that was! One of them offered to drive me straight to the frontier post at Arnéguy where there was a friendly sergeant on the Spanish side who was his brother-in-law. He might look the other way or he might not. But he would surely allow me to telephone Eibar and prove my identity.

I thanked him warmly. At the same time I may have looked a little hesitant. The other man slapped his kind and guileless companion on the back and winked at me.

"Don't you cross here, friend!" he said.

He was a typical product of the borderlands — thick-set, bluff, a trifle in wine, and with the nose of an Assyrian king. He was not a man to be easily deceived and would have made an admirable conspirator if only he could have kept his voice lower.

"Why not?" I asked.

He explained that over the frontier, in the province of Guipúzcoa, the people were a priest-ridden, Carlist lot of bastards. They would not betray a known and honest smuggler; but any stranger trying to cross into Spain was liable to be taken for a republican of the reddest, and would get no help at all.

His tone gave me a line on his own politics; and he did not care, in this or any other echoing café of freedom-loving France, who knew them.

"We're going to Mauléon," he said. "You come with us! Friends can't talk with the frontier on top of them."

The three of us got into his ancient Citroën. His name was Iragui, and I gathered that he owned a small garage on the outskirts of Mauléon. Zubieta, his older, discreeter and more trustful friend, grew artichokes.

On our way Iragui cross-questioned me loudly on my politics. I gave him a mixture of three parts Olura well shaken up with one of Paris Red Belt and a dash of Basque separatism. Lord help the psychology of lovers! There was I, mischievously and deliberately exploiting Olura, and suddenly brought up by a catch in my voice because I had created her too vividly. It passed as the generous indignation of an emotional socialist.

I was not allowed to see Mauléon at all, for Zubieta insisted on turning off the road to his farm. I am sure that he shrank, for my sake and his own, from entering still another café with Iragui and listening to him discuss frontiers at the top of his voice. As a *bon père de famille* he was not going to have us disturb his family either. He parked us on the turf with our backs against a walnut tree and came back from his house with a cheese and a liter of much better red.

A kindly man, he had a natural tendency to believe what he was told. But, once his suspicions were aroused, he was much more subtle in his questioning than the heartier Iragui. He agreed that I was a Basque from Vizcaya and not on my home ground; yet surely I had cousins, friends, namesakes in the Pyrenean districts who could act as a starting point for my inquiries? I had lost or found it inconvenient to show my passport — good! But what other papers had I got? Iragui, too, expected me to have some credentials. He had decided for himself that I was a courier from Spanish exiles to Spanish republicans.

I felt that Zubieta would be friendly to romance and that Iragui would appreciate sheer, fantastic impudence. So I took a chance and produced my British passport. Even if it was no help, I could hardly be arrested merely because I spoke Euzkadi and wanted to cross into Spain.

The exclamations! The astonishment! The laughter! I received a double dose of esteem. As Frenchmen, they had a respect for learning which is unknown among the English; as Basques, a respect for anyone who could master their language, for they all jealously preserve the absurd myth that it is unlearnable. I gave them the simplest possible explanation of my presence: that because of my left-wing opinions I had been expelled from Spain, could not immediately reenter it and wanted to see my girl.

They went into a huddle, and Zubieta came up with a promising plan. He delivered vegetables to the hotels of the little frontier town of St. Étienne de Baigorry and knew it well. From St. Étienne, where the French post was, a narrow road wound over the Izpeguy Pass and down to the Spanish post at Errazu. Nineteen kilometers of no-man's-land separated the two.

It was not this hopeful gap between officials which appealed to Zubieta, for the country was so broken and difficult that if you left the road you would only be forced back on to it. No, it was the fact that the road was closed for extensive repairs on the Spanish side. So tourists at St. Étienne were permitted to drive as far as the top of the Pass and the actual line of the frontier with few formalities, since it was impossible to go any farther.

That, he thought, might be a useful beginning. But I was bound to run into trouble, dressed as I was. I was plainly no tourist. I was a Spaniard with dubious intentions. Hadn't I any other clothes? Yes, I had, but at Bayonne.

Well then, I must return and put them on. I must go as far as I safely could in the character of a respectable professor with a love of the Pyrenees, change back into my present clothes whenever I had a chance and mingle unobtrusively with the gangs working on the road. At the actual frontier line there was a fixed post or a patrol, but the guards would not be alert since they had nothing to do day after day but smoke.

My two friends argued it out. Iragui boomed that it was an extravagance and that I hadn't a chance. Zubieta, as the originator of the scheme, insisted that it was child's play. I promised to send them a postcard to say which of them had been right. Both agreed — to salve their consciences — that if I were caught it could only mean a day or two in jail. I was not so sure of that. It could well mean jail until the Livetti case was cleared up. But I liked the plan. It was not too fixed, and lent itself to improvisation.

Iragui got me a free lift into Bayonne, where I recovered my bags from the railway station and spent an unexpected night of comfort. In the morning I put my baggage back in the *consigne* and took a train to St. Étienne, with a pack on my back containing my less respectable clothes.

By eleven I was on the road to the Izpeguy Pass. The guard on duty at the French post looked perfunctorily at the cover of my passport without making any note of it and told me that the road was closed and there were no facilities for entering Spain, but that I could certainly walk as far as the frontier.

I toiled uphill for an hour and a half over the hot and empty tarmac. I had not foreseen how conspicuous I would be. But after all and at last there was some traffic. Along came a convoy of three cars, bound for a pleasant picnic while looking down the valley into Spain.

The second car, containing only a Belgian holiday-maker, his wife and an appetizing basket with bottles poking their necks out of the white cloth, gave me a lift to the top, where I told them I would have a stroll round before returning to St. Étienne on foot. The two guards on duty at the border paid no attention to well-fed tourists, and indeed retired to eat their own lunch without bothering to count the numbers who had arrived in the three cars.

It was easy to vanish and cut straight down the hillside to the next bend. In case I met an unexpected patrol I strolled on as my academic self who had cheerfully ignored the frontier, secure in his innocence and the possession of a valid British passport.

I moved cautiously down the zigzags, keeping close under the slope of the mountainside. The only traffic was a pair of frontier guards on motorcycles, coming up to relieve their colleagues at the top of the pass. The roar of their engine in second gear gave me ample warning of their approach.

I still could not see the point where the road was closed for repair, since it was now twisting among crags. I would have walked round a corner slap into the middle of the first and highest gang of laborers if they had not chosen that moment to loose off four blasting charges which startled my guilty conscience into near panic.

To spot the exact position of the works was difficult. Where I was the road had been carved out of the hillside, leaving an unclimbable cliff on my left, and on my right a steep slope of debris without any cover. If I slid down that I should undoubtedly appear in full view of the blasting gang. So there was nothing for it but to go back up the road and take to mountaineering.

I arrived eventually at the top of the cliff, if one could call it a top when the damned thing merely leaned a little farther backwards. Traversing that alarming slope of loose gravel, I remembered how Olura at a rather tricky point of our attempted escape had exclaimed that I would call the ascent of Everest a cross-country walk. That, I imagine, is what an Everest climber would call my slope of scree. I was thankful when I reached a pinnacle of honest limestone where at last I could use hands as well as feet.

The flat and blessedly secure top of this rock provided an admirable view of the road. Just round the corner at which I had halted and turned back were two mechanical shovels loading lorries, a bulldozer clearing up the stone loosened by blasting and a gang of a dozen laborers gray with dust.

Farther down the valley was the main depot: huts, parked vehicles and more machinery with the bright colors and blunt, powerful lines which the Spaniards appreciate. For them a thing of purpose should look purposeful; elegance belongs to leisure.

The advanced party of roadworkers was no use to me. My sudden arrival in their midst could only lead to awkward and unanswerable questions. Obviously what I had to do was to reach a point below the main depot and walk innocently back up the road to it. There could not then be any suspicion that I came from France.

I worked out a route. From my pinnacle to the next bend below the gang was one long slide and scramble, most of it in dead ground. After that, trees began but seemed to end in nothing rather abruptly. Still, there must be some roundabout way back to the road.

There was, but only one and that a waterfall. It would have been utterly impassable in spring when the snow water probably shot out in an unbroken sheet. As it was, I could work my way down from ledge to ledge and pool to pool, soaked to the skin but preserving my knapsack by throwing it ahead onto dry rock whenever I had to take a shower bath.

I changed under the bridge where the road crossed the stream and slung my damp roll of clothes into the undergrowth, where it would soon rot away. My outfit bought in Bayonne was too respectable for a worker on the road. That did not matter, for I had decided that it would be fatal to pretend to be anything but a stranger. All the men in the gangs would know each other and their brothers, cousins, aunts and family friends. Mingling with them, as Iragui and Zubieta had hopefully suggested, would lead absolutely nowhere.

I plodded up the road and into the depot, where I waited around until I heard a foreman speaking Euzkadi. I asked

if he had any work. He replied that nobody was hired on
site; all his men had to be passed by the police, and he
ought to report my presence. That gave me an idea. I said
I really wanted to go over into France, and asked for his
advice as one friend and countryman to another.

"You'd be a fool," he said. "You'd get yourself shot at
before the next turning."

He pointed uphill to the frontier guards I had seen earlier, who were now standing uncertainly by their motorcycles two twists of the road above us.

"They are waiting for a foreigner," he told me, "who
was spotted coming down on foot. You can't move on this
road, day or night, without being questioned. My advice to
you, son, is to get on back. There's a truck going down to
Elizondo in a moment."

"The driver won't say anything when we pass the control post?" I asked anxiously.

"No. Why should he? How was it they let you through?"

"They didn't happen to see me," I replied with a grin.

"Jesus! Those chaps think they can take a holiday now
that there aren't any cars! And up here where we have to
work, it's just papers, papers, papers. Where do you come
from?"

"Eibar."

He took the trouble to check that, or perhaps he only
wanted to gossip. Either way I could content him, for I
knew several worthies of the town personally and a lot
more by name. So he put me in the back of an empty lorry
along with a poor devil who had had a couple of toes
smashed by a rock, and down we went into Spain with

nothing more than a wave-on from a sergeant at the control post who was digging potatoes.

So that was unexpectedly that. A loose, imaginative plan had cohered as it commonly does, whether in scholarship or commerce, into a solid with its own successful momentum. In order to get clear of the frontier before nightfall I walked on to the limit of my legs' endurance, following a tributary of the Bidasoa westwards and sleeping in the woods at the foot of Mount Eracurri.

The dew dried quickly, for it was one of those glorious mornings when the Basque country is motionless in Mediterranean heat while preserving the green of southern England. I crossed the watershed into the valley of the Urumea and struck down into a village where the morning's bread had just arrived at the tavern. I had tasted nothing but water for nearly twenty-four hours, and was ravenously hungry.

Full of eggs and red sausage, my aim undetermined, yet relieved for the moment of all sense of urgency and anxiety, I accepted the rest offered by the bank of the Urumea. I put my back against a rock with a twisted oak on it, peaceful as a Chinese painting, and began to think what on earth I should do with such liberty. Free from the hothouse of plots and interrogations, free — intellectually though never emotionally — from the beloved complications of Olura, I could at last draw breath and contemplate the past weeks. I was no longer trapped inside a ring. I was outside it, with time to see what it was made of.

Till then I had not begun to think clearly about Livetti. For one thing, I didn't like thinking about him at all. It was not that I cared what his relations with Olura had been — blindly indiscreet, if I knew her. She had mentioned trouble with the press over some Negro dancer in Rome, and Livetti might well have started to persecute her there. No, my aversion to that poor photographer was simply due to puppets, quarries, barrows, the sea and the smell of the boot which would sometimes return to me even in the open air.

In self-protection I had been forced to concentrate on the motive for killing Livetti. But that was futile. I had not the facts and could not know. Even the police, with all their evidence filed, collated and accessible, were reduced to wild guesses. The police magistrate considered it very possible that Livetti had been employed by Mgwana to get rid of Sauche. Gonzalez preferred the Cloud Cuckooland of Prebendary Flanders, the Group and London anarchists.

So leave murder alone and consider Livetti! By a photograph or blackmail he intended to exploit Olura and Mgwana. A private enterprise fully in keeping with his character. Need one look any further? Yes — since the trio of Sauche, Vigny and Duyker knew of his death and must have been responsible for his presence in the hotel.

How could they be sure that Mgwana would have no security guard? Well, cautious inquiries could have revealed that the Spanish Government had no knowledge of the visit. But governments act quickly and unexpectedly. Sauche couldn't be dead certain until Mgwana was nearly due to arrive.

Therefore no long-term, complicated plot was possible

at all. It was unthinkable that experienced conspirators like Vigny and Sauche should plan a murder without knowing what the security setup was going to be. It was as strong a point in their favor as the alibis.

Then tell me, clear light, clean air, Urumea on your way to the sea, doesn't the employment of Livetti look like rapid and able improvisation? Just a bit of foul, evil-intentioned mischief which Vigny had conceived after the third brandy and put into practice at once! He knew all about Livetti's specialty and could have whistled him up in a matter of hours.

The more I looked at this theory, the more I fancied it. A little block of highly probable fact was standing on its own legs like a conjectured word in an undecipherable inscription. And it asked an intelligible question. If Vigny planted Livetti in the hotel in a hurry, whom did he get to do his business with Araña? How could he lay his hands instantly on someone who spoke French and Spanish and had no easily traceable connection with Sauche and himself?

That looked like a good starting point for me. With all my local knowledge I ought to be able to uncover the identity of Araña's man-in-a-café. He was not an inhabitant of the district, or the police would have routed him out. But if he was not, he must have talked to someone at Maya familiar enough with the Hostal and its characters to recommend that unfortunate little crook.

Maya. The inn. Elena insisting that she *knew* Olura was innocent. When Olura reported that, I had taken it as the usual sort of interchange between two emotional women: in fact, mere politeness. But it was strong for mere politeness. Suppose the village did know?

Well, it would certainly keep its knowledge to itself. You wouldn't choose to land yourself in weeks or months of police interrogation just for the sake of a quarrel between foreigners. And a corollary to that. It would not be only the village which knew; it would be all the elders and the cousins and the in-laws in the immediate vicinity. Talk about the Mafia! The speakers of Euzkadi form an equally powerful secret society, never criminal but marvelously discreet and effective.

The Urumea had decided my route for me. I would walk to the outskirts of Amorebieta and telephone for a taxi. Echeverría must have made it his business to uncover as much of the story as he could, since he was indirectly concerned in it. While he might not say all he knew, I was sure he would be much too amused by my acquittal and reappearance to give me away.

I took the road to Tolosa, where Olura, sleepy, adorable and with a blistered heel which she had forgotten by midnight, had been dragged by me onto the last train. Nowhere had I any fear of recognition. The police were not looking for me, and I had few acquaintances in the province of Guipúzcoa. My dyed hair, bristly face and scruffy appearance were sufficient disguise to back up the native speech. When I stopped to talk by the wayside or entered a tavern to eat and drink I was easily able to account for myself.

It took me the best part of three days to arrive within striking distance of Amorebieta, for I had to give Eibar a wide berth and keep well to the south of all districts where I might be hailed in a loud and astonished voice before I could protest. Calling Echeverría was rather more tricky than I had foreseen, since village telephones are always very public and I was a most unlikely person to be sending for a taxi. I had to address him as cousin and merely say that I was on the main road if he happened to be passing. After blundering about at the other end of the line and demanding what cousin, he at last recognized my voice and shouted that he would drive out at once to fetch me.

He did not recognize me when I waved to him from the wayside — a heartening sign that I fitted into my environment — and was well away down the road to San Sebastián before he stamped on the brake. I came up to find him still exchanging remarks with the lorry driver who had been on his tail.

"Anywhere that's quiet," I said as soon as I had slid into the seat alongside him, "and ńo waiting by the side of a road."

Echeverría, though somewhat blunt, was always an interested conspirator. He ran back to a new, plaster-and-paint café put up to catch the motor trade by an Aragonese who did not speak a word of Euzkadi. There he could park the taxi without traffic police taking an interest.

He never drank during the day. When we had settled down with the singularly vile soft drinks of Spain, I said I hoped he had had no serious trouble with the Law.

"Not the slightest," he answered, "and no thanks to you! I just kept at it with that Gonzalez that you'd asked me to park where I could block the black Seat and pick up the very distinguished chief of the cannibals. And as you were a friend I did."

"He took that?"

"He had to. It was the truth. He threatened me with losing my license, so I told him to go to hell. If you have escaped, Ardower, you'd better get over the frontier. I'd know you anywhere."

I gave him my story: that I had not escaped, but had been turned loose and come straight back again. He made a noise of contempt and reminded me that all women were the same after twenty years. I agreed that his hypothesis was tenable, but that, as a man of learning, I could not accept it without the test of experience. He replied that I was an oddly shaped organ of generation and that if I were really his cousin he'd clear right out of Vizcaya and set up a garage for Madrid homosexuals. Meanwhile what could he do for me?

I started off to tell him that Olura was still under suspicion. He interrupted me to say he knew she was and, more than that, that she was innocent.

"Can anyone help me to prove it?" I appealed to him.

"Not in a court," he said. "Not any of us! We don't want to spend the rest of the year being talked at by a lot of police. When you were having a good time up and down the banks of the estuary, did you ever notice the *María de Urquijo*?

I said that of course I did. She was the fishing launch just settling on the sand when I first waded across the river with Olura.

"Well, Allarte is your man. Skipper Allarte. I'll ask him to talk to you. He'll do it for me because his grandmother used to sell sardines in Santurce right where the public piss-house is now."

Since Echeverría's own ancestors did not come from Santurce, I could not interpret this reference to some obscure obligation. In the interests of scholarship I ought to have asked. It is always profitable to explore the interrelationships between the Basques.

"Or if he won't," Echeverría went on, "he'll have to walk to Bilbao the next time he has a good catch and wants to buy himself a whore. On a day like this the *María de Urquijo* will have gone out on the morning tide, and Allarte will come into Lequeitio with his catch at dawn tomorrow. I'll bring him here to meet you at eleven. He likes a free ride."

I pressed money on him and had to show my well-stuffed wallet before he would take his costs and a little profit. Just for Allarte's morning thirst, he said. He did not approve of my spending another night in the open. He protested that my appearance was an insult to Vizcaya, and if I wanted to look like a decent person walking between villages it was time I had a shave. He knew a widow not far off who would put me up and be glad of anything I chose to give her except twins.

A typical bit of Echeverría's protective coarseness! When he drove me to his widow — a sweet, tragic woman in her forties, trying single-handed to run two children and a remote hilltop small holding — I heard him assure her that I was a good Basque and a man of honor and she had nothing to fear from me. She would not allow me to pay as much as I wanted, so for two hours I swung a mattock in the corn patch.

I said good-bye to her and her terraces with gratitude. To cultivate, like our far ancestors, a hilltop where the soft breeze from the sea dampens and rustles the leaves of the growing food is the next best way of living to my own. If there is the expected end to this business and never again any Olura, that is what I shall do when I regain my liberty.

Allarte and Echeverría were at the café fairly punctually. The skipper and I knew each other well by sight but had done little more than exchange greetings. I had been too occupied to frequent the bar and the foreshore; and Olura, as a reluctant observer, found nothing attractive in Basque fishermen, who were altogether too coarse and noisy for her. She should have seen them in winter when they endured poverty, often serious, with dignified patience.

Allarte was a big man in blue jeans, with an extravagant *boina* on his straight black hair and a large, almost circular face. He overwhelmed me with cordiality and unnecessary compliments, but seemed very shy at coming to the point. Echeverría had to help him.

"Go on, Allarte!" he said. "Ardower has his interests, but he is not a curate in charge of a Sunday School."

"Well, what we do I'd expect of a curate, not grown men," Allarte muttered, "and it's a fact that I'm ashamed to talk of it. But what the hell do they expect if they build a palace where there was nothing but a foul bottom and shrimping to amuse the children? It's reasonable to be curious about how the wealthy live."

I agreed that of course it was.

"And a little fun for us to laugh about during the long night," Allarte went on. "Where's the harm in that?"

It turned out that Allarte and his crew of three had been attracted by the lighted windows of the Hostal which they passed whenever they went out on a night tide, bound north or east. They discovered that guests were often careless in drawing their curtains, which was natural enough when the Hostal faced nothing but empty Atlantic and the uninhabitable rock of the Ermita. What they saw was generally a matter for ribaldry, but occasionally they had what Allarte — damn him! — called a stroke of luck. I gathered that Olura's casual habits had caused them to be late on the fishing grounds for three nights running. Their revolting form of entertainment had been materially assisted by an ancient telescope.

"She was there with a black man," Allarte said. "We thought at first that . . . well, you know very well that imagination runs faster than truth. In fact she was dressed as the foreign women dress for the beach. And if it's good enough for them it's good enough for me, and I see no reason why the Council of Vizcaya should send half-wits in peaked caps to patrol the sands.

"For all the black man was doing about it, she might have been the Mother Superior. She was writing and he was writing. Then she got up and opened a door, and you'd have thought she had seen a ghost. She called the black man over, and he saw it too. Mine is a good glass and, though it was hard to hold steady in the swell that was running under us, I could make out their faces as clearly as yours. When a man has traveled as I have, he thinks of many things. If we had all been in the Americas, I would have said that those two had found a most deadly snake in the room."

Allarte and his crew saw Olura pull the curtains. After that, by the light of the sea itself, they could vaguely follow our comings and goings along the balcony. They had not attempted to explain what they saw. Afterwards, however, they put two and two together, and made it their business to find out if the dates fitted.

"I have friends in the police," Allarte said. "It's sensible to drop a nice hake on the sods from time to time. So I learned that someone had tried to kill the black Prime Minister and got himself bumped off instead. About that I know nothing. But I saw the lady's face as I see yours. And I tell you that when she saw the corpse — for that's what she must have seen — she was surprised. And that's how all Maya knows she is innocent. Because I say so."

It did not get us much further, and I could well understand that Allarte was not likely to go to the police and confess to a launchload of Peeping Toms when what he had to report would be no proof at all to a magistrate — though good enough for the village.

"You know they arrested a crook called Araña for letting the man into the hotel?" I asked.

Yes, he knew that and Araña too. Then had he any idea who had bribed Araña and given him his instructions? It must be someone speaking French and Spanish who was a stranger to Araña and yet familiar enough with the district and the Hostal to choose him.

"My mate told him to try Araña!" Allarte exclaimed. "By God, I thought he wanted fish trays!"

"Who did?"

"The Breton, Bozec."

I think Allarte regretted at once that he had mentioned the name. He had been startled into indiscretion at finding himself unexpectedly involved. To avoid giving any information about Bozec — whose business must have been suspected by some of the inshore fishing fleet — he burst into a long and detailed account of the apparently irrelevant fish trays.

"Plastic they are. Lighter than wood and very practical. The manager of the hotel brings his own when he buys fish at Bermeo or Lequeitio. Well, we don't like the hotel, you see. It's a joke, you understand. So when Bozec said he wanted some of the plastic trays, my mate told him to give a few pesetas to Araña who could easily pinch a dozen from the stack outside the kitchen."

Clearly Bozec had been briefed by Vigny and then visited Maya to drink with the crew of the *María de Urquijo* and find out the name of any dishonest employee of the Hostal. The man in a café had been Araña's invention; it sounded more warmhearted than to admit he had been approached by a complete stranger in the hotel grounds and bribed then and there to put up a ladder against Olura's bathroom window.

Bozec's visit to Maya must have been on July 20, the

very day of Mgwana's arrival, the day that Olura and I so nearly passed each other on the beach. I remember that when she and I were eating prawns on the terrace there was a cheerful banging of bottles and glasses in the bar. I also remember that Spanish was being spoken, whereas I expected to hear Euzkadi. With that sea running, Allarte and his crew had nothing to do but drink and encourage any mischief that was going.

"What did he think of the trays?" I asked, in order to compel Allarte to go on talking.

"Only this morning I asked him if they were practical," Allarte answered sulkily. "He told me they were, but that he hadn't managed to collect some from the Hostal because he had no transport of his own."

"Where did you see him?"

"He is in Lequeitio. The propeller gland went, and the main bearings are out of alignment. So the harbor master gave him permission to refit. That's fair enough. He couldn't make Le Croisic if it blows up again like it's been doing for the last month."

Allarte's capacity for red Rioja, anchovies and bread was astonishing. When he rolled out to make room for more, I asked Echeverría if the Basque and Breton fishing fleets got on well when they met in the bay.

"They know more about each other than they would tell to you or me," he said.

"Allarte doesn't go out that far, does he?"

"I've known him go to Ireland for lobsters when he was broke. But it's not out at sea that he met Bozec, if that's what you are thinking, Ardower. Any of the skippers in

Lequeitio would tell Bozec to talk to Allarte of Maya if he wanted information about the hotel."

"Are the French boats allowed to sell their catch here?"

"No. But the port can't refuse repairs if the damage is as bad as Allarte says."

When Allarte returned, I asked him which storm it was that caught Bozec.

"The blow of July 10," he replied. "Came on with only a couple of hours' warning! The Breton fleet made for the Adour, but Bozec turned back too late. God knows why! He's a good seaman, and his radio was working."

Then I guessed a possible connection with Sauche and Vigny. Why had Bozec carried on for the Spanish coast when the rest of the fleet turned east to take refuge in the mouth of the Adour? To land Vigny, of course! The sudden storm was on July 10. According to Gonzalez, the police registered Vigny's arrival on the eleventh.

Allarte and I continued to drink a bit longer. He gave me news of Olura. She had looked so unhappy, her eyes always seeking the river, that Maya had been afraid she would romantically throw herself into it. But now a rich uncle had come out to keep her company, and taken the villa on the headland. A true *caballero* of the old school, speaking a simple Spanish slowly and correctly. Very courteous, very grave, said Allarte, but with the eyes of a dynamiter. An excellent description.

I hesitated whether to send her a letter or message by Allarte and decided against it, cursing myself for cruelty to us both. It was better that she should believe I was in jail or — if she had been told of my release — in England. As soon as she knew I was playing detective by ear and instinct within thirty miles of her, she would either make some rash and generous move or start feeling helplessly guilty because I might be rearrested or land myself in some collision with Vigny. Both were risks which I meant to avoid until such time as I had evidence worth putting to Gonzalez.

When Echeverría had driven Allarte off to Lequeitio, I staggered up the nearest hill for a couple of hours' sleep in the narrow shade of a loose-stone wall. After waking up I found a stream — never far off in that glorious country — and refreshed myself by a bath as well as by the thought that the water almost certainly ran past Olura into the sea. I took Echeverría's advice and shaved. There was enough moustache to be worth dyeing — a mere darkness, but making my upper lip look a bit shorter.

Then I started off for Lequeitio, keeping so far as possible to byroads and field tracks. It was an agitated walk. For an hour and a half of the early evening I was accompanied by a man of about my own age whom, once met, I could not lose. He seemed to fall in naturally with my intention of reaching the coast by avoiding main roads.

I told him that I was going to Lequeitio, where a lot of new apartment houses were being built, to see if I could get a job with a contractor — a story which was quite good enough when chatting to a passerby, but invited comment from any more permanent companion on why the devil I didn't take a bus. He said that he was a fisherman, which I was sure he was not. So we continued on our cautious way, each well aware that the other did not wish for too close examination by any public authority.

Crossing the coastal range, we were forced onto a secondary road. As we began the descent we saw a Civil Guard on a motorcycle, one bend below us, coming up. My companion dived into the scrub at the side of the road like a startled rabbit. After a moment's hesitation I did the same, for I should be instantly in trouble if asked for my papers. I was too late to avoid observation, but fortunately the Guardia had no chance to see my face.

He dismounted smartly and ordered the silence to halt. As it didn't answer, he strode towards a little ridge which commanded the inadequate cover where we were half hidden, crushing the heather with severity and unslinging from his back a complicated bit of American lethal machinery, less respectable for a servant of state than the old carbine and possibly less practical, but a lot more terrifying to the public, including me.

My companion, more experienced than I, saw what was going to happen and started to dodge silently from bush to bush before it was too late. I remained crouched in a wretchedly shallow, dry arroyo, dithering with indecision. When I dared to raise my head, old Spain was gallantly intent on its duty to smell out the disaffected, while new Spain, in the form of a motorcycle, glittered a few yards away by the roadside.

I did not wait to explore unfamiliar controls. I just hurtled down the road in neutral, getting a fair start before the Guardia heard me at all. As I reappeared on the bend below, my impertinence was too much for his patience and he gave me a squirt from his undignified weapon. Nobody in my quiet life had ever shot at me before. The experience was not so alarming as I would have anticipated. One has always, I suppose, something else to think about. In my case it was whether or not I was going to skid on the loose gravel of the verge at the pace I was taking the corners.

I left the machine for its owner at the bottom of the hill and vanished again into country lanes. There were several local inhabitants in the middle distance, but, after all, they could not know it was not my motorcycle. I hoped that in any case the outrage would be ascribed to my shady companion. It was quite likely that the Guardia was not aware that there were two of us.

All this meant another hungry night in the open. Since somebody looking rather like me at a distance was wanted by the police, I had to avoid villages and approach Lequeitio with extreme care. The little port, set in a bowl of the hills, could be entered by only three roads, easy to control. By waiting for low tide I found a fourth, scrambling over the rocky foreshore to the beach and then walking inoffensively along it to the harbor.

I enjoyed a huge, late lunch in a quayside tavern, where nobody used Spanish and I was just an insignificant part of the general noise. The Lequeitio fleet was out. The tall, brown houses with their splendidly timbered glassed balconies stared down on a harbor fairly empty except for the floating mess which fishermen always manage to leave on any smooth and enclosed piece of water. I

was conscious of too many unseen eyes for my comfort
— of bored proprietors and clerks looking out from the
dark entrances of the warehouses, taverns and chandler's
shops beneath the houses, of unseen women behind the
panes of the *miradores*.

I walked along the massive paving of the quay and
had not far to look for the Breton. Her name was the
Phare de Kerdonis, registered at Le Croisic. She was tied
up alongside the breakwater with a local boat, also under
repair, between her and the fishmarket. On her starboard
side was a small launch, about the size of Allarte's, called
the *Isaura,* her skipper busy with the maintenance of his
fixed rods and lines.

Out on the breakwater beyond the houses, where there
were no casual idlers, I felt naked and conspicuous. I had
not even any determined plan. These things are so much
easier for a cop; he can either employ some slimy individual to buy drinks for his suspect until the man gives himself away, or charge right in and detain him. What I
wanted to find out was whether Captain Bozec knew
Vigny. I was ninety per cent certain that he did, but conjecture was not enough. And what was the close association between the two? Close it had to be, for when Vigny
after that third brandy which I had invented for him was
wondering whom he could get at a moment's notice to
prepare the way for Livetti, the inspired answer was
Bozec.

Blue flashes of welding lit up the engine-room hatch,
on the edge of which an obvious Frenchman was sitting
with his legs hanging down. Unlike the Basque fishing

captains, he wore a peaked cap. Since he looked authoritative, I took a chance that he was Bozec.

"Have you been here long, Captain?" I asked.

"I've been here six weeks," he answered irritably. "And in any other hole of this coast it would be one."

He spoke idiomatic Spanish with hardly any accent. That explained one thing which had been bothering me: why Araña, who by and large had told the truth, had never said that the man who did business with him was a foreigner.

"What's the trouble?"

"The trouble is a son of a bitch of an engineer who can't learn to keep the screw from racing when we're halfway up to heaven."

"There were some nasty blows last month," I said.

"Where do you come from?" he asked abruptly — for it was obvious that I did not know what all Lequeitio did.

I told him that I lived in Fuenterrabía, which was right on the frontier and would account for my speaking French, if I had to, as well as Spanish. Then I asked him why he had not run for a French port, Hendaye or St. Jean de Luz.

"Because we were hove to in the gale, friend, with just the fishing jib to keep her head to it and glad to get in anywhere."

I am no seaman, but I thought his answer insufficient. If the sudden northwest gale had caught him fishing on the Biscay grounds it would have blown him, hove to or not, onto the French coast. He must have been very much closer than he ought to the merciless capes of Spain. It was true enough, however, that his choice of Lequeitio was forced. He would have found more efficient yards at the fishing ports of Bermeo or Santurce if he could have made either of them.

"It's the hell of an entrance with a high sea," I said.

"Well, it was that or the cliffs. Our only chance was to start up the diesel again and run it until something gave. By God, I didn't think I would be here more than a week! And then along came an inspector who wouldn't let me leave because the shaft wobbled. As if I didn't know it! But it would have taken us home."

I could guess what had happened. The harbor master, who must have wondered as I did why he was close enough to the coast to be driven onto it by the gale, was teaching him and his fellows a courteous Spanish lesson. Fish in territorial waters, would you? Right, you're a comrade of the sea and we do not want to be hard! But the red tape and mañana you'll have to put up with before we let you go will make you think twice about doing it again.

Bozec's troubles, however, were now over. His crew, whom he had sent home to France by train, were on their way back. The *Phare de Kerdonis* would sail in a couple of days.

He seemed to find me a sympathetic listener; so I switched to French to give him more confidence still. It was a mistake.

"You don't speak like a Gascon," he said suspiciously.

"Why should I? My native language is Basque."

"They say it resembles Breton."

An odd remark. Since he had been in Lequeitio for six weeks, he must have known that there was no resemblance at all. The half-smile on his face showed that he expected a reply from me. I had the feeling that there was a set answer — some sort of password admitting one to the club of contrabandists. So I made a downright deadly shot in the dark.

"I have friends at Zarauz," I said.

"Me, too," he answered casually, and signaled to the skipper of the *Isaura,* who pulled himself up onto the deck of the larger boat. I noticed for the first time that the *Isaura* was registered at Zarauz.

"Is this man a Basque?" Bozec asked.

Bernardino — that was what Bozec called him. I don't know his surname — engaged me in conversation. Where was I born? Where did I live? Whom did I know? I did not acquit myself very brilliantly, for I couldn't play Eibar, being already committed to Fuenterrabía. He reported that I was certainly a Basque, but that I did not come from the coast.

Bozec, still puzzled, tried me with a remark in Breton — evidently a final chance for me to give an acceptable reply. I couldn't give any at all. I have never studied the primitive languages of the Celts. So I just winked at him.

"Can you go back to Zarauz now?" he asked the *Isaura*'s skipper.

"It wouldn't be inconvenient."

"Then we'll all go together."

Five minutes later we were out of Lequeitio harbor and running eastwards along the coast. I knew what Daniel felt like; a den of lions was what I was going to get for praying to Olura three times a day. But no refusal was possible or wise. I assured myself that, after all, we were not in Algeria or Chicago.

During the three hours which it took to reach Zarauz conversation with Bozec flowed easily, though carefully keeping off the subject of our visit. Each felt, I think, that the other might be a person whose good will was worth having, but neither was giving anything away. In answer to my compliments on his faultless Spanish, Bozec told me that his mother was from Asturias and never spoke anything else with her children. Evidently she had the obstinate pride of many uneducated Spanish women, refusing to master French or Breton and quite content with some jargon which she spoke with her husband. He — Bozec's father — had been mate of a coaster trading between Nantes and north Spanish ports, and had fallen in love with a young girl — I did not like to ask where he had met her — left a helpless orphan by the Asturian revolt of 1934. By that and other remarks I inferred that there was a tradition among the Bozecs of jiggery-pokery in the Bay of Biscay.

Yet even Bozec could not have openly sailed the *Phare de Kerdonis* into a Spanish harbor, nor could he have launched and sent in a dinghy on the night of July 10; indeed he would have hesitated on any night, considering the deep-sea swell breaking on that rockbound coast. It was a job for a local man who knew the inlets and the few coves which were both remote and sheltered. Almost certainly he had a rendezvous with a Spanish fishing boat, to which he transferred his passengers at sea.

Could it be the *Isaura*, whose owner was plainly on intimate terms with Bozec? Bernardino was not communicative, prepared to join occasionally in our conversation, but reluctant to speak Euzkadi with me alone.

At last I caught him out with a casual aside, quite unknown to Bozec, as a calm, green, seventh wave lifted us ten feet and dropped us again. I remarked that it must be a change to have two French passengers who were not seasick.

"The poor devil!" he muttered.

Vigny's collapse on that night of July 10 must have been memorable and alarming.

The two of us left the *Isaura* at the fishing quay and strolled off along the front. I assumed that we were going to find our friends on some neat terrace above the beach umbrellas where there could be no uncivilized behavior. But Bozec walked away from the fashionable hotels and villas, through the old town and out to the edge of open country. We stopped at a square house, dating from the last century when thick stone walls and heavy timbering were fashionable, and standing in a small garden behind half a dozen thick-stemmed palmettos, ragged with age and neglect.

Bozec rang the bell. The door was opened by Vigny himself.

"I have brought this type along because he claimed to be a friend of ours," Bozec said.

Vigny took a second look at me. His speed of reaction was astonishing.

"Why, of course!" he exclaimed, warmly shaking my hand. "How are you, Professor? I am most grateful to you, my dear Bozec."

"Good! That's all I wanted to know," said Bozec bluntly. "We came over in the *Isaura*, but I'll have to go back by taxi."

Vigny pulled out a 500-peseta note and gave it to him. "Take a taxi down in the town," he advised. "Our friend will stop and dine with us."

I played his game, too, for want of a better, and said a warm and grateful good-bye to Bozec. He left convinced that we were all on excellent terms. Vigny's acting was so good that I myself felt he was genuinely glad to see me and that my suspicions might be wildly exaggerated.

He led me, chatting most amicably, through the hall into the dining room. It was full of great chunks of local carpentry in light-colored wood. Evidently Sauche had rented the house, furnished, from some family of local gentry. It had been built not as a summer residence but to live in all the year round. The small windows and massive walls were intended to keep out the chill damp of winter. It was a melancholy place, and the scarecrow palmettos made it even darker than it need have been.

The General sat in a tall leather chair, with a tray of drinks at his side. The two were living *en garçon* a little gloomily but in decided comfort. Slightly built and inconspicuous, the pair of them: one gray and clean-shaven,

one dark and moustached. But the major's slimness was
that of an athlete.

"A friend to see us," Vigny announced.

Sauche also was most cordial.

"From your appearance one would hazard a guess that
you are on the run," he said.

"In a way, yes."

"The professor did not come of his own accord," Vigny
explained. "Captain Bozec brought him."

"Bozec?" the General repeated with a military snort in
which there was some alarm. "Why?"

"That is what the professor will tell us. Meanwhile I
thought it best that Bozec should think we were delighted
to see an old friend — as indeed we are. Did you perhaps
wish to compare the grammar of Breton with that of
Basque and Berber?"

Feeling an inelegant clot in front of these two well-bred
masters of finesse, I pointed out that in the Basque country everybody knew — discreetly — a little of everyone
else's business, and so I had reason to believe that Bozec
might lead me to them.

Vigny let that pass, and poured me a whiskey.

"I don't think the moustache suits you," he said. "One
is no longer struck by the resemblance to Voltaire. But all
the rest is admirable without being exaggerated. I am experienced in security, yet I should pass you in the street
without a second glance."

"You know who I am?" Sauche asked.

"Yes, of course, General. In the hotel I did not. But under interrogation one learns as much as one gives away."

"I should hate to hand you over to the police," he answered reflectively, "after our short but most sympathetic acquaintanceship. But I am sure you will understand that in our position Commandant Vigny and I cannot afford to be compromised. Tell me first: how did you get onto Captain Bozec?"

"Through a certain Araña and a little imagination."

They were both silent, not meeting my eyes or each other's.

"We might be able to do a deal," Vigny said. "It's worth thinking about."

The interview was developing along most unexpected lines. They did not know I had been released and were assuming that I had escaped from prison.

"There is also the question of justice. Chivalry is so rare in these days that one should not have to pay for it too heavily," Sauche remarked with a sort of general-at-the-breakfast-table sententiousness. "Since you appear to know so much, I would ask you to give me a fair hearing. What we can do for you, frankly I do not know. But I would not like you to leave this house still thinking, as you must do now, that we are the lowest of canaille. What are your politics?"

I replied that I hadn't any, that as a philologist with an interest in prehistory I was accustomed to think of political development in units of five hundred years rather than units of twenty, and was overwhelmed by a sense of the futility of the purely ephemeral.

"You think there is never any point in resistance?" the General asked.

"As a historian I may think so. As an individual I support the right of any man to lose his temper with his government. One cannot stagnate."

"Then we can start from there. It is not only with General de Gaulle that — to adopt your phrase — I have lost my temper. It is with your government, too, and with all the irresponsible statesmen of our time.

"You, the British, have made the disastrous mistake of treating other races as your political equals, and you have compelled the rest of us to follow your lead. Yet never did you treat them as social equals. The French, on the other hand, have and had no objections at all to fraternity and intermarriage. Black, white, yellow — the ideal of the Revolution still lives. All Frenchmen are of equal value."

"I never understood that the Algerian and Indo-Chinese peasants had been so highly privileged," I said.

He begged me to spare him my irony and not to interrupt his apology.

"In any case, you know very well," he went on, "that it is impractical to treat a distinguished lawyer and his bare-arsed second cousin with the same consideration even though they are of the same race. It is the ideal which counts. Permit me to continue. The objectives of the Alliance des Blancs, of which you will have heard, are clear and logical. It maintains that we, the Europeans, had no right to surrender political power to states which are not viable, which had no unity before our administrators created it, which demand the services of the United Nations once a month. It is our duty to the future, as trustees of civilization, to preserve supremacy until such time as we can hand over to a responsible Confederation."

"To a French Empire, for example?"

"One could do worse. Or to the European Community, if you like. Or to any Great Power which is strong enough to save the peoples of Africa from themselves. Although I am a Catholic, I would prefer government by Moscow to the anarchy which must come from giving to innocents, cruel and happy as children, an independence for which they are not ready.

"Good! We now arrive at His Excellency, M. Leopold Mgwana, whose country for the moment — let us admit it — is efficiently administered. For the moment, I say. And if tomorrow he is assassinated? What future do you see when they have shot the bananas off the trees with their pretty machine guns and returned to the use of their excellent spears?

"Mgwana is an exception. His success intoxicates all Africa. The world would see the inevitable future more clearly if he were out of the way. But such a solution was not even considered. For that you have my word."

So Gonzalez's obsession with assassination was not so fantastic as I thought! When politicians claim that a proposal was not even considered, they invariably mean that it was — but rejected.

"It would not have been difficult," Sauche continued. "These dedicated liberals and pacifists accept as friends

anyone who can mouth their ridiculous patter. We therefore knew of the —" he searched for a delicate word
"— the escapade of Mlle. Manoli and M. Mgwana. When
we discovered the incredible — that neither of them had
asked for the routine protection of the Spanish police —
the situation was not without its temptations.

"Professor, what we did I ask you to see as an act of
war, regrettable but devoid of all personal considerations. The Alliance des Blancs serves humanity. Mlle.
Manoli and her Group make the same claim. I have decidedly the right to lose my temper with them. I chose the
weapons of scandal, a scurrilous press, ridicule. In fact I
took a leaf out of their book and used nonviolence. It is a
pity that you or Mgwana were so old-fashioned as to kill
poor Livetti."

"But neither of us killed him!" I exclaimed.

"Then who did?"

"That is what I have come here to find out."

"I think, my General, that we should telephone the police," said Vigny coldly.

Then I made a disastrous mistake. It was due to my
growing fury as the General blathered away about his
petty, pitiable "act of war." Suppression of that hatred
forced me into a sort of contemptuous triumph. I
told them that I had been acquitted of the murder of Livetti, released and asked to leave Spain. Partly led on by
the interest of that monomaniac Sauche and partly to convince them of the reality of my story, I even gave them
some account of the route by which I had secretly returned.

"Commandant Vigny," the General ordered, "this time you will tell me the truth."

"If you insist, my General. But I should prefer not to tell you in the presence of the professor. I have grown accustomed to him."

He shrugged his shoulders. I did not immediately see what he meant. But comment from me was not required, for there was no stopping the General. He was on his feet and loudly demanding the truth, determined to confront the pair of us as if he had been taking over from some incompetent Court-Martial.

"I offer you the excuse that it is the first duty of a Chief of Staff to spare his Commander unnecessary worries," Vigny said. "You had quite enough on your plate without the added complications of Duyker's folly; and it seemed to me unnecessary at the time that you should be bothered by the death of Livetti since the professor here had done his best to ensure that it would never be known.

"I feel that if he had been able to dispose of Livetti calmly and at leisure, that would have been the end of the affair. I genuinely wished to assist him, doubting if his experience could be as extensive as my own. But communication was difficult and dangerous. Like a fool I permitted Duyker to speak to Mgwana on the telephone. His tone of voice was hardly engaging. He insisted that he knew how to deal with natives, that Mgwana was helpless and would do whatever he was told. As usual he was wrong.

"But let us begin at the beginning. Duyker picked up Livetti at the rendezvous. You will remember, my General, that Livetti's instructions were to photograph His Excellency with his girl friend, if possible in some pose which would leave no doubt what their relations were and at the same time would be fit for publication. That was his specialty. In case there was a row, he was to make the most of it and yell for the Liberty of the Press. The worst that could happen to him was a day or two in prison and expulsion from Spain. I admit I hoped for something of the sort in order to gain still more publicity.

"What happened is hard to believe," he went on. "I have done my best to disentangle it all from Duyker's account, which consisted of little more than exclamations of indignation. And even when I have constructed a coherent story, I cannot make it fit the known character of Livetti. In my dealings with him I saw no sign of immoderate sensibility. So what you will hear, my General, has been filtered out through Duyker's mind and then through mine. The truth may be simpler.

"Duyker and Livetti stopped by the roadside not far from the hotel to run through the arrangements. It was then that Livetti first heard the name of Olura Manoli. He at once launched himself into an Italian passion. Duyker, as you know, has no great respect for Italians. For him the only white men are Dutch, Germans and the objectionable English. We, the French, qualify or not according to our political opinions.

"Livetti said that she was too beautiful and that he would not do it. That much is certain. Duyker quoted the exact words. He has not the imagination to invent them. And Livetti, I understand, spoke English perfectly.

"Duyker told Livetti with his customary tact that he had been paid to undertake the job, and that it made no difference whether he was photographing a cow's backside or a woman's. Livetti insisted that it was an outrage. He seems to have accused himself with tears, saying that he had no use for morality or honor since neither existed; but he respected beauty. He said that Olura Manoli with her clothes on was an angel, and without them a saint to whom any artist would pray.

"What had passed between Livetti and Mlle. Manoli we cannot know. But there it is! She appears to have plunged him into an abyss of sentimentality."

Vigny shrugged his shoulders and offered no further comment. He made it clear that he was reporting with proper military accuracy what Duyker had told him, and that he himself believed it to be somewhere near reality.

At the time I could not make head or tail of it. All this high-falutin' stuff about beauty and innocence sounded to me like the jabberings of some noble and bearded pre-Raphaelite waving an empty bottle. Only after my brief meeting with Olura could I guess at an explanation. Livetti had been damnably ashamed of himself. But he was not capable of privately retching with remorse like the rest of us and telling Duyker to go to the devil. Shame was not an admissible word in his vocabulary. It couldn't be. The moment it entered his conscious mind he would have to confess to himself what a degenerate little horror he was. So his Italian imagination invented all this pseudo-aesthetic fantasy which had in fact just enough truth in it to serve as an excuse.

"Duyker of course made nothing of all this excitement, but he is easily shocked," Vigny went on. "I do not know if he ever has a woman. The thought appalls me. I feel that he would carefully cover her up and say grace. It is perhaps understandable. He has shown me snaps of his family and female friends. That he should associate women with bovine backsides does not surprise me.

"Livetti must have seen right through our good old Duyker and deliberately provoked him, playing like a cruel little cat with all Duyker's suppressions and phobias. He had a mind like a dagger when it came to twisting the point about in anyone's faults but his own. He seems to have told him that male Negroes were far more beautiful and affectionate than whites. When Duyker whispered that to me, I could see that he had taken it in a heterosexual sense which horrified him quite enough anyway.

"Then Duyker hit him. He says that Livetti hit back. I dare say he did, but what could the poor devil do? Duyker got him by the throat, forced his head out of the window of the car and thumped it up and down on the sill.

"Finding to his surprise — they must have remarkable skulls in South Africa — that Livetti was dead, he acted with the daring that one expects from a colonial. He carried out the whole plan with Livetti dead instead of Livetti alive. He drove quietly into the garage under the hotel, drew up alongside the door into the shaft and hoisted Livetti up the ladder which this Araña had left in position. He took out the screws which I had loosened and shoved the corpse through the window.

"In five minutes Duyker was away and in forty minutes

mote he had joined us here. When that night he told me
the whole story, I was alarmed but considered he might
have done worse. He had never been seen with Livetti and
there was no connection between the two. He had been
driving from Madrid to Zarauz and would appear to have
taken a normal time for the journey. Over the plateau he
propels that car of his as if he were the only man on the
road. His departure and arrival were both witnessed, and
he wasted only half an hour in picking up Livetti and dis-
posing of him. His alibi, though not so unbreakable as our
own, is good enough."

Sauche's air of melancholy increased. Clearly enough he
disapproved of his brilliant subordinate and that intolerable ally, Duyker. But what could he do? I had the impression of a man deprived of hope and compelled to accept violence. What was his futile Alliance des Blancs
against the Napoleonic splendor of the ruler of France
with his patriotism, right or wrong, and his fearless
search for a modern cadre within which that patriotism
might be expressed? While still in France or Algeria
Sauche may have deluded himself that he was an equal
and alternative. After a year of exile, only an effort of
will could persuade him that he was anything of the sort.

By a similar effort he put aside all the disgraceful implications of the story which Vigny had told with such
ironical detachment — by God, his hand sketching in the
air had almost illustrated it too! — and turned to a subject which might excuse his intended treatment of me.

"I ask you again," he said, "what do you know of Bozec?"

"What everyone knows — that he had no business to be

where he was or he would not have been driven into Lequeitio by the gale."

"Why was he there?"

"I had thought for fishing. It is only your insistence, my General, which makes me suspect there may have been other reasons."

"The problem posed by this gentleman is very difficult," he sighed to Vigny.

"Disagreeable, yes. I should not say it was difficult."

"Why not?"

"Because he has no existence."

This time I had no trouble at all in seeing what he meant. Except for the brief meetings with Echeverría and Allarte I did in fact have no existence. All the police were ever likely to discover was that I had left the North Express at Bayonne and stayed a night there. Even if Iragui and Zubieta volunteered statements in answer to some appeal for news of a missing Englishman who spoke Euzkadi, they could only report my intentions; they could not explain why I had never arrived in Spain or been returned to France. I might have fallen over a cliff, or been shot by a frontier guard who was keeping quiet about it.

"One could perhaps trust to the professor's word of honor," Vigny suggested helpfully.

"Normally, of course," the General replied with exaggerated courtesy. "But since his object is to clear Mlle. Manoli of all suspicion . . ."

"But you? Have you any suggestions?" Vigny asked me.

"I suggest you sacrifice Duyker. I should not say that his attitude to colored peoples precisely reflects the ideals of the Revolution."

"I agree. It does not. But you are far from a child, Professor. You know very well that the financial supporters of a political movement are always more fanatical than the front line. The treasurer of a party commands obedience; the leader's problem is how far he can safely disobey."

Sauche, looking stern and unhappy as a commanding officer at a military funeral, murmured his approval. He added that it was out of the question to sacrifice Duyker; yet the alternative, so far as he could see, was that he and Vigny would be returned to France as undesirables.

"There is always South America," Vigny said. "In these days of air travel it is not far."

I could appreciate what he was up to. He was not going to have it said afterwards that the solution was his. He was forcing the General to decide.

"This damned Livetti!" Sauche exclaimed. "It is humiliating to be compromised by a common murder."

I fear I am inclined to be provoked by sloppy thinking.

"The murder of Livetti was plainly political," I told him. "It is my own which would be common. You propose to remove me merely to protect yourself."

"But at the same time I protect France," he answered superbly.

"To which your freedom of action is really essential?"

"Without doubt. I see you understand."

I was now very frightened indeed. I exclaimed that he

couldn't do it, that we were civilized men, that it was unthinkable.

"I admit that it was once unthinkable, my friend," Vigny said with a weariness which I believe was sincere. "But we have grown accustomed to the unthinkable. Your life? My life? Do they matter so much to your units of five hundred years?"

Inconsistently I thought that mine at least did, and that it was time to take immediate action and crash out through the window. But one cannot be expected to perceive under the façade of a most intelligent hotel acquaintance the former major of parachutists in Algeria. My arm which had just lifted the heavy vermouth bottle dangled painfully at my side. Vigny was so fast that he even caught the bottle before it hit the floor.

"You seem to think we are all alone in the nest," he said, "just because we sometimes prefer to open the door ourselves to visitors. But we do not cook for ourselves and clean the house. French officers were by no means always disliked by their subordinates."

He tapped a bell. Two scoundrelly North Africans entered the room. I say scoundrelly; yet I admit that in other circumstances I should call them faithful and devoted retainers. Are we to despise the havildars of the Indian Army, the Moorish sergeants of the days of the great Lyautey? They were soldiers to the very bottom of the loyalty which they preserved instead of a soul. Loyalty for them. Obscure aesthetic values for Livetti. Learning for me. Illusions of grandeur for Sauche. Our excuse for being alive. Blessed are the simple.

"This gentleman will not be dining in mess after all,"
said Vigny. "He will be served in the room behind the
kitchen. Please show him the menu and take his orders if
he should desire any small alteration."

The two closed in on me with the cordial smile of male
nurses and led me to the room behind the kitchen. At one
time it must have been the summer larder. Ventilation
was from gratings set high up into the thickness of the
north wall. It was furnished with a washstand, camp bed,
table and chair. I do not think that Sauche's limited activity in Spain ever called for the use of a cell. More likely,
this was very discreet accommodation prepared for over-
night visitors who might arrive by the *Isaura*.

I approved the menu and hoped that the cook could
perform its promise. He did. I was somewhat ashamed of
consciously enjoying my dinner when it did not look as if I
was going to have another; but I was hungry and one cannot change one's tastes. Did the official reports of execu-
tions in former days ever state that the prisoner ate a
hearty breakfast, or is it just a comic-paper joke?

The coffee was excellent, and the Armagnac out of this
world — no doubt a present to the General from some
Gascon admirer. I always knew that he and Vigny liked
me. I wonder if it would have shocked them to learn that I
hated the pair of them with a savage, contemptuous,
bloody hatred for what they had done to Olura. But there
was no object in revealing it or indulging it. When I raised
between my palms the balloon of brandy I instantly sup-
pressed the sweaty thought that Vigny's heart in the hands

of an Aztec priest would be much the same shape and size.

About nine Duyker came in, punctiliously shook my hand and asked me to accompany him. I suppose he had been summoned from some hotel in Zarauz where he was staying. The rather blank moon-face with its deep tan and fair hair, which I had seen only in the café at Amorebieta, somehow reminded me of an albino. His manner was what I could have bet it would be — a headmasterly grief that there should be nigger-lovers in the upper forms, coupled with a hearty acceptance of unpleasant facts. We might have been off to shoot some large and unfortunate animal in each other's company, and he exhorting me that it was the duty of a white man to follow his wounded buffalo into the bush; or it may be that I read into him thoughts which he never had because I myself shared the feelings and was not averse to the intentions of the wounded buffalo.

In fact he was taciturn and I remained in a suitably academic calm. In view of what happened I can see he felt distaste for what he had been selected to do or to see done. But Sauche's demand must have been unanswerable. Duyker had made the mess and could not avoid being chosen to clean it up.

"I should like you," he invited, actually smiling, "to give me your solemn word of honor that you will not call out when I take you to my car."

I replied that I refused to give him anything of the kind.

"I only wished to avoid humiliating you," he said.

He let in the two North Africans and pointedly looked the other way. No gag. No injections. No scientific nonsense. Just common sense and sound colonial administration. One of them pointed a pistol at me while the other swathed my head in tight bandages so that my jaw was firmly fixed. I must have looked like an illustration in a Red Cross manual. They did not tie my hands — in case, I suppose, someone looked into the car — but hobbled my feet. When I had been installed in the back seat of Duyker's Chrysler, my knees covered by a rug, alongside me an attentive Algerian, the whole setup was convincing. I was recovering from, let us say, a car smash and being taken to hospital to have the dressings changed.

Duyker took the corniche road to the west, and turned off it into the mountains when we were some miles short of Deva. He did not hesitate at the obscure corner and seemed to know where he was going. I am sure that the General did not grossly abuse Spanish hospitality until I presented him with the dilemma of either removing me or being expelled, so that it was unlikely that he had a well-reconnoitered spot for regrettable incidents. Possibly it was a quiet meeting place recommended by Bernardino. The byroad was so remote that even I had not heard of the villages at its far end.

Duyker stopped the car and told the Algerian to unpack my head. The faithful fellow did not bother to unwind the lot, but skillfully used a razor blade — which suggested that there would be no further need for the bandages.

"I am sorry for the inconvenience," Duyker said. "I

hoped you would be the kind of chap who wouldn't whine."

I shook my ears like the hobbled pony that I was and heard a truer silence, the mountain silence. The car had been climbing slowly through oak woods on the side of a steep hill. So far as I could tell by the general lie of the land and a moon in the third quarter we were now on a saddle of fairly even ground where the trees stood more sparsely.

"Beautiful country," I remarked conversationally — for it seemed that Duyker admired coolness, and he was my only hope. "I imagine that you get a view of the sea from here in daylight."

"You do," he replied, turning round in the driving seat and apparently glad that there was no ill feeling. "You're some kind of university lecturer, aren't you?"

I agreed that I was.

"We don't know your name as being active against us."

"I am not. I have no interest. I think you have a case for your apartheid if you don't grab too much. But economically and politically it won't work. One can't just stand on historical rights."

"Then what in hell were you up to with that black swine, Mgwana?"

"Getting him out of the jam you put him in. I might have done the same for you."

"And that criminal decadent, the Manoli woman," he said with a shudder of disgust.

I reminded myself that my love for Olura was no business of his and unseasonable, so I merely remarked that I maintained her right to sleep with anyone she pleased.

Hardly tactful, perhaps. But it brought him to the point without more ado.

"I am going to beat you and let you go," he said.

"You're going to what?" I asked, amazed.

"Beat you."

"But what good does that do?"

"I consider it sufficient punishment for what you have done and approved."

He reached under the seat and drew out a sjambok. I believe they are made of rhinoceros hide. The lash of the blasted thing was a good three-quarters of an inch thick, and the handle much thicker. It added to the African atmosphere already expressed in his car by two leopard-skin cushions and other small pieces of animal debris.

"I should have thought that would have been quite enough for Livetti," I said, feeling my way.

He replied that it was for punishment, not man-to-man fighting. So that was how he excused murder to himself. Poor little Livetti!

"But I take it you don't find many punishable citizens in Spain?"

"I keep it as a symbol," he said. "When you go abroad, don't you carry something with you from your home?"

"Not a damned thing," I told him. "But then I never feel abroad."

It was no good arguing. From the point of view of any intelligent European, Duyker was as mad as a hatter. One wonders if a Boer psychiatrist would agree. Vigny at least

I could understand, but I could not get this. If he turned me loose, I should be on the telephone to Gonzalez next morning.

"And when you have beaten me you will let me go?" I asked as if I were eager to have it over.

"I shall."

"Where to?"

"That has nothing to do with me. I shall let you go."

There was some kind of echo in the back of my mind. Pilate washing his hands? Or the Holy Office? Hand over the culprit and look the other way while they burn him? It couldn't be. But it was. That was what he was going to do. If he just delivered me to the Algerian to be murdered, it was sin. But if he punished me first for his own account, he was no longer responsible and the score was even and his conscience was clear.

The hypocrisy of it was unbelievable. I remembered, however, that Duyker was active, according to Gonzalez, in affairs of the Reformed Church. No wonder he had to invent a convenient angel with whom he could do some sinewy Calvinist wrestling. The solidity of Christianity continually astounds me. It seems to have no difficulty in shrugging off the eccentricities of South African pietists or a Prebendary Flanders or the comic vicars dragged from under the stones into daylight by the Deighton-Flaggs of the popular press.

"I will not be beaten with the native looking on," I said, boldly entering through the Looking Glass.

"That stands to reason."

"Well, where will he be?"

"He will stay in the car."

The Algerian, who spoke no English, listened stolidly to this conversation. He must have had orders to obey Duyker absolutely. No doubt his past career had familiarized him with many different preliminaries to execution. He lit a cigarette and showed no particular interest as I hobbled off between the trees, closely followed by Duyker running the lash of the sjambok through his fat fingers.

On this fairly level ridge where we had halted the timber was old and in control of the ground, clear of the saplings and shrubs which compete for every pocket of soil on steeper slopes. It was a place made for rest and contemplation which, if I had to die, I would prefer; one could end with dignity, conscious of being a part of that nature which is continually dying. What I resented was that I should be a torn thing, unfit for death. I do not think that I was particularly afraid of the coming pain, but very much aware that, mad and irrelevant though it was, it would hinder my communion with that Divinity which included Olura and the hills.

I did not look round at Duyker. He said nothing, content for the moment to follow me wherever I wanted to go with my little two-foot steps. Perhaps he thought I would fall, when it would be easier to go to work at once than to make the futile gesture of helping me up. Perhaps he too was remembering silence under stars at a time when race and religion had been matters of easy, kindly pride instead of secret torture.

I bore a little to my right towards the tinkle of water. I

could just distinguish the shape of a noble chestnut, beyond which streaks and patches of gray moonlight suggested that the sparse woodland opened out into a glade.
Over the mold of last year's leaves I hobbled to the bank
of a shallow, clear stream, a couple of yards wide, which
any long-legged man would normally cross by a jumping
stride from one sloping slab of stone to another on the far
bank.

Normally. Yes, if he didn't know the sweet, cold waters
of my Vizcaya. My heart began to beat as if I were running. I thought Duyker must see me quivering. I was, as I
have tried to explain, in a pantheist mood of unity with
my surroundings; so prayer was easy and instant without
the necessity for any Name and Address. I begged whatever could hear me that Duyker would do what he ought
to do, and that this special moss did not grow by the sun-
baked tributaries of the Vaal. Meanwhile I hobbled meekly
over the gravel just downstream from the stones, and took
my time over it.

I had nothing to lose if I were wrong, so I turned on him
before his foot hit the other side. That solid-looking moss
under his shoe stripped off the slope and disintegrated in
slime. As soon as his outstretched hand hit the ground, I
grabbed the sjambok out of it. It was the only weapon I
had so I used it with full force and fear while he was still
on one knee. That awful lash took him across the mouth
and immediately widened it to double the size.

Spouting blood, he sprang straight at me from his half-
up position, hard and low as if in a football tackle. I went
down, for I could not use my feet. Quite what happened

then I hardly know. There can be little rememberable thought in the speed and instinct of the cornered buffalo. Instead of falling on top of me, he must have jumped back and taken a revolver out of his pocket. At any rate he widened the distance between us, either despising me because of his weapon or forgetting that though I was down on one elbow I still had the sjambok in my other hand.

I struck upwards, again at his face. He got the flick of the tip this time, and the effect of it on the open wound was hideous. Gasping and choking, he gave me time to fasten on his hand and force it down. I could not loosen his grip on the gun. He was too strong for me to bend his arm. In the course of this I was on the ground again with him on top of me and the blood coming down as if one had knocked over a jug of warm milk. It is really very difficult to be academically exact.

My concentration was entirely on where his gun was pointing. At one moment it was wavering over my feet, so I suddenly curled up and brought the lashings round my ankles close to the muzzle. He didn't see what I was trying to do. Even when he was coughing, his arm locked in my grip was surprisingly steady. I forced a finger over his and pulled the trigger. The rope was only grazed, but enough for a jerk to break it. He was no match for me as soon as I had a proper purchase on the ground, so I threw him off and ran for it.

It must have been all very quick. At any rate the Algerian did not leave the car and come to the rescue until the sound of the shot. Or perhaps he didn't interfere because two blows of the sjambok, some grunts and a bit of a struggle were what he expected to hear. By the time he came up I was an impossible target, a shadow vanishing into the trees. Once safely out of the clearing I waited to see what would happen, mopping myself up with leaves. I had a sudden revulsion against Duyker's blood getting into my various abrasions. About as sensible as his horror of miscegenation!

Duyker was now lying on his back, quite still. The Algerian glanced at him, jumped into cover and stayed quiet. After five or ten minutes he came out. It may have occurred at last to his ultramilitary mind that the revolver was still in Duyker's hand and that I had possessed no arm of my own. He knelt down by Duyker and delicately felt his heart. Then he stood still for a moment, looking all round as if to impress the precise scene on memory. I could almost hear him thinking whether he ought to take any initiative without orders. He decided to risk it. No doubt there had been sufficient precedents. He removed the gun, put it in his pocket and started to lope off down the road. I heard the soft strides die away, and there was at last an awkward silence.

I, too, left Duyker lying, for I had had quite enough of practicing as an unregistered mortician. It seemed to me that the runner was right to leave the body untouched and the car on the roadside, and to report with the utmost speed to his superior officer. What Vigny would do I could not imagine — presumably invent a credible story to account for Duyker being where he was and call in the police to investigate his murder. They could not pin it on me, since I was not in Spain. With that thought I took to the hills, not caring where paths and tracks and guesswork led me so long as I reached some other stream than that by which Duyker lay.

No soap so he died, and she very imprudently married the barber. The childhood nonsense ran round my head as I tried to wash away the bloodstains from my clothes in a cold depressing dawn which only emphasized the brown and purple. But when the sun came up and my clothes were drying on the grass I saw that my fate need not be so bad as all that. My dirty blue shirt and trousers might have been stained by anything — dark, thick Rioja for example. My coat I painted with a wisp of grass and the last of the hair dye. They hadn't bothered to empty my pockets. The reason why I had no soap was simply that I had not had time to buy a fresh cake in Lequeitio.

Echeverría would have been more shocked than ever by my appearance. I tried to look like an unemployable laborer recovering from a three-day binge. The cheap cotton pullover I buried together with the sjambok. Don't ask me where! I wandered off, dazed with the sensation of being an outcast.

Every half hour I argued with myself so fiercely that I had to sit down to do it. I told myself that I had killed in self-defense and was plainly guiltless; but the blunt truth, so soon after the shock, would not stick. I had no proof that Duyker's life was not worth more than mine. What had I preserved for the world by killing? A minor authority on Comparative Philology. What had I destroyed? A man of action who appeared to my fallible judgment to be mentally unbalanced but might be a prince of good fellows out in his native bush. A totting up of human values gave no certain answer. As for religion, it should hold us both equally guilty. But there I grope. Religion is like rhubarb. Years must pass before anyone educated at an English boarding school can taste again the freshness of either.

All my fault? In a way it was. I accused myself of utter folly in ever accompanying Bozec to Zarauz when nothing prevented me from making a jump onto Lequeitio quay and leaving Bozec and Bernardino to wonder uneasily who the devil I had been. Yet philologists are not conditioned to realize that an active minority of their fellows lack any sense of the sacredness of human life, and that for a Vigny the only valid objection to murder is that it may be inconvenient.

Instinctively I was heading west for Maya. When I had been released from Madrid just seven agitated days earlier — days which had telescoped themselves into an uncomputed, animal memory of trees, hills and movement — I could only complicate matters for Olura by impulsively trying to arrange a secret meeting. Now, however, it was essential that she and you, the unknown guardian, should know the true story of the death of Livetti. Afterwards I intended to recross the Pyrenees and return home secretly, where I hoped to find some friend to swear that I had been in England since my release. But I did not really believe that I should ever be accused of killing Duyker. It seemed so unlikely that Sauche and Vigny would mention my name if I did not mention theirs.

Again I had to walk. I would have broken my rule and

risked public transport, but I was too filthy and questionable a character for even the most ramshackle country bus. So I played up to my appearance, eating and drinking in dark, foul taverns and pretending to be a lamentable bum permanently pickled in alcohol.

After two days striding along the high ground — except when there was anyone about to observe such an unlikely sense of purpose — I crossed our river where it was still a fast mountain stream, and cautiously approached Maya from the west. The village and its estuary were hidden, but through a gap I could see the Hostal de las Olas, the island of the Ermita and the curve of the great open beach where first I had talked with Olura.

By six in the evening I was in the woods where we had started our futile attempt to escape. I avoided the estuary, for it was Sunday; the sands were dotted with picnic parties just packing up before returning to Bilbao and the miniature industrial centers of the valleys. More with the intention of catching a glimpse of Olura than of reconnoitering possible approaches, I climbed a pine tree which overlooked the villa and the cove on its southern side. There was no sign of life in house or garden, and no guard at the gate. It seemed as if I could walk straight in after dark, but I was determined not to be impatient.

On the sands immediately below me were two men leaning against a beached dinghy. Though dressed as if they belonged to the foreshore, their appearance was unfamiliar, and they ought — at that hour and after a calm week of profitable fishing — to have been in the inn. It was possible that they had come to Maya for a Sunday outing, but they showed no intention of starting home.

I distrusted them even more as soon as I spotted a Pair of the Civil Guard who were sitting and smoking behind a screen of bushes just above the road into the village. They might have been enjoying the chance for a quiet cigarette or keeping an eye open for cases of Sunday evening immorality, but it seemed wiser to assume that the authorities were employing a lot of tact and money on the surveillance of Olura.

If so, the watch need not be so discreet after dark and would close in on the villa. In any case an unobserved entry was not going to be easy. The man who leveled the top of that miniature promontory and built a house on it had an eye for a charming site but did not consider the convenience of illicit visitors. Perhaps he had a wife or daughter whose standards became too relaxed when on holiday.

The low cliff on the south side, which faced me across the cove, would have offered an easy scramble up if not for the two figures, still unaccountably there at dusk, on the sands below it. The north and east cliffs dropping straight into the river were stepped by convenient ledges and could be reached by swimming or wading downstream. But both seemed to me then to be far too public. Allarte and his fellows might be loading gear into their craft by the light of flares, and there would be faint luminescence everywhere from the open doors of houses and the terrace of the inn.

So the best bet was to enter from the west: in fact by the normal way in. By a cautious approach across the

sand, well above high-water mark, I thought I could reach
the low wall to the right of the entrance, avoiding the road
and the gate itself. The trouble was that there seemed to
be a small light burning above the front door. So far as I
could tell in the gathering dusk, it was very inadequate,
yet probably sufficient for all my movements to be dimly
glimpsed once I was over the wall and in that exposed
front garden.

I came down from my tree and walked back through
the woods to the ruined cottage on the banks of the river.
After stumbling about among the brambles in the last of
the light I discovered the stone under which we had buried, three weeks earlier, Olura's Red Riding Hood cloak.
She had never retrieved it. I did not think she would, even
if she were allowed to walk that far.

It was still in fair condition. I shook out the cocoons,
ants and woodlice and carried it off. In spite of the whiff
of mold I could still detect the fragrance of Olura. That
was an incentive rather than a misery, for I was sure that
I would be with her in half an hour.

By the time I returned to the cove it was dark. The villa
was showing no lit windows on its southern side, but there
was a gleam in the air above the terrace, possibly from
the living room, possibly from flares on the village beach.
That damned light over the porch was stronger than mere
optimism had reckoned. I grumbled to myself that if there
were anything in telepathy Olura would have inexplicably
got up from her chair to turn it out.

The powdery sand at the top of the cove was two or
three feet below the level of the road. I crawled along it on

hands and knees, popping up my head at intervals to keep track of the movements of the few pedestrians. The two suspicious characters by the dinghy, which I had to pass closely, were no longer there. When one of them obligingly lit a cigarette, I discovered that they had moved across the cove until they were immediately below the villa. I again wondered what the devil you and Olura had been doing to attract such keen supervision. Allarte had given me the impression that you were more or less on parole.

At last I came up against the corner of the west wall. The ex-dinghy party was thirty yards away near the edge of the water and could not possibly distinguish anything at that distance. The only risk I ran was that someone in the tavern across the road or one of the Pair — if they had left their screen of bushes for the dark alley alongside the tavern's pool of light — might have his eye on the wall at the moment when I slid over it. That, after all, was unlikely. First I threw the cloak over; then I pulled myself up, keeping as flat as possible, and dropped down into the garden.

In the darkness under the wall I put on Olura's cloak. It was of course too short, but the flower beds and their edging of low shrubs hid my legs. In any case nobody out in the road could see more than a moving figure, whose identity would be taken for granted so long as the outline was familiar.

Insensate daring? A typically academic contempt for the common sense of plain humanity? Well, I agree with you that perhaps it was speculative; but in normal cir-

cumstances I should have got away with it. In fact I did,
so far as that particular maneuver was concerned. If you
will house your goddaughter on the sort of peninsula
which would be chosen by a robber baron in a small way
of business, you compel anyone who desires access to her
into some degree of imprudence.

Drifting slowly up to the house and stopping at intervals as if to enjoy the night scent of flowers, I reached the
flagged terrace on the east. To my bitter disappointment
there was still no light to be seen. The French windows
were unlocked, so I went in, closing them behind me. Nobody was about. It seemed early for Olura to have gone to
bed — and, if she had, at least one window would be blazing with light.

I explored the passage down the middle of the house
from the living room to the front door. As my only means
of illumination was a box of wax matches and I did not
dare to switch on the lights, I could not tell whether you
had just left the house for a stroll or were no longer living
in it.

I was just about to return to the living room when a
sudden draught blew out my match. Someone had opened
the window. Immediately afterwards I saw the beams of
two powerful torches playing over the room. I squashed
myself into the corner between the walls of living room
and passage. A second later a beam lit up the whole length
of the house.

It was the Pair of the Civil Guard — presumably the
same whom I had seen earlier watching the road into the

village. I could hear their low-voiced conversation. One of them asked if they should search the house.

"Better not," the other replied. "There is politics in this."

About the only time in my life that I have thanked God for politics! If they came down the passage I hadn't a hope.

"Was he sure?" the first asked.

"Quite sure. He said that the poor señorita was in the garden in tears."

"She'll have something to cry for. Headquarters believe she is an English terrorist. You saw her too?"

"No. But since I knew she and her uncle had not come home . . ."

"Good! You take the front, and I'll stay on the terrace."

They went out, leaving the French window open. I returned to the living room, and from the cover of an armchair watched the man on the terrace. He shone his torch on the rocks and the water, and then appeared to be signaling across to the sands. Soon afterwards I heard a horse cantering over the beach.

This was hell. Evidently you would both be back at any moment. Ought I to stay or not? So far as I was capable of any constructive thought, I decided that my discovery and arrest — both pretty certain — might compromise Olura. I blamed myself for impatience. I should have waited until I knew more of her routine and why she was being guarded by horse and foot.

So the only thing to do was to get out and get clear. It was a hard decision to take — the more so, since I doubted if it were possible. With a man at the front door, the garden route was out. So was a climb down to the cove. If I slipped or dislodged a stone, the two chaps on the sand below would hear me; and if I fell, it would be slap into their hands. The only practicable way was from the terrace, silently down over the rocks into the water of the estuary.

Somehow I had to get rid of the guard outside the window. One obvious trick was to switch off the light over the front door. That ought to bring both of them into the house to investigate. However, they could then be sure that there was really somebody about, which I wanted to avoid. So fuse the circuit? Difficult without any light to work by, but the wiring of any villa of that age was sure to be rather slaphappy. I was inclined to put my trust in the local electrician and to hope that he had not been an efficient Basque.

First I folded up the red cloak and deposited it among the cushions of the living room couch. The Pair had only flashed their torches round the room and could not possibly be sure how many cushions there were. Then I tiptoed down the passage to the front door and had a look at the switch. My luck was in. The screws which held it to the wall were loose. With a handkerchief round my hand — memories of Mgwana and silk stockings — I wrenched it out from the wall a little and stuck the blade of a knife underneath. Sure enough the insulation had worn off a wire, or a wire had been pulled partly out of its terminal by the loose switch. There was a satisfying pop, and darkness outside.

The guard at the front door ran round to the terrace to tell his colleague — a silly move of which I took instant advantage, slipping out of the door and shutting it behind me. Then I crawled round the north side of the house, reckoning that if they ran back to the door that way they would pass me in the pitch darkness without spotting me. But in fact they went straight inside through the window, politics or not, to catch the unknown who had switched the light off. As soon as I saw those great beacon beams of theirs searching the rooms I went over the wall of the terrace and down into the estuary.

I had intended to swim upstream and go ashore on one of our hidden beaches. It could not be done. The tide was racing out too strongly. To swim across to the open sands seemed to me to be asking for trouble. Even at night they showed as a paler expanse against which my figure might be black. If the mounted man or men had good night sight, I could be chased and captured before reaching the distant cover of the sand hills.

So there was little else for it but to go down on the tide. I didn't like that either. Flares, as I expected, were on the beach. A head floating down past the boats, the village and the inn would probably be spotted — and, even if I got past the lot, there was no future but the open Atlantic. An exaggeration, this. I could have worked myself ashore on the right bank well below the village, and perhaps got away by following the beach towards the Hostal de las Olas. But one is not at one's best when hanging on to a piece of seaweed, with the current, let alone the Pair, demanding instant decision.

Downstream I could just make out the bow of Allarte's launch. It was anchored only a few yards from Maya beach, but the far side of it must be in darkness. That was what I chose. I allowed the current to sweep me down on the *María de Urquijo,* and climbed aboard just opposite the engine housing where my silhouette would not stand out against sky or white sand.

I remember thinking that I could be seen from the bedroom windows of the inn, but no lights were on and it was unlikely that anyone had yet torn himself away from pleasant digestion of the Sunday night supper and gone up to bed.

The glory hole in the forecastle, packed with bits of net, lobster pots and miscellaneous gear, offered a refuge. It was heated, I should guess, by the decay of small pieces of fish. The smell was unspeakable, and I was very glad when Allarte and his crew of three came aboard. As soon as the forecastle began to thud into the sea, I knew we were clear of the estuary and came out.

Allarte was far from welcoming. He swore copiously and told me that I had no right, friend though I was, to hide on the *María de Urquijo.*

I apologized for the necessity and asked him why he was fussing, since he knew very well that nobody was looking for me.

"What I know is that you are wanted for murder," he said bluntly, "and the whole place is crawling with police. For God's sake, Ardower! It's likely the boat will be searched wherever we put in!"

I asked incredulously if all the excitement which I had noticed around Maya was just for my benefit.

"Of course! What did you think? They knew you would come."

It is humiliating to find one's behavior predictable. The criminal will visit his girl. Normal police procedure. Picket the house and you have him. It drives home the truth of Olura's insistence on the unity of mankind. Dons or juvenile delinquents, the first thing we do after committing murder is to call on our young women.

I could not make out how my return from France was known. Even if Sauche and Vigny had managed to give a hint without compromising themselves, why should police be so sure I was in Spain?

"What murder?" I asked Allarte.

"How do I know? A foreigner, they say. And they have no doubt that it was you. Look, man! We have families! This is a risk we cannot take."

Allarte throttled down the diesel. He and his crew left me sitting on the break of the forecastle, while they went into a huddle like mutineers deciding what to do with an awkward officer.

At last he called me over.

"None of us want to take you back to Maya," he said. "It would be uncivilized behavior to a friend. But we cannot afford to have trouble with the police. What we will do is land you on the Ermita. After all, you could have swum there, though God knows how you would have got ashore."

"And you won't talk?"

"Not us, by God! Not drunk or sober! I tell you, we have families."

The Ermita is not quite such a fearsome island as it appears from your terrace. The top, if one could roll it out flat, would cover some four acres. There are patches of turf and heather wherever there is shelter from the salt spray. On the far side, which only the fishermen ever see, the slope facing the open Atlantic is more gentle and the cliffs much lower. There is a just possible, indetectable landing place which can be used on the rare occasions when there is no swell booming in from the Bay of Biscay.

We came up alongside this low rock, with all fenders out, and Allarte told me to jump. He threw after me a loaf of bread and said that he would be back, weather permitting, the following night with more provisions. He warned me on no account to light a fire or to let myself be seen from boats or on the skyline, and told me that I should find water behind the hermitage which gave the crag its name.

I climbed up to the hermitage very carefully, for it was no place to be helpless with a broken ankle. I found four thick, loose-stone walls enclosing a small room, and a bit of roof left. It was horribly cold, and I did not attempt to sleep or to occupy the hut. Too many odd vegetable growths — odd at least in darkness — poked out from the walls and encumbered the floor. The enclosure seemed inhabited by a sad spirit of loneliness, which I felt might become visible and unpleasantly conversational at any time. So I sat down on a patch of turf with my hands round my knees and my dripping clothes spread out alongside me. Nakedness is a glory of love and the sun, even an emblem of virtue in a nudist camp; but civilized man, pitched into night and nature with no clothes on, feels singularly defenseless.

My spirits rose a small point with the dawn, both taking the devil of a time to develop into any sort of warm lucidity. Then I slept a little, and woke up convinced that jail had been more friendly than this freedom. The only comfort was that I felt pretty well. Ever since the police magistrate had turned me loose on the public I had become remarkably tough, even for a much-traveled and impecunious don.

There was, as Allarte had told me, a rock pool of rainwater at the foot of the bare slope behind the ruined hermitage. Whoever the hermit was — I know nothing of him except that he is supposed to have been a soldier in the Thirty Years' War — he had smoothed a primitive catchment area to feed the pool.

After a breakfast of bread and water I explored my refuge. On one side was nothing but the sparkling semicircle of the Atlantic; on the other, my love and very dubious future. The whole scene of my happiness was spread out for me as I crouched among the eroded rocks at the top of the island: the Hostal de las Olas, Maya, its inn and its beloved estuary, and your villa where it pleased me to think that I could see Olura in the red cloak. But the distance was more than two miles, and I insisted that it was probably the massed geraniums in the tubs of the terrace. When I and my clothes were warm and dry I spent the long hours lying in the sun and reviewing the feverish days since first I met Olura. I marshaled all the facts as if for a thesis. It was then that this narrative was prepared rather than in the actual writing.

In the evening I saw Allarte's launch coming round from Lequeitio. He and his crew had certainly dumped me on a spot where they themselves ran no risk of ever being accused of complicity. As soon as the *María de Urquijo* passed behind the Ermita it was out of sight of Maya and the mainland; a watcher on shore would only see it disappear and reappear two or three minutes later. Allarte did not even stop. He brought the launch up alongside the landing rock and flung ashore a bundle of old ragged net containing more bread, a kilo of cold, grilled sardines and a leather skin of Rioja.

I ate ravenously and made myself a bed of heather on a patch of sheltered grass. It was one of those soft, clear nights when a man in the open wakes often to full consciousness and then falls alseep again without intervals of drowsiness. There was no sound but the splash and suck of the sea, no light but the brilliance of stars and the phosphorescence of ripples and bubbles beyond the streaks of foam. In one long, peaceful interlude of wakefulness I thought I heard Olura call my name. That was not surprising. My thoughts were obsessed by her. During the afternoon I had childishly lined up two sticks so that in the early darkness I should know which were the lights of the villa.

The beating of the sea itself was high-pitched and feminine, agitated rather than militant. That I should hear a falsetto *Phi-i-ilip* from the sucked pebbles of some deep cleft was not beyond imagination. I got up and started to prowl restlessly above the water. There could be no doubt that the cry was reality, or at least that I was really hearing it. I make the distinction because hair was prickling at the back of my neck. In such an emptiness the siren or the wandering spirit does not appear so impossible as when listening to the positive biochemists of my College.

I threw off my few clothes and dived in. The freshness of the sea dispelled the fear of it. Whatever it was that I had heard and was still hearing, I settled down to swim indefinitely towards the thin sound. But it was much nearer than I thought, seeming to come from a whale-backed rock, soft with long weed, away to the west of the landing point. The rock was just clear of the falling tide and I came ashore as gently as on a beach. My mermaid was there, stretching out her arms and calling into the limitless night.

Beyond uttering each other's names I doubt if we even spoke. We clung together like the two last seals on earth, herded up by nature to reproduce from desolation a happiness of the sea. *How did you get here? How did you know?* — I believe that some time I must have asked those questions and received some incoherent reply about Elena and the stars. But speech has so little to do with ecstasy.

"Take me to the Ermita, Philip," she said at last. "I couldn't find a place to land."

It was only then that I realized there might not be one. Something of the sort had passed through my head before I dived in, but that had been no moment for caution. Together we swam to the landing rock, keeping such close contact that often we went under and rose laughing. A sensuous journey, easier for furry flanks and pulsing tails. But perhaps seals cannot laugh.

No lonely swimmer could ever get ashore unhurt on the Ermita except in dead calm and at the top of a spring tide. The landing rock, falling sheer to deep water and the restless Atlantic, was out of reach. But we felt absurdly sure that two could do what one could not, and we were right. Round to the south we explored a dark fissure, sheltered from the direct battering of the waves, where a patch of foam-flecked water heaved sullenly up and down. I hung on to the weed while Olura stood on my shoulders and pulled herself up to a wide ledge. From there two long legs with frog flippers on the end of them — which I had not even noticed before — came down to me, and we were on the Ermita.

I led her to such hospitality as I could offer — a dry and filthy coat, the heather and Allarte's gift of wine. We kept each other warm as she told her story.

She said that on the night I was in the house she herself had been at the inn, taking a late supper after driving her godfather as far as the frontier. She was not allowed to cross it, but otherwise was free to do what she pleased. In the middle of her lonely meal she felt a sudden compulsion to run back to the villa and turn off the light over the front door. She reminded herself firmly that she couldn't turn it off. It had been burning day and night since Friday.

Feeling more desolate than usual, she had sought out

Elena for the inarticulate warmth of her comfort and together they had gone up to her former room. While looking out into the night they had seen, as they thought, one
of Allarte's crew go aboard by swimming. At the sight of
such masculine folly they stopped crying and cheered up.
There was nothing out of character in a Basque fisherman, after a heavy evening's drinking, impulsively taking
a swim with all his clothes on to clear his head. Elena
accepted it quite naturally, described by vivid gestures the
quirks of the indomitable drunks of her country and
merely remarked that she hoped he had a warm sweater
on board.

When Olura returned to the villa, the Pair was in possession and insisting that somebody had been in the
house. She replied that the fellow who claimed to have
seen her in the garden must have seen her ghost, for she
was always in two places at once. She giggled happily in
my arms remembering her effort to express this obscure
thought first in pidgin Spanish, then in French which one
of the Pair vaguely understood.

After searching the house and apologizing profusely,
they tried to mend for her the wayward bulb over the front
door, blew the fuse twice and left, promising to order an
electrician in the name of the law to pay Olura a visit. It
was clear that they had been enchanted by the English
Terrorist.

When they had gone, she found the cloak and put two
and two together. Next morning she harried Elena to get
hold of Allarte as soon as he returned on the evening tide.
The two cornered him in a private room and wore down

his denials by threats and supplications. The threats at any rate worked. He could not stand up to Olura's bluff when she swore she would tell the police immediately if he didn't confess what he had done with me. She must have reduced him to pulp with an obstinate determination to be understood.

Allarte, however, had refused to take her out to the Ermita. Everybody would notice it, he said. Everybody would want to know what he was doing. And the tide was anyway too low to put her ashore.

That much Elena confirmed, and Olura had to accept it. But she managed to persuade herself that a swimmer could go where a boat could not. Except for a low cave or a very narrow entrance I cannot imagine such a place, for timber is less breakable than bone. The night was comparatively calm, and a couple of miles in her frog feet were well within her powers.

Horrified by her recklessness, I exclaimed that she could have missed the island altogether in the dark.

"No, I couldn't," she replied casually. "Through all those long nights wondering where you were I had time to notice so much. There was a great star low down on the horizon which I called yours. And it used to disappear behind the top of the Ermita. So I knew that if I kept the lights of Maya behind me and couldn't see the star I must reach the island."

"Jupiter," I remarked pedantically.

The planet blazing in the northeast sky had been my companion for many lonely hours, but I had not paid much attention to it. My rainbow's end was the tail of the Milky Way hanging over Maya in the west.

"Is it?" she answered with feminine indifference towards giving a name to something which was too important to need one. "Well, I think my navigation was pretty scientific."

It was. She had hit the target bang in the center, below the savage crag on the southern side. Then she had swum round, looking for any place where Allarte could possibly have landed me and calling out. But since she was so close under the cliffs and out of breath I never heard her until she stubbed her toe on the reef of the whale-back and came out to rest.

"Does anyone know where you are?" I asked.

"Nobody. My godfather went to Paris this morning."

"And the police?"

She chuckled happily as if they had suddenly become a mere casual annoyance.

"I was very careful. If they miss me tomorrow, they'll think I made another bolt for the frontier."

I left the details of my own story for next day, for I did not know whether she had heard that I was wanted for murder. I refused to spoil the hours of unity by a description of violence which I believed was bound to shock and repel her.

The sun was clear of the ocean clouds before we awoke. She sat up and yawned like a newly created Eve, exploring with little-girl eyes her immediate surroundings.

"What a lovely place!" she exclaimed.

That certainly was not how I myself would have described the Ermita. After the black water and waving weed of the night, our patch of green probably looked to her eyes more like a sunken alpine garden than a rock cap pickled in salt and the wind. I said that I might appreciate it more if we had a full picnic basket.

"It will do you good," she retorted. "You'll have time to pay some attention to me."

That gay, ironical jealousy of a mere thought! I thanked God in all humility that it was I who had worked the change in her — not that I was in any way responsible for her content of joyous femininity, but at least I had unwrapped the parcel right side up.

However, I was now to see her for the first time in that maternal mood which everyone else — her touchy young Africans, her Group and even Leopold Mgwana — considered the natural expression of her character. While we lay in the sun and ate the last of Allarte's sardines, I perceived that she knew far more than I ever suspected and that I had not been so clever as I thought in avoiding all detail. It was she who had refused to encourage me.

I gave her the whole story of my rash visit to Zarauz and the attempt to remove me. Livetti and his death had to come in. She told me rather distantly and formally how and when she had met him. I got the impression that after so much cross-examination by an incredulous Gonzalez — and perhaps an incredulous guardian? — the whole episode had become unreal to her.

It was not her fault that she had inspired a muddle-headed decency in the man which had cost him his life, but I feared that, with her readiness to accept guilt, she might think it was. Not a bit of it! Livetti was a thing in a wheelbarrow, a thing which threatened her lover who could do no wrong, a thing which had led to the humiliating exposure of an intimate and difficult folly. It was by exaggerating all this resentment, I suspect, that she protected herself from any feeling of responsibility.

When my story arrived at the end of Duyker, it was my turn to be reticent. I skated over the struggle, just saying that I had inevitably knocked him about but that I could not understand what had caused his death.

"You drove his false teeth down his throat," she said, "and he suffocated."

A macabre and faintly comic end for that bully of the open spaces. Civilization had caught up with him at last. Olura's voice had an edge of hysteria. She too must have sensed the contrast between the man and his death. She pictured, of course, a nasty smack in the mouth, not the savage effect of the sjambok. I did not disillusion her.

"It was my only weapon," I said.

"But he meant to kill you! And you really fired that shot at your feet?"

"Well, yes. I had to get away."

"You had no right to expose yourself like that! Suppose he had gone on shooting?"

I replied that it was dark and that he was hardly in a state to aim accurately. I was almost apologetic. Don't women have any constant principles at all? I had expected to be a pariah for indulging in bestial violence, and there I was being gently rebuked for not killing Duyker

when I had the chance and preferring to take a very slight
risk with my own life.

"How do you know so much?" I asked.

"Gonzalez. He has been keeping my godfather informed."

That sounded very hopeful. It might, I said, be impossible ever to prove Vigny's account of the murder of Livetti, but there could be no doubt that the rest of my story
was true. I could describe the house, the room behind the
kitchen, the car, the journey, everything.

"It's much worse than that, Philip."

The car and the body had been discovered in the morning by a passing farmer. When the police got in touch
with Vigny, he must have brilliantly played dismay and
ignorance. He took the offensive at once, stating regretfully that I had called at the villa to accuse him of killing
Livetti and planting the body in a bathroom window of the
Hostal de las Olas. I had apparently persuaded myself into
an *idée fixe* that he was responsible, ever since he and
Duyker had happened to pass Miss Manoli's car on the
road. I became excited and violent and even picked up a
vermouth bottle with the intention of smashing General
Sauche. Damn him! Of course my fingerprints would have
been found on it, and wrong way up.

They were unwilling to cause annoyance and scandal,
of which they had had quite enough already, so they put
me under temporary restraint and did not send for the police. They even wished me to have a chance to continue,
as they thought, my escape. Very wrong, but it would be

understood that they had a sporting sympathy for any fugitive. So Duyker kindly took me up into the mountains and turned me loose. I must have grabbed some weapon and killed him.

This was appalling. I could not see any answer. It was quite as good a story as the truth. The Algerian would swear whatever he was told to swear. Nobody could ever prove that he was in the car that night with Duyker.

"There was just one shot?" Olura asked.

"Yes. Why?"

"I was thinking of Vigny," she said vaguely. "I saw something. Wait a minute! Yes, what Vigny would believe. It would never occur to him that you wouldn't take life when you could."

Her opinion of me was romantic. If I could have got the muzzle of that revolver to point at Duyker instead of my feet, I am sure I would have tried to pull the trigger. My life was at stake and I was very frightened.

"What difference does it make?"

"It means that Vigny thinks you never had control of the gun, and that Duyker fired the shot. He could have killed you."

"No body. No evidence."

"Duyker bled all over you, Philip. You left that out. Those revolting clothes of yours over there — you don't spill wine. Tell me the truth! Wouldn't the police have found blood all over the place?"

I admitted reluctantly that it was a common result of deep face wounds.

"And where you hid to watch the Algerian?"

"Plenty. I remember trying to wipe some of it off with leaves."

"It would look as if you had been hit."

"Not to police. They don't know there was any gun."

She exclaimed against the stupidity of police. It wasn't them, she said, she was thinking of.

"It's Vigny, Philip, Vigny!" she insisted. "He must have been taken by police to look at the ground. I wonder if we couldn't persuade him that you crawled off to die."

I still could not catch up with all these jumps which were more instinct than thought. Justice, police, evidence — one is accustomed to consider crime in those terms. Olura, however, despised the lot as a sort of game which the participants treated very seriously but had nothing to do with essential truth. Take Civil Disobedience, for example! She would expect her Prebendary Flanders to be acquitted on the grounds of his excellent character and idealistic motives however many statutory offenses he had willfully committed. Her contempt for the majesty of the law was now working the other way round. She saw nothing whatever wrong in faking evidence against the guilty.

She was feeling her way to what lay on the other side of the hill through people, not through facts. The maddeningly feminine way of influencing events! Still, she was onto something. Vigny, puzzling out the Algerian's report, must indeed find the struggle difficult to reconstruct. If Duyker always retained possession of the gun, why hadn't he fired again and again? If it was I who had control of it, why didn't I kill him while he was still very much alive?

Anything might have happened, but certainly the possibility existed that I had been hard hit, not worth another shot, yet managing to crawl off while Duyker was choking. The police, since they did not know there had been any gun, would not look for my body. And Vigny dared not be caught hunting for it.

So far as my trial for murder was concerned, all this got us nowhere. I could not prove there had ever been any shot. The bullet, fired more up than down, might have gone anywhere. And I had not the faintest notion where I was when I buried the sjambok and untied from my ankles the two halves of the hobble which would show how the rope was severed.

"You keep fussing about evidence, my darling," she repeated. "It's Vigny we must think of. Suppose your body were found, where's his story then? And who took the gun which killed you out of Duyker's hand?"

It wasn't worth arguing. Unless my body *were* found — and at the moment I found it far too pleasant a possession to part with — her fantasies contained nothing but vague possibilities of playing on the nerves of the military. I pointed out that if I could not show a motive for assassinating me, Vigny's story was as good as mine. What would really shake him was evidence proving he had planted Livetti in the hotel — which he hadn't.

"Oh, that!" she said as if it were just a minor inconvenience. "We could have that."

"Where from?"

"Mary Deighton-Flagg."

I rolled over indignantly and sat on a sea thistle. It

added to the force with which I expressed my opinion of Mary Deighton-Flagg's character and reliability.

"It's never worthwhile being rude to people, Philip," she said primly. "All that is quite true. But in her way she likes me and she badly needs money."

"But, Olura," I protested, "I can't understand you. If it were a policeman who proposed to fabricate false evidence, you'd be the first to say nothing could justify it."

She answered that I should not be stupid, that she was not a policeman but a woman very much in love, and why were we wasting precious hours in talk?

She insisted that I should stay for the time being on the Ermita, where I was safe. She would try to swim out again on the first calm night. Meanwhile we could even see each other. Kneeling behind a rock and holding my arm as if I were likely to be inattentive, she pointed out where there were specks of red on the terrace and where there were not.

She could persuade herself that I was near her and camping out on an unconventional summer holiday. Sky was blue and water silky. I do not think she realized the hostility of the place when wisps of cloud squirmed over it and the spouting of the sea was orderless, without even the tranquillizer of rhythm. She was even glad for my sake of the ruined walls and crazy roof of that homemade cell which nothing on earth would induce me to enter.

At dusk I made her leave, for I disliked the look of the weather. So did Allarte. I could tell that. We watched the *María de Urquijo* nose her heaving, fendered bow right up to the landing rock while Allarte flung ashore three packets. He could have no idea that there might be two to be fed; so extra food meant that he foresaw a period when the island would be unapproachable.

I saw the last of Olura with every miserable kind of foreboding, though there was no reason to be afraid for her. When she put on her swimsuit and frog feet, dived clean from the landing rock and rose to wave good-bye, the sea was calm enough and the lights of Maya clear. An hour and a half later I saw the signal of safe arrival which she had promised to give: a light flicking on and off in her bedroom window.

Next morning the wind carried spurts of drizzle and the sea was getting up. With no handy cave, no fire and no tool but a small pocketknife I was in a worse state than Paleolithic man when the coast was nearer to the continental shelf and the Ermita a pleasant knoll in temperate forest. All I could do for shelter was to choose an overhanging rock and build up on the open side a tight-packed hedge of heather and brush.

For two days the weather closed down, and Maya was simply a gray horizon where even the red of roof tiles was hardly distinguishable. The next two — of sun and high wind — were endurable, for I could at last feel dry and clearly see from time to time the dot on the terrace which was Olura.

On the fifth and sixth days she was no longer there, and I tortured myself with the thought that she might have been mad enough to steal a dinghy and try to row to the Ermita. I knew very well that she would not attempt to swim. No doubt my morbid imagination was partly in-

spired by hunger. Nothing remained of Allarte's food par-
cels but a few stale, damp rolls. I was down to trying raw
mussels, limpets and shrimps — all of them equally revolting.

The whole scheme of hiding began to seem to me mere
cowardly procrastination. With increasing melancholy I
saw that I must make my way at once to England. They
could extradite me if they had a case, and to hell with it!
But first I must see Olura again. I gave myself all of a fifty-
fifty chance of spending a few hours at the villa unde-
tected. The police must long since have grown tired of
waiting through wet and windy nights for their predictable criminal.

At nightfall the rain came in again from the Atlantic,
gentle but reinforcing my decision to get out. The surf was
still formidable. On the western side of the Ermita the
landing rock was curtained by spray, and the whale-back
where I had found Olura was certain death for ship or
man. But under the lee of the island there was nothing
much wrong with the sea if I could reach it. The fissure
where we had come ashore was a vile maelstrom of leaping foam and driftwood. So there was nothing for it but to
go in from a ledge of the cliff — a much higher dive than
I had ever taken before. I was, I can see, so damnably
depressed that I did not much care whether I lived or
drowned. An exaggeration, perhaps. But life meant life
with Olura, and I had persuaded myself through too many
lonely days and nights that it was out of the question.

With the wind behind me I swam for the beach, not the
estuary. The breakers got me, but only once; and when

they couldn't smash they helped. I landed fairly close to the Hostal, shaken and dazed but able to stagger out of the surf. When I had rested and coughed up the water, I walked along the sands — Leander's old journey to daily paradise — towards the estuary.

There was light behind the curtains of the living room. Evidently you were at home. I could neither see nor hear any police by the edge of the water. They would not have needed a mounted man to catch me. Allarte's launch was rocking at anchor in the driving rain, and Maya beach was empty.

It was slack water at the top of the tide. I walked a little upstream, putting your promontory between myself and the village, swam down to the rocks below the terrace and dragged myself up. I waited some time with my head over the wall until I was sure there was no one about. The lamp behind the curtain beckoned. I crawled to the French window, for it seemed to be the easiest way of progressing. Anyway I did not want to be seen against the light. When I tapped, you opened; and the sad thing from the sea crawled over the threshold to be told that Olura had been arrested and removed.

Secret and Personal

I HAD sat through the long evening in a mood of sullen anger, directed as furiously against Ardower as the persecutors of Olura. Pity did not immediately overcome it. This down-and-out derelict who writhed across the threshold was Olura's lover. The culmination of all the Utopian delusions of her short life was to give her heart to a half-drowned, exhausted murderer on the run. Humiliation was complete.

He was unamenable to any suggestions for his comfort until I had answered his questions. I informed him shortly that Olura had been arrested the previous day on a charge of concealing a felony, and that I personally was surprised that the authorities had held their hand as long as they did.

Refusing my recommendation of brandy and a hot bath, Ardower mentioned that he was very hungry. Perhaps I would be so good as to lend him a razor? Steadying himself by a grip on the table and with his ironical eyes holding mine, he explained this obscure addition to the menu by announcing that he preferred to shave before dinner. I did not appreciate this veiled insolence.

I escorted him upstairs. He needed my arm. To support a much younger man creates a greater intimacy than being supported by him. That too I resented. While he shaved and rubbed himself down, I impatiently collected such provisions as were in the house and laid them out in my bedroom. With so many idle Spanish police about, one's privacy downstairs was always uncertain.

He ate and drank enormously, becoming slightly intoxicated. Though too tired to give me more than a bare outline of the facts, he would not rest until he had confirmed Olura's story. When he became incoherent in his determination to explain himself, I led him to her room and expressed my hope that he would accept her hospitality. He appeared unduly moved, so I left him.

I must now append some account of the machinations of my dear and unaccountable goddaughter which indirectly led to her arrest.

On August 19 Lieutenant Gonzalez called at our villa and informed us that our movements and communications were now free of all restraint, but that Olura must remain in Spain as an essential witness. The authorities regretted that her passport could not yet be returned; they would, however, make all necessary arrangements if she wished to leave for some resort with more opportunities for society and entertainment. She refused to make any move whatever until she had news of her Philip.

Gonzalez, who had developed a soul in duplicate, one for use as a security man and the other for private life, pleaded ignorance. He said that the Livetti case was now in the hands of civil police, where it ought to have been all along, and that the political branch was no longer in the picture. It is possible that liaison between the two organizations was limited and cumbrous and that Gonzalez had shown no curiosity after handing over his prisoner; it is also possible that he did not tell us of Ardower's release because it would deprive him of a further opportunity to call.

My next move was to obtain information as from one reasonable man to another. As Madrid had proved difficult, I approached the Provincial Government of Vizcaya after telephoning London and Paris for the necessary introductions. Among the projects which interested our consortium was the modernization of the Spanish steel industry. I was therefore persona grata.

A small wine was held in my honor, at which I had arranged that the Chief of Police should be present. With these officials and others I normally spoke French. If they found it an effort, I had recourse to the sixteenth-century language — after all, the Spanish of Cervantes — which my family has always preserved as a proud tradition of the home, though abandoning, rather than changing, its religion.

When I was alone with the Provincial Governor and his Chief of Police, I mentioned that Olura appeared to have become involved, as rich young women on holiday will, with a certain Philip Ardower and that I was much exercised at learning that he had been under suspicion of violence to a press photographer. Would it be too much to ask what had happened to him?

To my surprise the question aroused a note of mischievous geniality. Dr. Ardower, they said, was a serious scholar of Basque language and literature. He had, it was true, hidden the body of this photographer, but he had no more politics than a monkey. His motive was clear, even chivalrous; and in fact he had saved Mr. Mgwana and my goddaughter from a scandal which the Government would have been the first to deprecate.

Preliminary examination having established his innocence, he had been temporarily expelled from Spain — this in view of the delicacy of the investigation and its possible repercussions. He had left an impression of audacity which might be termed impertinence if not redeemed by a gracious courtesy and the fact that he showed no resentment. They regretted that he preferred the society of the lower classes to that of more influential people who would have been charmed to entertain so distinguished a scholar.

I could see faintly appearing the character which Olura had drawn for me. But then the faces around me became sterner. Ardower had secretly returned. Nobody knew how or when, and they were all most uneasy about the why. The motorcycle of a Civil Guard had been — for a mere matter of ten minutes — impudently stolen. Without much hope it had been examined for fingerprints. The department had expected, if any, those of an enterprising and badly wanted agitator who had been illicitly organizing the port workers. Instead, it found Ardower's. Apparently he was unfamiliar with motorcycles and had not lifted the machine off its stand by the carrier, but by the tank — on the underside of which was a complete set of prints of his right hand.

Affronting the Civil Guard, they said, was a most serious offense. If my goddaughter or I knew where Dr. Ardower was to be found, would we please advise him to get back over the frontier the way he had come and thus allow them to forget about the case?

The effect of this news upon Olura was a most difficult mood compounded of joy and restlessness. She treated me, with the best will in the world, as an encumbrance like the table which got in the way of her stride and the meals which annoyingly had to be eaten at expected times. Her conversation — or that small part of it which deserved the name — largely consisted of impossible schemes for letting Ardower know that she was not in danger and would join him in France. She was also in that sensitive mood when, if a man makes a general remark of some intelligence, the woman takes it as a personal remark of none. Both sexes, if intelligent, passionate and in love, are sufficiently insane to be shut up like cats. In the case of Philip Ardower I should also block the chimney.

This tension was abruptly dispelled by Lieutenant Gonzalez when he called on us a week later with the news that a South African named Piet Duyker had been brutally done to death not far from Deva and that Ardower was wanted for the murder. He had been deputed, I suppose, to confirm that Olura knew nothing. After a few formal questions to which she quietly replied, he sensibly left her alone.

Over his usual sherry-and-bitters he gave to me such details as he knew. It seemed more than possible that the impulsive Ardower had commited this act of utter folly, believing the South African to be responsible for the unpleasant episode in the hotel. We both assumed that there had been a violent quarrel, though reserving judgment as to why either of them should have been so unwise as to accompany the other into remote fastnesses of the mountains.

I at once telephoned Paris, requesting my partners to arrange for me a conference with one of the departmental heads of the Deuxième Bureau whose name I need not specify, and flew up the following day. The fate of Ardower did not concern me so much as the charges hanging over Olura and the threat of more to come. I desired to express my conviction that General Sauche and Major Vigny were responsible for the murder of Livetti, and to inquire whether the French Government had or could be persuaded to have any interest in the case.

My private démarche was politely rejected. In fact I was told that Sauche and Vigny could stew in their own juice until the Spaniards were tired of them. Paris was sensitive. The recent kidnaping from Germany of one of Sauche's fellow conspirators had not only disturbed the love affair with the old enemy but had suffered a bad press throughout the world.

I was not proposing any such illegalities, but was treated as if I had. The French have still a nineteenth-century view of the power of a financier. It was impressed upon me that Sauche must not on any account meet with

an accident in Spain unless the innocence of the French
Government were obvious and transparent. Private enterprise would be unhesitatingly denounced and the agents
who were watching the General — discreetly and at a distance — would be instructed to prevent it. I was gratified
to learn that there were such agents.

I returned to Maya disheartened. There was no help to
be had in Spain or France. The only consolation was that
all the details of this unsavory case still remained hidden
in ministerial files. I thought it best that they should stay
there. It would be time to call in our own diplomatic rep-
resentatives when publicity was no longer avoidable.

I told Olura something of my failure. She hardly listened. She was unrecognizable. Never had I seen her so
serenely beautiful. There was about her an air of determination, of having grown up and yet of feverish gaiety. I
was haunted by some memory as exasperating as a tune
which one can neither recapture nor dismiss. Her expression, I at last decided, had reminded me of contemporaries in 1917 returning from Paris leave to the Western
Front.

She told me that she had spent a day with Ardower. I
exclaimed against such folly when he was wanted for
murder. She laughed and replied that she was absolutely
certain she had not been followed, and that I had better
not know where he was. When she had soothed me into
such a state of comfort that I was prepared to pay attention, she gave me Ardower's version of the death of
Duyker — which struck me, I must admit, as less credible

than the common-sense account which Vigny had rendered to the police. It is always hard for my generation to believe in unprincipled private violence. God knows we have lived through enough of it! But a man is conditioned by the ethical standards prevailing in his youth.

I said that the courts must decide between them. To that she replied that the courts couldn't, because Ardower was dead. She rolled her eyes at me in a soulful imitation of grief which I found in poor taste.

I shall now permit myself to adopt the convention of direct speech which Ardower frequently employs in his narrative and appears to me worthy of sedulous imitation. His verbatim records of conversations are of no value as evidence, being merely remembered and edited, but I find them economical.

I answered her with some impatience, probably saying: "Well, who the devil killed him?"

"I haven't decided yet whether it should be Vigny or Duyker. I thought you might advise me. You're such an old fox."

"But what, my dear Olura, is the point of a deception which must inevitably be exposed?"

"The point, Uncle Henry, is that these cruel crooks know that they cannot be found guilty of the murder of Livetti. But they can't be at all sure that they won't be tried for the murder of Philip."

I told her that the whole idea was preposterous, and that I flatly refused to tamper with the administration of justice.

"Philip was shocked, too," she said.

"If he's the man I hope he is, he will take his medicine. The innocent have nothing to fear."

I have never seen her so angry. I really was not surprised that otherwise sane people suspected her of being an active anarchist. She let me have her opinions of Justice. In England ignorant magistrates, the Establishment, wigs, black caps, medieval mummery to stop fools thinking! In Spain secret police, civil guards shooting on suspicion, torture, military law!

"You're all content to play at Justice by the rules!" she cried. "Since they meant to kill Philip, what does it matter whether they did or not? They are guilty!"

A wholly irrelevant tirade! The rules might or might not suit her, but the penalties for tinkering with them were severe. She would only make matters worse, I said. At least we could trust the Spanish censorship to handle so delicate a case with caution. And in London I would see that it was made clear to the papers that any unjustified inferences founded upon her behavior in Spain would be met by ruthless actions for libel.

She retorted that she did not give a damn for the Sunday papers, but that I did. Her attack on me was wholly unjustified. I will quote what I remember of it:

"Think of all those faces in your club trying to pretend they have heard nothing! Olura again! Bribing Livetti to assassinate Leopold, or is it Sauche? Persuading her lover to commit murder to cover it up! Are you a fit person to conduct a great merchant bank, Uncle Henry, and advise the Church Commissioners on their investments? And the French partners! *Méfiants!* Beautifully, Frenchly *méfiants!* I've laid you open to blackmail by the enemies of de Gaulle. I'll bet that has occurred to them already!"

Naturally these considerations, though not so grossly exaggerated, had also occurred to me. I replied that I was prepared to excuse her hysteria, understanding that it was due to her anxiety for Dr. Ardower, but that she would do better to appeal to my affection. What steps exactly did she wish me to take?

"The first thing is to persuade Gonzalez that Philip is dead."

"I have no evidence."

"Those French agents you mentioned told you about a man with a bandaged head leaving the Zarauz villa."

I was on the point of asking how I was to know that so unlikely a story was true, but thought better of it. I remarked instead that what Gonzalez believed would depend on how well she could act.

"Don't you remember me when you first arrived?" she asked. "Don't you see that time and again I have tormented myself with the thought that Philip might be dead? And now when he could be garroted by the public strangler? I don't have to act at all, Uncle Henry. I only have to be a half of myself."

With deepest misgivings I gave way to her. One should not at my age be faced by such a distasteful alternative — treachery to the enduring object of one's senile love or treachery to one's social responsibilities and class, which

must be above suspicion. My only comfort was that I
could swear I had been misinformed if the police un-
earthed Ardower alive and showing his teeth.

When Gonzalez arrived in answer to my telephone call,
I at least had no acting to do at all. I have no doubt that I
appeared peevish, pompous and reluctant to talk.

"You are aware that your Don Felipe is dead?" I asked.

He was greatly shocked — and not only, I think, because justice had been defeated. Half jealous, half romantically unbalanced, he was emotionally involved with
his pair of criminals.

"And Mlle. Manoli?" he asked anxiously.

I showed him Olura. She sat at a corner of the terrace
with her head on her arms, buried in the folds of a shabby
red cloak which she insisted on wearing day in and day
out. To my mind she looked far too much like a Racine
heroine in the last five minutes of a Comédie Française
production. But she knew her man. Gonzalez, all the unofficial part of him Latin to the core, expected a dramatic
expression of grief from a dramatic character, and he got
it. A simple English policeman would have suspected in-
sincerity.

He requested the source of my information. I made a
mystery of it, implying that Mr. Mgwana was bringing
pressure to bear on the French Government and that I was
collaborating with their agents.

"I do not see what interest the French could have in Dr.
Ardower," he replied stolidly.

"No? When your government has extended its hospitality to de Gaulle's bitterest enemy? When you know that he

and this Major Vigny planted Livetti on my goddaughter?"

He did not cross-question me. The file at police headquarters which recorded my past activities and international connections was sure to mention that our Paris house was in close touch with some of the Ministers who preserved in the Chamber the tradition of French democracy. That I should have reliable informants was easily credible.

"We cannot prove they planted Livetti," he said. "Mere suspicion against an incontestable alibi is not enough. Please go on, M. Sequerra."

"I will tell you exactly what happened. Ardower knew that one of them killed Livetti. When he illegally returned from France, he was fool enough to call at their villa in Zarauz and threaten them with exposure. I do not know what proof he had. Whatever it was, they decided that he was too dangerous and must be removed. Vigny and Piet Duyker took him out and executed him."

"Then who killed Duyker?"

"Take your pick! Vigny to ensure his silence? Ardower in self-defense?"

"What evidence have you?" he asked.

"That is your business. I am just a reliable and anonymous source. The police have only to find where Ardower's body is buried. Meanwhile can you obtain authority to interview Sauche?"

He replied that he did not need any, that he was still in charge of the Livetti case so far as it concerned Mr. Mgwana.

"Then I suggest, my dear Lieutenant, that you tell him you are inquiring into the death of Philip Ardower. Ask him who was the person with a bandaged head who was driven away from their house about 10 P.M. on the night of August 25th! The reactions of Vigny and the General to that simple question may well interest you professionally."

Gonzalez extracted a few unimportant details from me, which I gave with reluctance as if fearing to compromise the French agents, and appeared very ready to show himself a more subtle interrogator than civil police. He delicately requested that I would present his compliments to Mlle. Manoli whenever I considered that she was in a fit state to receive them.

For the next three days Olura did not leave the villa. Once or twice the good Elena came up from the inn to visit her. I assumed that she had heard the news and, in the absence of any other female companionship, felt it her duty to support and comfort. They were both very clever and did not allow me to guess that Elena was in the secret.

After the energy of her dispute with me, Olura had become indecisive. She wanted to visit Madrid and interview that Mary Deighton-Flagg. She asked me if I believed Miss Deighton-Flagg's story of the anonymous telephone call which sent her up hotfoot to the Hostal de las Olas. Ardower and Gonzalez had both accepted it; but Olura, who knew the woman well, thought it most unlikely that she would spend money — which might compel a week without a decent meal — on so slender an indication of scandal. A lie was there anyway, she said, so we might as well have one which would be helpful.

I could not pretend to be shocked, for I had heard exactly the same remark from a distinguished and punctilious Queen's Counsel. So I merely suggested that the coaching of witnesses should be left to professionals. That she accepted this pusillanimous advice was, as I now see, due to her inability to tear herself away from the proximity of Ardower.

Meanwhile Lieutenant Gonzalez had interviewed our two military men. He was under no obligation to report the result to me, but he did. He told me that they had been shaken by the news of Ardower's death and that their reactions had been compatible with guilt, though perhaps to be explained by surprise. They blankly denied any knowledge of a bandaged patient in a car and could only repeat what they had already stated to the police: that Ardower and the late Piet Duyker had driven away from their villa in the late evening, that they believed Ardower had escaped from prison and wished to help him in spite of his aggressive and difficult attitude.

Gonzalez was ill at ease. No doubt about it. I had the impression that the real purpose of his visit was to give me some friendly warning which conflicted with duty and could not, when it came to the point, be boldly inserted into a silence. I wondered if I were about to be interrogated in less pleasant surroundings by one of the chiefs of his service. He looked more than ever like the manager of a small branch bank refusing a perfectly sound loan because it was against the policy of the head office.

What he had heard from his superiors and did not say was only too plain next morning. A tedious functionary of police named Captain Feria called on us indecently early and arrested Olura on a charge of concealing a murder. I protested that if such was the prerogative and necessity of the Law, it should not have waited a month before taking action.

Olura was magnificent. I half expected the practices of civil disobedience, but she showed the good civic manners of her upbringing. She was guilty of a felony and there was no more to be said. She absolutely refused to allow me to accompany her, saying that it was essential I should stay. She told me quickly that Ardower was on the Ermita and that Elena and Captain Allarte knew it. If there was little or no chance of her release I must try to get him out of the country.

So long as she was unafraid, I was ready to remain in Maya. I looked forward to being free to dictate terms to Ardower and extracting for myself, once and for all, the truth. Meanwhile I thought it best to tell this Captain Feria that I refused to allow my goddaughter to be escorted only by a male policeman. He assured me that there was a respectable woman of his service in the car. I looked out, and there was. To my eyes she appeared considerably more villainous than he did.

Left alone in the villa, I understood that there had been a covert declaration of war. Any more mention of bandaged heads, and Olura Manoli stands trial! It was highly improbable that Vigny and Sauche knew who was Gonzalez's informant. Ardower, if he were after all alive? French agents? Myself? Even Mgwana? But whoever it was would appreciate the threat and perhaps offer a profitable bargain.

I do not suggest for a moment that Sauche alone could influence the Spanish Ministry of Justice. What I think may have happened was that after Gonzalez's questioning he called on any friends he had in high places, pretending alarm and renewed plots against his life. That was the last straw for authorities already in the mood to damn all foreigners and their obscure intrigues. No doubt the excuses which had been good enough to keep the Italian Embassy quiet went nowhere near satisfying the Consul-General of South Africa. So the police were instructed to hold Olura until the truth came out for the crime to which she had confessed.

I now return to the night of Ardower's arrival. When I had left him to sleep, I cleared up the puddles on the floor and wondered for how long I could conceal his presence if I decided to do so at all.

Our domestic arrangements were simple. A respectable old body named Concha came in every morning to clean the villa and prepare our breakfast and a light lunch. She then returned home to her own responsibilities. I could think of nothing better than to stage an exhibition of elderly distrust and obstinacy and refuse to allow her to clean Olura's room on the grounds that it contained an unknown quantity of valuable dresses and jewelry.

This worked more effectually than I had foreseen. She screamed at me that she had always been a woman of honor and that she would rather steal from the Church than the poor señorita. She then left the house with dig-

nity, bursting into tears as soon as she was in the garden.
Poor woman! I would have trusted her with a bookmaker's
bag of unidentifiable pound notes.

Meanwhile Ardower had stayed quiet in the locked
room. When Concha had gone we had breakfast. I found
him less emotional — indeed clear-sighted and self-dis-
ciplined. I was prepared unhesitatingly to sacrifice him
if there were any benefit to be gained for Olura. Though
my thoughts had remained unspoken, I was taken aback
to find that he agreed with them. He declared that he
could never marry Olura, that the vast discrepancy of
income could only lead to never-ending strain on their
mutual affection, however much each considered the sus-
ceptibilities of the other, and that though one could love
eternally one could not be an eternal lover. He personally
would prefer long absence studying the languages of
Mgwana's forests to a long sentence in a Spanish jail, but
one or the other was probably the right solution for Olura.

I let this pass. He had constructed for himself out of
lonely introspection too simple a world. He also underrated
the character of the Manolis. He would have to put up
with Olura renting a beehive hut in the nearest village or a
flat right opposite the jail, unless I could get rid of him out
of her life.

He faced me across the breakfast table, thin, worn and
with very watchful eyes drained of all emotion. He was an
unnecessary complication, for I saw no difficulty in freeing Olura as soon as Mgwana knew she was in jail; nor
was I seriously afraid of adverse publicity now that I had
had time to weigh up the risk and to recover from Olura's

extremely unjust attack. Everything could be arranged except the killing of Duyker.

One resents disturbance in the early morning at my age. One is accustomed to swear at humanity in general. One is also well aware from experience that such thoughts are never translated into speech or action, and that a certain sour amusement may be extracted from analyzing the silent outburst of resentment. It occurred to me that an excellent reason — among others more ephemeral — for blasting Ardower to hell was that he had the effrontery to love Olura as much as I did.

A forgivable sin. Serener contemplation of it led me to put him at least into the class of a diamond bracelet which Olura wanted — if, that is, she had been a woman to set her heart on anything of the sort. In that record which she wrote for me there had been a passage which I found moving. She said that she knew little of my youth and begged me to remember.

While Ardower drank his coffee, I did the remembering. In a long memory there are so many selves. The young Henry, his love and his misery are no longer vivid. I remember far more clearly what the man in his middle forties thought about him, and how the pompous fellow was impatient of such a waste of time in loneliness and suffering. And so one arrives at the present self, the pantaloon, who has forgotten so much that forty-year-old Henry remembered, but disapproves of him all the same and is very sorry indeed for young Henry and his romantic obsession.

I said to Ardower, breaking a long silence, that Olura

had not mentioned to me — or only very vaguely — his Breton captain.

"I don't suppose she did," he replied. "I doubt if she got hold of it at all. Her emotions were naturally a little overwhelmed by Zarauz and Duyker."

I questioned him about Bozec and Bernardino. Applying myself to his answers, I was mortified to find that I had decided to intervene and that I was meditating just that sort of skulduggery which Olura and her woolly friends expect of International Finance when in fact it is the most unlikely section of society to indulge in it. But what use is power unless employed for those we love?

I confess, too, that as the general shape of a counterattack began to form I felt a sense of enjoyment: comparable, let us say, to that of regulating a market and sending off the speculators to lick their wounds. Perhaps I recovered something of youth; or it may have been that I welcomed a reversion to the ethics of my early ancestors who were trained in statecraft at the courts of Córdoba and Constantinople and accepted revenge as a moral duty. Those two military nuisances, Vigny and Sauche, deserved no mercy; and none would be given them right to the end.

"Can you endure more loneliness?" I asked.

Ardower replied that he was near the limit, but that he would have to. Meanwhile might he rest for a day?

"I want you to remain here in the house, in such comfort as we can arrange, for about four days," I said.

My own ruthless handling of poor Concha had suggested an idea. The old fool of an admiral from whom I rented the villa at a price which must have doubled his yearly pension had been bothered about his valueless valuables. He had them all locked up in an airless cubbyhole under the eaves, which was then sealed by the local notary public.

I proposed to pack Olura's things and call in police and the same notary to lock and seal her bedroom with its adjoining private lavatory and to register the fact that the room contained eight unexamined suitcases of ostrich skin. Having observed the antics of this public functionary during the almost religious ceremony, I thought it safe for Ardower to remain hidden under the bed.

He considered it an intolerable risk, but I overruled his protests and explained that the plan depended on the most trustworthy constant in our world: professional character. Notaries do not look under beds unless engaged in matrimonial cases.

Cheering up a little, he said that a cheese, some fruit, half a meter of Pamplona sausage, bread, butter and anything there might be in the cellar, not forgetting a corkscrew, would keep him comfortable for a week if my estimate of four days turned out to be optimistic. To these requirements I added Olura's typewriter and a quantity of paper, requesting him to spend his enforced leisure in drawing up for me, and me alone, a very frank and detailed statement of his relations with Olura and Mgwana, of his movements and his interrogations.

That is the origin of the document which forms the bulk of this file and is divided for the sake of clarity, as I have already explained, into two parts by Olura's narrative. I assumed there would be revealing discrepancies between the written account and his verbal report. There were few. I also assumed it would be short. I did not then know that he was a practiced writer who had even succeeded in the nearly impossible task of popularizing his obscure linguistic research.

I sent at once for the notary public. As I expected, his ridiculous self-importance facilitated our business. He was registering the presence of eight unexamined suitcases, the property of the arrested spinster, Olura Manoli, and nothing else concerned him. He displayed no emotion or curiosity, nor did the policeman in the passage, except when they found it necessary to calm my simulated distrust and indignation. It seemed to me astonishing that the notary public did not smell the sausage which was under the bed with Ardower. It is possible that even at his age he was more occupied by the delicate and lingering perfume of Olura.

I locked up the house and the same afternoon flew up again to Paris. Confident that I had not come empty-handed, I insisted on a second conference with officials of the Deuxième Bureau. I was received, though with pointed impatience.

When I related what I knew of Captain Bozec of Le Croisic, my distinguished friends became more excited, and I was asked to repeat my story at the highest level. It was already known that Sauche and Vigny had escaped by sea, and that correspondence was shuttling back and forth. Bozec was one of half a dozen very vague suspects.

I went on to the question of Bozec's rendezvous with the

Isaura, explaining that her owner was a plain fisherman who would not be capable of complicated navigation. Therefore the position of the rendezvous must be simple — two Vizcayan peaks in line or something of that nature — and would be well known to the crew of the *Phare de Kerdonis* as well as the master. If they were quietly arrested, what was the chance that one of them would talk?

Inevitable, I was told. Bozec and his crew were all in it for money, not from political conviction. An offer of ten thousand francs would produce the rendezvous and the method of communication, especially if the alternative was a five years' sentence for treason.

So at last I was free to come to the point. If I could frighten the former General Sauche, I said, into arranging his urgent retirement from Spain, would it not be easy to sequester the *Phare de Kerdonis,* put a trustworthy crew from Naval Intelligence aboard her and pick him up at the rendezvous without anyone being the wiser — except possibly the skipper of the *Isaura,* who would never dare to talk?

Yes, they liked it. There were a lot of "ifs," but in principle they liked it. They were kind enough to say that the Services always benefited from the fresh thinking of the financial world. But what was to be done with Sauche and Vigny? They could be kept secretly on the ice for a week or so; but never, in such doubtful circumstances, could they be brought to trial or caused to disappear.

Leading them step by step towards the solution I had in mind, I suggested Algeria. Could they not turn up accidentally in Algeria, where the Government would know what to do with them and could be trusted to keep it quiet?

No, but no, but no! Even if it could be shown that they had visited Algeria voluntarily, no one would ever believe it. Sauche and his *plastiqueurs* had been and still were a real danger to the Head of State. He and Vigny deserved to be squashed like the bedbugs they were. But there was no way of hiding the mess.

I then revealed that there was, pointing out that all they required for the ultimate disposal of the pair was a government which would not be suspected, which had no kindly feelings for them, which was in absolute and efficient control of its police and security services.

"These two gentlemen," I declared, "have insulted and offended M. Leopold Mgwana beyond bearing."

They needed confirmation. I told them that if they could get me a clear line to Mgwana and scramble the conversation at their end — I knew that Mgwana could deal with it at his — anyone who for reasons of state wished to listen in might do so. I added that the cost of the operation which I envisaged — above the line, that is — need not be more than one obsolescent, long-range, propeller aircraft.

When that evening I had Leopold Mgwana on the other end of the line, I told him that Olura was in prison and Ardower on the run. At first he misinterpreted my circumlocutions and was firmly convinced that I had bad news about the financing of his prestige airline; then, when he understood, he was continually interrupting me with exclamations of grief and anger. Yes, I assured him,

I knew of his statement to the Ministry of Justice; but it
simply had not been believed. The police could not make
up their minds whether he had merely hit a press photographer too hard, or whether he was trying to protect Olura
from the consequences of a plot to assassinate him in
which she had been involved.

Then I let him know who were responsible and somewhat exaggerated the danger to Olura if the pair remained
at liberty. I explained why the French Government was
unable to help me and added that favors would be recipro-
cated all round.

Mgwana understood our problem by instinct, though it
was certainly the first time that he had been asked to bury
an international embarrassment in the mysteries of his
Africa. He asked if anyone in authority were listening to
our conversation. When I replied that on my invitation
there was, Mgwana assured him in his sonorous, somewhat biblical English — which the unknown, though no
accomplished linguist, understood without difficulty —
that he, Mgwana, would be personally responsible for all
security measures. His only conditions were that the aircraft carrying Sauche and Vigny must be cleared from a
foreign airport and that the pilot, as sole survivor of an
accident, must be able to answer the questions of press
and diplomatists with every appearance of sincerity and
emotion.

A preliminary planning outline and a routine of communication were agreed. For me, too, communication was
made direct and easy — an obvious necessity, since I had
no wish that the Paris partners should have any clear idea

of what my business with the Deuxième Bureau had been. One of the French agents employed to report the movements of Sauche was ordered to accept and transmit my messages — a gratifying gesture of trust, considering that only a week before I had been threatened with his interference.

That done, I could afford to indulge my anxiety for Olura, and boarded the first plane for Madrid. I knew that reverence for the Manoli balance sheet would ensure that she was treated with respect, and it was not the imprisoned part of her which worried me; it was the free Olura, which no cell could confine, wandering out to the Ermita in ignorance and despair.

Her eyes had nothing in them but a question. I told her guardedly that a friend had arrived by sea and was occupying her bedroom in excellent health. She splendidly controlled any expression of emotion which might have given away the secret, leaving it to the touch of arms and cheek to say what she thought of me. Guiltily remembering my hesitation, I may have been outwardly the more moved of the two. At the end of our conversation she reminded me to call on Miss Mary Deighton-Flagg.

Prejudice, such as Ardower's, against the Press is absurd. It is not the object of journalists to instruct the public, but to entertain it. I have always found them excellent and helpful people whose gratitude can easily be earned by giving them information which, for forty-eight hours, will be near enough to the truth. Miss Deighton-Flagg was not of course in this responsible class, but obliging in every way and very ready to sympathize with the limited

demands of a much older man, though initially she mis-
understood their nature. As a free-lance society correspondent there was no abnormality I could see in her to
criticize.

Intimacy, in the conversational sense, developed with
most satisfactory frankness. It had been Livetti himself
who telephoned her. He had two motives: to get a background story for his photographs and to have a lady of the
press on the spot who would and could scream in print for
the Liberty of the Photographer if there were a row.

What she said confirmed Vigny's account of the murder. Livetti, when he spoke to her on the telephone from
Zarauz, was aware only that Mgwana had taken some
London deb down to the Hostal de las Olas. She herself
had not known till she arrived at the hotel that Mgwana's
companion was not a juvenile with a taste for publicity,
but Olura. What, she asked me, had happened to Livetti?
Had he called the whole thing off and returned to Rome?
When Gonzalez and his service desired to interrogate
without giving anything away, their technique must have
been masterly.

I found that the young woman, in spite of a very credit-
able pose of bright courage, was in fact appalled at the
prospect of indefinite exile. She saw no hope of remaking
her life except by devoting herself to a novel. As I had no
doubt that it would be of modish and profitable obscenity,
I offered to serve the cause of literature by financing two
years of comparative comfort while she wrote it. All that I
wished in return, as her disinterested patron, was that she
would swear in any court of law whenever required that

the telephone conversation which brought her up to the
Hostal had been in French.

"Of course it was," she said at once. "How stupid of me
to have forgotten!"

In the morning I flew to Bilbao to see Gonzalez. The
complexities of the case were now beginning to have their
own intrinsic interest, so that I was no more tired than if I
had been engaged in any series of delicate financial negotiations.

I gave him Olura's compliments, and asked whether it
would be possible for me to have rather obvious police
protection if I were to call in person at the Zarauz villa. He
agreed at once, and was glad that I wished it to be obvious.
It would be extremely embarrassing to the authorities, he
said, if there were any discourtesy to me.

I stayed the night at a most comfortable hotel where, in
the bar, I met a French tourist and his pretty, school-
teacherish wife who were collecting Basque folk songs on
a tape recorder. The ingenuity of these devoted servants of
state both delights and disturbs me. I had previously
thought it utterly absurd that Ardower, a transparent don,
could be suspected by Gonzalez of being a security officer.
The two naïve folklorists, equally transparent, gave me
the news that Bozec and his crew had been arrested, that
the rendezvous with the *Isaura* was known and that the
Phare de Kerdonis was ready to sail whenever I gave the
word.

On the morning of September 4 I drove over to the villa
at Zarauz. The chauffeur of the hired car was accompanied, as chauffeurs often are, by a friend. His stern and

closed solidity made it plain to any observer that he was not the normal type of friend. There was also a uniformed policeman lounging at the villa gate.

Sauche received me very cordially. Both officers in their manners and tact were an advertisement for the French Army. One regretted that there was no war to occupy them. My name meant nothing to Vigny. Sauche had heard of me and was searching memory. I assisted him by mentioning several common acquaintances. Before his defiance of de Gaulle, the General was noted for his excellent political contacts.

As soon as I explained that Olura Manoli was my goddaughter and ward, they assumed that I had called to do business. That, at least, was what I judged from the faintest possible air of mercantile rather than military insolence. I admit that I prefer the French generals of my youth who looked immensely stupid and distinguished and in fact were neither. Sauche reminded me of a shop assistant who had taken a correspondence course in management. I simply do not believe that Ardower recognized him straightaway as a professional soldier.

"You are naturally aware, gentlemen," I asked, "that you are under surveillance by agents of the French Government?"

"They are even very well known to us," Vigny replied.

"Yet it is not likely that out of three murders they would not have noticed even one."

"Only three?" Sauche retorted. "In France I am never accused of less than a dozen."

"The police are often excitable, my General. But here

we know of only three: Livetti, Duyker and Ardower."

I suppose that as a corps commander Sauche could deal effectively with a surprise attack in the field. In conversation he could not. His face and his hesitation invigorated me.

"Livetti, of course, was no great loss," I admitted casually.

He strolled across to the window. To his practiced eye there could be no doubt that the police had taken precautions for my safety. It seemed to me that I might now usefully refer to them.

"The authorities have been good enough to inform me that Ardower visited this house on the evening of August 25. He has never been seen since. Two witnesses state, however, that a man with his head bandaged was driven out, accompanied by the late Piet Duyker and a third person: presumably yourself, Major Vigny. I suggest that on the orders of General Sauche, Duyker executed Ardower. You then buried the body and killed Duyker to ensure his silence."

"This is a monstrous figment of the imagination!" Sauche exclaimed. "The police will never find any such burial!"

"They will, my General. In the next day or two they will. My friends and I lack experience. It is taking us a little time to find a convincing spot for the grave which the police have not already searched."

I felt that with this remark I might have overplayed my hand, encouraged to the edge of fantasy by the pleasure I

took in crossing swords with them. But not at all! To them
graves and their contents were instruments of policy.

"It would help our negotiations if I knew your reasons for killing him," Sauche said. "A question of Mlle.
Manoli's present difficulties, or perhaps of her estate?"

Oddly enough neither of them ever doubted that Ardower was dead. After all, the admirable Gonzalez had interviewed them in all good faith.

"The bullet which cut the femoral artery is still in
place," I told them. "Somebody, therefore, removed
Duyker's gun."

"And if Duyker fired in self-defense against a lunatic?"

"You will still have to explain why Ardower left this
house with a bandaged head, where he found the rope
which he tried — too feebly — to use as a tourniquet and
why the other half of the rope is still knotted round his
ankle."

After a short pause, Sauche very sensibly remarked:

"M. Sequerra, I observed that my enemies have persuaded you to collaborate with them up to a point. But
since you thought it worthwhile to call on me with this
story, I must assume that you personally are prepared to
offer terms. What are they?"

"Not very hard. I only want your signed confession to
the outrage upon my ward, and I will allow you to say that
Duyker killed Livetti. Whether he did or not, he is no
longer here to deny it."

Vigny burst into protests, insisting that he would fight
this nonsense to the last. He said with a strained smile

that he himself was prepared to face any court and to prove that the quarrels between Duyker and Livetti and Duyker and Ardower, whatever they were, had nothing to do with the General or himself.

"And the press of the whole world will be in the court-room," he added. "What about La Manoli and her distin-guished nigger then?"

An intelligent man! He had attacked the point of least resistance. It seemed a very good moment to throw in the reserve which Olura had provided.

"You would succeed in creating all that publicity which I prefer to avoid," I admitted to Vigny. "But you would find yourself accused of complicity in the murder of Livetti. We know that you arranged for the presence of an English newspaperwoman in the Hostal de las Olas."

He denied it furiously. It was curious how those two always sounded less convincing when they told the truth than when they were lying.

"So far she has admitted to the police only that she was sent there by an anonymous telephone call. But she is now prepared to swear that the conversation was in French and she will recognize your voice."

"We are finished," Sauche said as superbly as he could. "We are perhaps a little to blame. But that little, when inflated by bankers and the agents of the so-called Fifth Republic . . . I take it that you have made some arrangements for our safety in return for the statement you require?"

I replied very truthfully that I had not. I suggested that

they should escape as they had come in, across the Pyrenees.

Vigny, white with fury, was about to exclaim that they had not crossed the Pyrenees and could not return to France. Sauche, the more discreet of the two, silenced him with a gesture.

"I think we shall be able to leave tonight," he said.

That certainly was rather sooner than I dared hope, allowing me to fulfill the optimistic estimate of four days' confinement to bedroom by which I had encouraged Ardower. I learned afterwards that they had paid the skipper of the *Isaura* to stand by in port ever since the death of Duyker.

What their plans were I did not know and could not ask. My guess is that they meant Bozec to drop them in Portugal, where no unnecessary questions would, I think, have been asked so long as they declared their intention of taking the first plane to South America and actually took it.

The document which we drafted was dignified but satisfactory. We had, however, some difficulty over the timing. Sauche was willing to accept my word that I would not deliver it to the authorities until the following morning. Vigny disagreed. So we compromised by taking, all three of us and my plainclothes escort, an amicable stroll to the post office where I sent the envelope, registered, to my address in Maya. They on their part dispatched an apparently innocent telegram to St. Nazaire, a town conveniently large but only seventeen miles from Le Croisic.

After calling on my folklorists at the gay little *camping* where they had set up their car tent and private transmitter, I was back at Maya in the late afternoon with a basket containing the most luxurious picnic that the very civilized shops of Zarauz could produce. When my car had left, I broke the door seals of the notary public and displayed to Ardower, I fear too pretentiously, a copy of the confession.

Left alone so long with only a diminishing sausage for company, his morale was at low ebb. Looking over again the sheets which in my absence had poured from Olura's typewriter, I can distinguish the point at which he began to be overwhelmed by this cruel brooding on his difficulties and to be convinced that there was no way out.

He congratulated me with warmth and simplicity on my success in freeing Olura and said that he would now give himself up and stand his trial. All that bothered him was what story he could tell of the death of Duyker which would omit all mention of Olura and Mgwana. His unselfishness seemed to me as remarkable as his temporary want of intelligence.

"My dear Philip," I said, for it was ridiculous even to my conventionally mannered mind not to experiment with his Christian name, "it does not appear to have occurred to you that you can tell any story you please, since there is nobody to accuse you of lying."

And I pointed out that the Livetti case was closed by the confession, the authenticity of which was assured by the signatures of Vigny and Sauche as well as by their sudden flight. As for the evidence against him, there wasn't any beyond Vigny's statement to the police, now hopelessly discredited. The Algerian, well out of the affair, had no incentive whatever to talk. Bozec did not come into it at all, and did not know the identity of the caller he had escorted to Zarauz.

However, to avoid being arrested on a charge of Affront to the Civil Guard and held for six months in case any other charge could be pinned on him, I recommended that he should immediately try to return to France. He interrupted me, exclaiming in unacademic language that illegal crossing of frontiers was not a job for amateurs.

In that I agreed with him. If it is necessary to disobey government regulations, one should always employ a professional. Still, it seemed to me that his friend Allarte would have some inkling of the proper way to set about it and could put him ashore at night on the beaches of the Landes. Philip objected that Allarte had a family, never far from hand-to-mouth existence in the winter, and that he could never afford to pay him so much that he would risk a jail sentence.

I did not tell him that Allarte would be in no danger whatever, that indeed I could arrange for them to be unofficially welcomed. The less that he knew of Bozec and Naval Intelligence, the better. So I contented myself with saying that if he thought Allarte's price beyond his personal means I would lend it to him and his children could repay me.

He laughed dutifully at what he thought to be the tasteless remark of an insensitive tycoon. I felt that I ought not to develop the actual proposal I had in mind until he was more used to the conception of a future. So I opened the picnic basket and was glad to see in his eyes that guilty light of a mourner who, through the last of his tears, has just caught sight of the bottles and cold collation on the dining table of the deceased.

When he was sufficiently mellowed to appreciate that there were other loves in the world beyond Olura's and his — mine, for example, for her and for her father — I explained to him that Theodore knew her better than either of us. His blasted daughter, he called her. I remember his exact words, for on that same morning he had warned me that he had less than six months to live.

"That blasted daughter of mine," he said, "is as likely as not to enter some kind of nunnery run by Californian Hindus, and we'll tie up her money so that they don't get a penny of it if she does."

I thought he exaggerated and told him so. Olura's sixteen-year-old obsessions with Church of England vestments, compulsory education of unmarried mothers to university level and the rights of every minority to overrule any majority would probably be superseded by the delights of debutantcy and marriage into whatever class was replacing the peerage as the most desirable.

Theodore would not agree. A fortune, he insisted, was a nuisance to a girl like Olura, who would always resent it and misuse it. She would never marry into society, money or power but follow her nature in deciding that truth could only be found through the embraces of a Chinese boilermaker or in trying to reform an alcoholic missionary. He could not bear to think of the unfortunate fellow

trailing after her round the world and being allowed to
save his face by writing the checks for the hotel man-
agers.

So the trust which he required for his darling was eccentric. All his money was left to her children, if any. She
had the full use of the income until marriage, when it
could be reduced and the income reinvested at the pleasure of the trustees.

I explained these provisions shortly to Philip and
awaited his comment.

"You are suggesting, if I understand you, that I fall into
the class of alcoholic missionary," he said. "A little hard
on a devoted scholar with a taste for good living. But I see
the analogy."

That was more like him, and I was encouraged to proceed. I proposed that Olura should have enough to be able
to taper off her enthusiasms gradually, but not so much
that he would find himself in the position foreseen by her
father, and I asked him to name a figure.

He replied that he had not the faintest idea, that I had
better put it up to Olura. I told him that he still did not
know her. She would be so impatient at being asked such
a question that she would insist on living on his salary.

"Well, what does it cost to keep up that sort of thing?"
he asked, pointing to the eight unexamined suitcases of
ostrich skin.

"At least ten thousand a year."

"Make it five, and I should have a hope of equaling it
some day."

That was one difficult negotiation settled. A second was

more embarrassing: to extract Allarte from the inn and persuade him to accompany me to the villa. I could not manage it without attracting the curiosity of all Maya — which, on his return, he allayed by pretending a discussion over the rent of his moorings. His evident joy at seeing Philip and their satisfactory jabberings in Basque predisposed him to accept my offer. On the falling tide before dawn Philip left the house by the cliff below the terrace, as he had come.

I was glad to see in the morning, when I had received my registered letter and was waiting for the car which would take me down to Madrid, that the sea was shimmering in the heat as far as the misty horizon. Philip would be saved from an uncomfortable day of seasickness and the new master of the *Phare de Kerdonis* would have no great difficulty in picking up the *Isaura*. It was the first time that I could really appreciate what attraction my pair of romantics had found in the coast.

I have no firsthand knowledge of the further adventures of General Sauche and Major Vigny. Two gentlemen, bearing their passports, boarded at Madrid Airport a plane which they had chartered to take them to South Africa. At what discreet point these two were exchanged for the real owners of the passports I do not know.

It will be remembered that the plane got off course and made a forced landing in mountainous country where Mr. Mgwana had not yet been able — owing, he claimed, to the negligence of British colonialism — to introduce all the benefits of civilization. The pilot fortunately took a route which led him to the nearest Government Officer.

His passengers were regrettably lost in the thick bush, and little more of them was discovered than was essential for identification.

When I last saw Mgwana, I ventured to hope that Vigny's end had been of a nature to satisfy his intelligent interest in the arts of the table. Some years ago he would have taken this as a reflection upon his people. He now retorted, as any of the more confident members of my club might do, with an unrepeatable jest upon the manners and morals of the City of London. Africa will go far with such a man for example.

This was at the christening of his goddaughter, little Theo Ardower. I was relieved that Prebendary Flanders had not been invited to perform the rite, though this may have been due to the fact that it took place in the sane, gay and decorous atmosphere of the College Chapel. I noticed that the beautiful gravity of Olura was attuned to perpendicular architecture and that, happily, she was well aware of it.